from SWG from
Wendy !

Stone's Gems and Murder

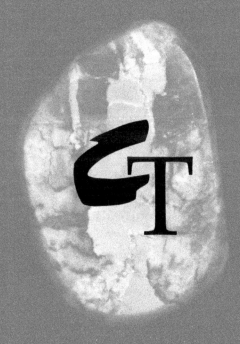

Cheryl F Taylor

A Rock Shop Mystery

Copyright 2016 Cheryl Taylor
FIRST EDITION December 2016

Cover Design by Cheryl Taylor
Cover Photograph by Cheryl Taylor

ISBN-10: 0-9982122-1-0
ISBN-13: 978-0-9982122-1-0

Printed in the United States

Published by:
CT Communications
9535 E. Marilyn Ln.
Dewey, AZ 86327
cfaytay@gmail.com
cherylftaylor.com

Edited by: Linda Schwandt
Schwandt Editorial Services

To
Greg Peterson and Jim Peterson
Thank you for all that you tried to teach me about rocks and minerals. Hopefully I didn't screw things up too badly!

Books by Cheryl Taylor

Gone to Ground

Up North Michigan Cozy Mystery Series
Up North Murder (Book One)

Rock Shop Cozy Mystery Series
Stone's Gems and Minerals (Book One)

1

Hospital smell, thought Amy Stone as she paused just inside the visitor's entry way of Mountain Regional Medical Center, *you just can't disguise it*.

She looked around the entry, noticing the soft lighting, and the beautiful artwork lining the chocolate colored walls. A large desk graced the left side of the spacious lobby, and dominating the center of the room was a large copper fountain, water cascading down its corrugated surface only to fall into a rock strewn basin at the bottom. If Amy hadn't known better, she would have thought she'd wandered into the lobby of a plush hotel, not the county hospital. The smell was a dead giveaway, however.

The nose knows! Amy thought with an internal laugh.

Pulling herself out of the contemplation of the olfactory essences of the modern hospital, she moved forward, heading for a bank of elevators at the far side of the lobby. She glanced at the scrap of paper in her hand.

Room 354.

Taking a deep breath, she punched the up button on the stainless steel plate mounted beside one of the elevators.

Room 354 turned out to be at the far end of a sterile looking hallway painted with a variety of colored stripes each leading off to the depths of the hospital, presumably to the different available departments. Amy glanced at a wall plaque listing various ranges of room numbers, and headed off down the left-hand branch toward a distant exit sign. She walked past a nurses' station on the right-hand side, nodding to the dark-haired woman in rose pink scrubs who was sitting at the desk, writing on a chart. The nurse glanced up at Amy's presence.

"Nick Stone? Room 354?"

"Last room on the left." The woman smiled at Amy and nodded in the direction Amy was heading. "He was awake a little bit ago when I checked on him. He said his daughter was coming. Are you...?"

"Amy Stone." Amy interrupted the nurse. Then, noticing the startled look in the woman's eyes, she smiled to soften the rudeness. "How's my dad doing?"

After a moment's hesitation, the nurse smiled in return. "He is doing very well. His surgery was successful, and he'll probably be moved to a rehab facility in a few days." The nurse, her name badge said Rose Ann, grinned at Amy. "We'll be sorry to lose him. It's not often that we get a patient who is so cheerful and so funny, in spite of all the pain he must be in."

Amy gave Rose Ann a rueful grin. "Yep, that sounds like my dad. Always one for a joke." She paused, and then tilted her head toward the end of the hallway. "I guess I'd better go check in. He's expecting me and I wouldn't want to be late."

With a nod at Rose Ann, Amy turned and continued down the hall until she reached the bright blue door with the number 354 on an engraved sign in the center, and the words "Stone, Nick" written in blue ink on a card mounted beneath.

She paused briefly outside the half-open door, then taking a deep breath, knocked, and stuck her head in through the opening, calling in the forced-cheerful voice Nick would expect, "Is anyone home?" As she stepped inside her eyes were immediately drawn to the hospital bed where a man lay, leg encased by what seemed to be an enormous cast supported by a metal cage. Her eyes traveled up to the head of the bed where her gaze met those of the occupant.

Bright blue eyes under a shock of snowy white hair met Amy's dark violet gaze, and the resident of the bed grinned at her appalled expression.

"Well, Amethyst, what do you think of the body work?"

Amy shook herself out of her momentary hesitation at the name. "It's Amy, Dad. I go by Amy, remember?"

Nick Stone's grin grew even broader at the scowl on his daughter's face. "I remember things very well, Amethyst. I broke my leg. I'm not senile. I remember your mother and I wrote the words 'Amethyst Gem' on your birth certificate, didn't we hon?" Nick looked over his shoulder at his wife, who had so far been sitting quietly in a chair near the large window on the far side of the room, book open in her lap.

Crystal Stone smiled as she looked at her husband, and then her daughter. "Yes, that's how I remember it, but I was on pain medication at the time, so my memory might be faulty."

Amy groaned, and shook her head. Amy, as well as her younger sister and brother, had all been victims of their parents' sense of humor regarding their last name. Amethyst Gem Stone, Opal Jewel Stone, and Jasper Onyx Stone had all caused some laughs in the classrooms as they'd been growing up. It didn't help much when Amy decided to pursue geology, her sister became a jewelry maker, and Jasper a mason.

Knowing from experience that arguing with her dad just encouraged him further, Amy decided to drop the whole subject of her name, and walked across the room, grabbing a chair as she passed it, and pulling it with her to the head of the bed. She sat and reached out to take Nick's hand.

"So, Dad, how are you doing? The nurse said you might be moved to the rehab facility soon."

Nick grimaced briefly, as though a flash of pain momentarily grabbed his attention away from his daughter. "Yeah, I hear the same thing. I'm going to miss the Jell-O here, but I'll be glad for a change of scenery." He nodded toward the huge window which looked out on an identical window across a forty-foot span. When the hospital expanded a few years ago, they didn't exactly take aesthetics into consideration.

"What on earth happened, anyway? When Mom called, she just said that you broke your leg falling off a ladder. What the heck were you doing on a ladder, for cripe's sake? I thought you'd hired Carl to do that kind of stuff." Amy showed her exasperation by shaking Nick's hand as she spoke. Sure, Nick was a young sixty-five, but when was he going to start to learn his limits?

Nick's eye's took on a distant expression, as though he were looking back to that moment, five days ago. He frowned and shook his head slightly.

"I really don't know what happened, Amethyst. It was hot. Hell, it's July in Arizona and it's always hot, but something seemed to be blocking the outflow vent on the air conditioner. So I got the ladder to climb up and see what it was. Carl was in the back, sorting out a new shipment of crystals, and I didn't feel it necessary to bother him. It's not like I'm decrepit after all, despite the evidence to the contrary." Nick looked at Amy as if daring her to argue, which she considered, but knew it wouldn't serve any purpose.

The old George Bernard Shaw saying about wrestling with a pig came to mind when dealing with her father. According to good old George, "I learned long ago to never wrestle with a pig. You get dirty and besides the pig likes it." That pretty much summed up her life with Nick, and while she'd never been able to totally resist the verbal "wrestling matches," she did try to avoid them whenever possible.

"I was up on the ladder, unscrewing the vent cover, when I thought I saw something move behind me. I swear I could feel it brush past my head. The next thing I knew, I'd lost my balance, and I was waving my arms like a windmill. Then I came crashing down. I landed on a new order of thunder eggs." He grinned up at her. "At least they weren't damaged. Gorgeous pieces. I got lucky finding them, and the guy gave them to me for a great price. Still, I don't remember much after I fell until I woke up in the hospital."

"Did Carl come out of the back room? Did you figure out what you saw?" Amy looked at Nick and frowned. Stone's Gems and Minerals was housed in an old rundown building from the early 1920s, and was periodically subject to invasions from pack rats and other vermin. Nick did everything he could to maintain the old building, but it obstinately refused to be modernized, almost as if it enjoyed its dilapidated status.

"Carl says he came out when he heard me hit the ground. He's the one who called 911." Nick looked off into the distance, and if trying to see a memory that was hidden from view. Crystal got up from the chair, and moved to the side of the bed where she took his hand, patting it lightly. Her pale blonde hair swung over her shoulder in a shimmering cascade which always reminded Amy of a waterfall. Concern filled her dark blue-green eyes.

Nick's focus sharpened, and he looked back at Amy, a rueful expression on his face. "Sorry honey, I just don't know what distracted me. Maybe a bat? We've had a couple get in recently. I've had the pest control people out, but they can't seem to find any access points. It doesn't make sense." Nick shrugged, and then seemed to banish the question from his mind.

"How long are you planning on staying?" Crystal asked, looking at her daughter. "You said in your message that you'd be able to help out at the shop for a little while, until your dad is able to get back up and running."

Amy felt the rock in her stomach tighten and she caught herself chewing on her lower lip and running her free hand through her short curly brown hair. She forced herself to drop her arm, but it was too late. Her mother gave her a worried look, and Nick was studying her intently. This was the moment she had been dreading, explaining to the parental units the recent changes in her life.

"Uh, actually, I can stay as long as needed. I don't work for Gila Geologic Consultants any longer. I turned in my resignation last week." Amy cringed, knowing that a barrage of questions would descend on her in a matter of seconds.

Instead of questions, however, there was complete silence which seemed to stretch on for an eternity in Amy's mind. Finally Nick cleared his throat, and glanced at his wife. Crystal met Nick's look and nodded slightly, that invisible communication that existed between two people so close to each other coming into play. Then Crystal looked at Amy, care evident in her gaze.

"Okay, honey, what happened? You must have had a good reason."

"Several when it comes down to it, but mainly there was a problem with the big dam project in northern Arizona. A key feature was missed, or... well, it wasn't disclosed in the geological survey of the construction site. So a huge, multimillion dollar dam was built and now, less than two years later it's cracking. There is a lawsuit pending and I got thrown under the bus so hard that I still have the tire tracks on my butt."

"Then you fight it. If you didn't do anything wrong... if it wasn't your mistake, then you don't accept responsibility. Who was the supervisor for the project? Who were the team members? Why aren't they on the hook?" Nick's face was clouded with anger and his voice was harsh. He, better than anyone, knew what a reputation was worth in this business.

More than anything in the world Amy didn't want to answer Nick's question, but she knew there was no avoiding it.

"Jeff was the senior member of the team, and Dean was supervisor."

Jeff. Jeffery Donaldson. Currently Junior VP at Gila Geologic Consultants. When Amy started working at the company, he worked with her on the huge Elk Canyon dam project. On top of that, he was Amy's boyfriend... *well, ex-boyfriend now. Damned if I ever want to speak with him again.* Dean Donaldson was his father. Hard to say which one engineered the cover up, or even why it was engineered in the first place. Amy suspected pressure or kickbacks from higher up in the construction hierarchy, since it would have added significantly to the cost to move the dam site up the river, but would someone have been so stupid as to want to gamble that the dam would be fine and pay off the inspectors? It really didn't make sense to her. Yet her name was on the report, and as she remembered it, Jeff had kindly let her sign as the lead... her first big project with Gila Geologic.

"That sorry...!" Nick started to push himself upright, as though he was going to try and get out of bed in spite of his leg. Crystal put her hand on Nick's shoulder, and he settled back, although Amy could still see the tenseness in his jaw indicating how angry he was.

"What are you going to do now?" Crystal asked. "What about the apartment? Is he still living there?"

"Yes, he is. I'm not. I've moved out and packed my stuff into storage. The management was willing to take me off the lease for a small fee. I don't care what Jeff does now. He's on his own. You've got me as long as you need me." Amy's chin lifted in defiance.

Crystal looked at her daughter, and then shook her head slightly. "Okay, Amy. You still have the key to the house, right?" Amy nodded. "Good. There are fresh linens on your bed."

"It will be good to get you in the store, Amethyst. I'm not sure I trust Carl to run things by himself. That man doesn't know obsidian from agate for pete's sake," Nick grumbled, obviously still upset by her tale.

Amy laughed, and the tension in the room broke. "I don't know why you keep him, Dad. He's pretty hopeless as far as the specimens go."

"He's great at maintaining the online presence of the store. You know, photographing the specimens, putting up listings, making sure that the shipments go out. If I see something, he makes sure we get it at a decent price. He's just got no sense when it comes to the stones themselves. It doesn't seem to sink in. It doesn't matter too much when I'm there. You'll be able to take care of that part of the business until I get back. Just don't go buying any fancy pieces without talking to me first." Nick grinned at Amy, knowing her obsession with rare specimens.

"No promises, old man. What time do I need to be at work in the morning?"

Seven o'clock the next morning Amy pulled her Wrangler into a parking spot in front of Stone's Gems and Minerals. Turning the key, Amy studied the facade of the building. It was nothing fancy; old wood and dated brick, with a solid front wall and no windows to be seen. It was a two-story building, but built with a four-sided hipped roof and dormers, the actual eves at the level that would exist for a single story structure. Huge bushes of climbing roses brushed those eves on either side of the front door. Amy had always loved those roses, and the scent that blew into the shop every time the door opened during the blooming season.

On each side of the small rock shop were cute faux adobe structures catering to the increasing tourist trade. To the left was a small strip mall that billed itself as a "trading post," fronted by a large parking lot. Several years before, some enterprising business men bought a huge tract of land just outside the Hualapai Reservation, and built a large campground and RV Park. With the increasing interest in traveling 'Historic Route 66,' as well as other various attractions, the developers counted on campers and other travelers visiting the area in greater numbers. The building to the other side of Nick's shop was another modern adobe-style building, housing an art gallery and a high end jewelry store. For years Nick had been fighting the town of Copper Springs which felt that his little shop brought down the tone of the neighborhood. Nick always won, but Amy wondered for how much longer. The scruffy exterior of Stone's Gems and Minerals certainly didn't fit in with the new buildings going up in the area.

Amy felt the thrill she always got when visiting the little

shop. As a girl, spending time in the small, cave-like store had always felt like visiting another, subterranean world, and even as an adult she'd never lost that feeling. She opened the door to the Wrangler and climbed out, whistling to Jynx, her Australian shepherd border collie cross, to follow. Amy was walking to the single glass door in the middle of the front wall, fishing in her front pocket for Nick's key ring, when she heard another vehicle drive up. Jynx, who had been sniffing at the bases of the rose bushes uttered a soft bark and froze. Turning, Amy saw a small, two seated sports car, modified and lifted for rough roads, pull into the parking area. A tall, almost scarecrow looking man opened the bright yellow door of the coup and climbed out, making Amy think of an origami crane unfolding itself in the process.

Carl.

Great, Amy thought, a little bit of her excitement dissipating. She'd been looking forward to exploring some of the store's recent acquisitions for an hour or so without Carl's mosquito-like voice buzzing in her ear. What had persuaded the man to come in early today of all days? Nick might have a lot of reasons for hiring Carl, but he'd always given her the creeps. Not only did he have an obsequious air which caused her to grind her teeth, but he couldn't tell one stone from another most of the time.

These days, and with a business like Stone's Gems and Minerals, an online presence was vital. A town the size of Copper Springs simply didn't have the population to support a shop like her dad's, even during the tourist season. Hence Carl. Nick hired him for his computer and photography skills, ability to maintain the website with all the current stock, sift through and maintain online auctions, as well as take and ship orders. It was the kind of detail work that tended to drive Nick up the wall in Amy's experience.

Years ago, when Nick first retired from the Forest Service and opened the shop, it had been solely a rock shop, carrying various display specimens, large polished bookends, spheres and other decorative pieces made of natural rocks and crystals. Many of the items he'd created himself in the large workshop behind the family house outside town. Amy remembered sitting in the shop as a little girl, watching Nick turn a large rough piece of amethyst geode into a smooth, beautiful sphere, the druse, or crystal, creating a rough canyon through the center. She still treasured that piece, and it always sat in a place of honor wherever she lived. She could picture him carefully shaping the cube, and then cutting the edges over and over again. Next came the grinding and the polishing. Few understood the amount of work that went into that simple shape, and with the influx of cheap spheres and other shapes from countries which used child labor, few understood the cost in time involved.

Stone's Gems and Minerals wasn't just a rock shop, however. Nick had made sure to stock the equipment needed to create these items as well, and over time it became the "go to" spot for the numerous rock hounds in the area, as well as popular for the tourists traveling down Route 66 in Arizona. Gradually Nick had added a section with stone and mineral beads and jewelry findings, partially under pressure from his daughter Opal, who frequently told him that he needed to expand his customer base.

"Hey, Amy. Good morning! It's great to have you here!" Carl's high, nasally voice piped, making Amy's skin crawl. She felt the irrational urge to knock him alongside the head. Still, he was her father's employee. She might not care for the guy, but hopefully she wouldn't have to deal with him for long.

"Hi Carl, it's good to see you. How's it been going?" Amy could feel the fake smile plastered across her face tighten to the point that she thought her cheeks might break.

"Not bad, not bad," he grinned at her, the annoying bleached soul patch wiggling below his lip like a fuzzy caterpillar. "Other than Nick's accident, of course. Darned shame about that. Still, it's good to have you here. There was a query on that beautiful blue, gold and red pietersite sphere, and I wasn't sure how to respond."

Amy felt her stomach clench. Some of the specimens in her father's shop were rare and valuable. The exceptionally large chatoyant pietersite sphere in question was valued well over a thousand dollars.

"You didn't sell or buy anything did you?" The question came out strangled, and Amy felt like her chest was being squeezed in a vise. Nick wasn't totally joking when he'd told Amy not to buy any fancy pieces without talking to him first. Some of the rarer minerals and meteorites could run into the thousands or tens of thousands, and if she bought a counterfeit accidentally, or sold something too cheap, or, heaven forbid, dropped and broke a rare piece, it could cost the shop a bundle. Even worse would be the blow to the shop's reputation, and in the world of gem and mineral collectors, reputation was everything.

"Nah. There was just a guy in asking about that sphere, wanting to know about its history and where it came from. What's that term? Its provenance? I wrote his name and number down. It's inside. Nick was pretty adamant that he didn't want any of the big display pieces sold without letting him know first." Carl smiled at Amy apparently oblivious to her agitation.

The vise released, and Amy was able to take a deep breath again. She cleared her throat and turned back to the door. Sliding the large brass key into the lock, she turned it and pulled the heavy door open. Jynx slid past her and into the dark expanse beyond the hall. Carl had moved up behind her, grabbed the edge of the door and held it for Amy to pass through.

"Uh, thanks, Carl." Amy tried to subdue the internal squirm at Carl's proximity and hurried through the door and down a short hall into the dark interior of the store. Several emergency lights did little to illuminate the space, and Amy groped along the left-hand wall for the bank of three switches. The wall, as usual, was covered with various items hung on display and the light switches eluded her for a moment. Finally she hit on the switch plate, and threw all three on at once. A soft light bathed the main showroom of the store.

Amy stood for a moment and looked around. She shook her head, torn between exasperation and love. The front room of Stone's Gem's and Minerals looked as though an earthquake hit... repeatedly... followed by a hurricane and maybe a tornado. Boxes were stacked upon boxes. Shelves lined the walls and were layered thick with display trays filled with various specimens of crystals and semiprecious stones. There was no way anyone could find anything in here, yet Nick always knew exactly where each piece was located and could tell a customer everything he or she might want to know.

"Sort of a disaster, huh?" Carl had come up behind Amy and was looking over her shoulder. Amy moved to the side and Carl walked into the room. "I have no idea how on earth Nick ever finds anything in here, but if someone comes in and asks for labradorite slabs, he can lay his hands on them in a matter of minutes. Absolutely amazing!" Carl grinned at her, and then headed toward the small office which housed the computers and shipping materials.

Amy smiled to herself. When she was younger coming to the shop always held the aura of going on a treasure hunt. She looked around again. Of course, back then, when the shop was new, there weren't nearly as many boxes or shelves, she thought ruefully. If she had to guess, there were probably unopened treasures from the first year the shop was open. How Nick ever managed to do an inventory, she had no idea.

Amy glanced at her watch: Seven-fifteen. The store opened at eight, so she had a little time to reacquaint herself with the place. Over the last ten years, ever since she'd graduated from Northern Arizona University and went to work for Gila Geologics, she'd only been home on short visits. She'd always made time for the shop when in town, and at times had met her father at various rock shows around the state, as well as in the neighboring states of California and Nevada. However, she hadn't spent any concentrated time here, and was feeling the need of a refresher course.

According to the history that Nick received when he bought the building, Stone's Gems and Minerals used to be a "speakeasy" back in the day. Amy could imagine the small dark building as a bar. In fact, if rumor was correct, somewhere in the building was the entrance to a tunnel, used when the revenuers raided during prohibition. Amy and her siblings had searched and searched, but had never been able to locate it. She shivered slightly at the memory.

In spite of its past, Nick had made the building his own.

On either side of the front door stretched long, thin offices, taking up the entire front wall of the shop. Back when the building was first built, these long thin rooms housed the bar. Now they housed the computer office, Nick's private office, to the right of the front door. On the left, behind the counter, was a small storage area where Nick kept some of the more valuable items, such as the silver and gold jewelry findings and wire, as well as faceted gemstones. He also had a small, lighted table there where he could work on projects while waiting for customers to venture in for a visit.

The main showroom of the store was a huge L-shape, and was stacked with smaller pieces. The long leg of the L also held all the rock working equipment such as saws and polishers, while in the short leg of the L, the one running parallel to the front of the building, hung every type of natural stone and semiprecious bead imaginable. Every square inch was taken up with strands in a multitude of colors, and what wouldn't fit on the walls or the central partition was piled in various display trays piled on the shelves or the floor. Nick's philosophy was "no flat spot shall go uncluttered" from what Amy could see.

The back right corner of the shop was Amy's favorite room, and she headed back there, eager to see what Nick had added to the collection since the last time she'd visited. In this one room there was slightly more order, although Amy emphasized the word "slightly" in her mind. Once again the lighting was soft, and the walls painted a dark gray. But in this room the walls were lined with glass cabinets and shelving, each with their own lighting source. Inside rested all the larger specimens, natural crystals, spheres, sculptures and bookends. In Amy's mind, it was this room that made the rock shop, Stone's Gems and Minerals.

At the extreme back of the building, covering the entire width, was the store room, and the back entrance of the store. Amy studied the front room, seeing the ridge in the ceiling between the legs of the L, where the outflow from the air conditioner was located. It was there that Nick had his accident. She looked around, trying to imagine what could have distracted him to the point that he'd fallen. Nothing that she could see. Dark gray walls, subdued lighting for the most part. The ceiling wasn't high and the acoustic tiles had been stained by years of persistent leaks.

I guess a bat or two could have gotten in. They wouldn't be easy to see if they got under the tiles. Amy looked up. Really, Nick needed to do something. It seemed like the shop was in an even more decrepit state than usual. She'd have to get the pest control people in again, just to be sure. Nick would have noted which company he'd hired last time. It would be in his office, or maybe Carl would remember. Jynx was sniffing around the boxes sitting on the floor across from the main entrance, but from what Amy could tell, she was just simply curious, not on the trail of any unwanted creatures.

"Jynx, come here." The dog lifted her head and looked at Amy, then spun and ran across the room and sat expectantly at her feet, the intense border collie eyes fixed on her face. "Good girl, you're going to stay over here." Amy walked to the counter, and gestured for the dog to go past, behind the counter. There was an attached gate, which could be closed to block passage. Nick frequently brought his corgi, Bess, to work with him, and this was her spot. *She'll just have to share for a little while* Amy thought.

"You need to stay here Jynxie. No pass." Amy ran her hand across the top of the gate in a gesture Jynx knew well. It meant that was the border, and she was not to go by. The dog looked at her, and then went over to the foam dog bed and lay down, putting her chin on her crossed paws, eyes fixed on Amy's face, seemingly saying, *Yes Ma'am, awaiting further instructions.*

Amy turned and headed back to the computer office where Carl had gone a few minutes before. She stuck her head in the door and saw Carl busy on the desktop computer, studying the monitor intently.

"Hey Carl, do you happen to know which pest control company Nick used?"

Carl looked up, seemingly distracted. Then his focus sharpened. "Oh, hey Amy. What was it you needed? I was just checking on our current auctions. There are a couple ending today that are getting a pretty good bid run."

"Bidding or selling?" Amy asked. Even though Nick had forbidden her from buying any pieces without his input, and there was no way he would ever trust Carl to judge the true value of a piece, it was possible that they'd started watching one more than a week ago when Nick was still hale and hearty.

"Bidding on a couple of nice pieces. A gorgeous labradorite free form. Great blue, purple and gold flash on that one," Carl said, referring to labradorite's trademark reflection of light off surfaces within each stone. Since these surfaces varied from stone to stone, no two were exactly alike, and those differences made them very popular with collectors, as well as very expensive. "Labradorite always sells well, and Nick set his top price several days before he fell. The rest are selling. A few pieces that haven't been moving and with which Nick is willing to part." He grinned up at Amy, referring to Nick's tendency to get attached to certain pieces so that he pushed the price up, making it unlikely that anyone would buy it away from him. Of course, those few times that someone else fell in love with a piece, and offered him the asked for price, Nick was torn between accepting much more than the specimen was worth, but losing ownership, or keeping it and forfeiting an outrageous profit.

"What was it that you wanted, anyway?" Carl looked at Amy curiously.

"What was the name of the pest control company that Nick used? It's probably in his office, but you know what his paperwork is like."

Carl gave a wet chuckle that caused Amy's skin to crawl. *Maybe the pest control people can dispose of Carl as well. Urgh!*

"Yeah, I getcha. I think it was Valley Pest Removal. Think we've got something crawling around?"

"My dad said that something moved and distracted him. That's why he fell. I don't see or smell anything in here, but I think it would probably be a good idea to get things checked out."

"Sounds reasonable. Here, let me find the number for you." Carl turned back to his computer and hit some keys in quick succession, then grabbed a pen next to the keyboard and wrote a number down on a note pad, tore off the page and handed it to Amy. "Here you go. Hope they do a good job this time. The city has been after Nick about the condition of the place."

"Bad?" Amy looked around at the clutter. As much as she hated to admit it, the shop was beginning to look a little like a rock hound's version of "Hoarders."

"I hear that someone wants to put in a high end restaurant, but your dad won't sell. The way the story goes, some members of the town council are 'encouraging' him to move the business out so that the building can be torn down, and a more 'tourist friendly' business can be brought in. I don't know, maybe they're right. After all, more than fifty percent of the business is online anymore. My source says there's a lot of money involved. You'd be an heiress." Carl leered at Amy and she thought she'd gag on the spot. Her temper finally boiled over.

"Dammit Carl, knock it off! That is the most disgusting thing I've ever heard anyone say. Especially after Nick's accident. I don't care how much someone is offering for the shop, and neither do my brother and sister, and it's none of your business how much the place is worth anyway. I swear that if..."

The sound of the chime at the front door drifted in, and Amy whipped around to see Gladys Sanchez and Emily James standing there looking wide-eyed in shock at Amy's tirade. Amy took a deep breath, choked and started to cough. The look on Gladys' face started to shift from shock to concern, and she reached out to take Amy's arm.

"Are you okay dear? Just come over here and take a seat. Come on now." The older woman led Amy over to the stool in front of the counter and urged her to sit. Amy caught her breath and the coughing fit subsided.

"Thank you, Gladys. I'm so sorry you had to see that."

"It's fine honey, isn't it Em? I'm sure you're under a lot of stress with your father's injury. I... Oh my goodness!" Gladys gasped and took a step back from the counter as Jynx's head popped over the edge, paws on the glass surface.

"Sorry again Gladys. Jynx, get down. I'm okay. Everything

is okay." Amy gestured for Jynx to drop back behind the counter. Jynx gave Amy one final look, head tilted to one side, then pulled her paws off the glass and dropped back out of sight.

"It's just my dog, Jynx. Bess, Nick's corgi, is at home," Amy explained, feeling flustered. "I hope she didn't scare you too much." Amy looked up at Gladys, then at Emily. A stealthy movement pulled her attention away from the two women who were shaking their heads. Over Emily James' shoulder she could see the door to the computer office. Carl was standing there, watching the three women, a look of such hatred on his face that Amy felt herself shrivel inside. He must have noticed that her gaze had shifted from the women to him, and he quickly schooled his features into the bland aspect he usually presented to people, but Amy was sure of what she saw. Carl nodded at her once, and then returned into the office, quietly closing the door behind him.

Amy's attention returned to Gladys and Emily. In typical fashion, Gladys was buzzing away about how worried she'd been about Nick, and now about Amy, and was she all right. Periodically she'd make a comment, and then turn to her best friend and say, "Right, Em?" and Emily would nod silently. As long as Amy could remember, these two women had been some of Nick's best customers, maybe not monetarily, but support wise. They frequently bought jewelry-making supplies, and even more importantly, often recommended to others that they visit the shop. Since the two friends owned a small diner on Route 66 where it passed through Copper Springs, they often ran into new "friends" with whom they wanted to share the joys of Stone's Gems and Minerals. It helped that they had decorated the Copper Springs Diner with various mining and geology memorabilia.

"Uh, I'm sorry Gladys. What did you say?" Amy asked.

"I was just saying how concerned we were when we heard about your father's accident. How is he doing?"

"He seems to be doing okay. He's in Flagstaff still, but they're getting ready to move him to a rehab facility in a few days if things continue to go well. He'll hopefully be over in Kingman, but it could still be in Flag, or down in Prescott, but at least he won't be in the hospital."

"It's so wonderful that you're able to come and run the shop for him while he's laid up. Are you staying out at the ranch?"

Amy beat down an internal laugh. Her parents' place was in no way a ranch, only encompassing sixty acres, and housing a few cows and horses, but some people insisted on referring to it as though it was a huge spread consisting of thousands of acres.

"Yes, I'm staying out at the house. Saves Mom from worrying about having to get back and take care of things. She's planning on renting a short-term apartment in Kingman. Now, what can I do for you ladies?"

"Nothing, dear. Em and I were just going by and we saw your Jeep and wanted to say hello, didn't we Em?" Gladys beamed at Amy, and then glanced over at her friend, who nodded.

"We really must be running, though. Chastity Lyons, one of our high schoolers, opened this morning, and I'm sure that she could use some help. It was good seeing you, Amethyst. I'm glad you're home."

With that the two women turned and hurried out of the store, leaving Amy with the sentence, "I'm called A...." hanging unfinished. *Great, I'm never going to live down this damned name!* Amy sighed and got off the stool and stood next to the counter, looking at the closed door of the computer room. What was she going to do about Carl? She couldn't very well fire him, although that's exactly what she wanted to do. Besides, she was only going to be there a few months at the most, just until Nick was able to take over the reins again, and she was able to find a new job. Surely she could put up with him for that long.

"Well, Miss Jynxie, I'd better get the pest control company called, and then start familiarizing myself with the inventory. It's almost opening time." Jynx's head popped up from behind the counter and she uttered a soft woof... her indoor voice Amy had always called it.

Glancing at the agate clock hanging over the counter, she headed toward Nick's office. First things first. Set up the cash register, or what passed for a cash register in Nick's world, and then pest control. Maybe while she was at it, she could find out what was going on with the town this time, but the cash register definitely had to come first.

3

The day went by in a rush, and before Amy knew it, five o'clock had rolled around and she was locking the front door. Copper Springs had a booming tourist trade, and at the end of July it was in full swing. In between visitors, Amy started going through the various papers in Nick's office, looking for anything related to the town, or ordinance violations.

Nothing.

Amy wasn't too surprised. Nick's record keeping followed his own convoluted rules and she figured she'd be lucky to find much of anything in the expected locations. She did find an old inventory from several years before, which she figured gave her a starting point in figuring out what was in the store. More importantly, it gave her a starting point in pricing, since there were many things in boxes or trays that didn't have the price marked. If Amy knew what Nick had paid for the specimens, or the beads, then she could figure out what the price was supposed to be. Otherwise she'd have to call him each time a customer came in.

Amy sat at the desk, head in her hands, fingers clenched in her curly brown hair, dark violet eyes squeezed shut. A knock on the office door pulled her from the contemplation of Nick's organizational shortcomings. She looked up and saw Carl standing in the doorway. They hadn't spoken since that morning. In fact, he'd barely set foot out of the computer office, only emerging for lunch, and to use the bathroom occasionally. Now he was staring at her with a wary look on his face, as though he expected her to erupt like a volcano at the slightest provocation.

"Yes, Carl. Can I help you?"

"I'm going to take off now. It's after five. There are a couple of auctions we've got bids in on that don't close until later, but I'll monitor them from home on the laptop." He gestured down at the computer case he was carrying over his shoulder. Amy remembered Nick complaining that Carl had convinced him to buy a laptop for just such situations. Nick did it, seeing the necessity, but he hated anything that took him further from the point of action, since he didn't trust Carl. They had a strict understanding that only those things Nick okayed would be bid on, and only to the amount he said was acceptable, but there was one time when Carl thought he was doing Nick a favor, and bought a very expensive piece of rutilated quartz, a clear quartz with small hair-like structures inside, only to find out that it was a glass copy. Even the fact that they were able to dispute the purchase and return the item didn't help soften the blow much.

"No problem, Carl. Thank you. Maybe some time I could take the 'evening shift' so you don't always have to worry about it. I know Nick didn't like the auctions, but I don't mind taking care of them at times." Amy looked up at Carl and was surprised so see almost a look of panic cross his face.

"No, that's fine Amy. I appreciate it, but I enjoy the auctions." Carl forced a laugh, but hugged the computer case even closer to his side, as if he were afraid that Amy would rip it out of his hands. Amy looked at him in confusion.

"Okay," Amy dragged the word out with uncertainty. "I don't want to step on your toes. I know when Nick hired you a couple of years ago it was specifically for your technical expertise, but surely you want some evenings off."

Carl relaxed marginally, although he seemed to remain wary. "It's not every night. Actually it only happens a couple of times a month, but really I'm fine. Nick said he really wasn't interested in posting or watching auctions, especially on the different platforms which are out there now. It's what I'm paid for, you know." Carl laughed again, but it seemed no more real than the first time.

"I guess if that's what you want to do." Amy yawned and stood. "I suppose I'll take off too. Have a good evening, Carl. I'll see you tomorrow."

Carl nodded, then gripping the computer case tight to his side; he turned and hurried out of the front door. A few seconds later Amy could hear the roar of the sports car starting, and the squeal of tires as it pulled out of the parking area.

"Well alrighty then. I don't like being around you much either," Amy muttered to herself as she walked over to the counter.

"Are you ready to head home, Jynx?"

The dog lifted her head from where it had been resting on her crossed front paws. Her golden brown eyes met Amy's dark violet ones. She scrambled to her feet and walked to the gate which Amy had opened for her.

"Okay, Jynxie. Come through." Amy gestured that Jynx could come through the barrier that was previously in place. The dog walked out into the shop and stopped to sniff at some of the boxes. "Just let me put the cashbox away, and we'll get going."

Amy grabbed the steel box, and headed back to the office where she locked it into Nick's private safe. She glanced at the general safe, the one Carl had access to, then decided that since she would be there in the morning, there was no reason to leave the box in that one.

Nick's idea of a "cash register" actually involved a cashbox and a calculator, as well as numerous pads of receipts bought from the Walmart in Kingman. When he was there, he generally removed all but a hundred dollars in small bills and change from the cashbox each night, and put the reminder in an envelope to go to the bank. Unless it was an exceptionally busy day and he needed to replenish the change, he usually only made a deposit run once or twice a week.

If Nick knew that Carl would be opening in the morning, he would leave the cashbox in the general safe, but the remainder of the money would go into the private safe. Over the past six days, however, since Nick had been injured, the amount of money in the general safe had built up to the point that Amy was feeling antsy about getting into a more secure location.

"Too late now," she told herself, looking at the clock. "First thing in the morning for sure." At least the majority of their customers paid by either debit or credit card. Thank goodness for plastic, she thought.

Cashbox stashed away for the night, Amy called to Jynx, and headed for the front door, dog close on her heels. She hit the switches on the way by, returning the store to the ineffectual emergency illumination, and proceeded out the small hall created by the computer office on the left and the space behind the counter on the right. Pushing open the heavy glass door, she heard the cheerful tinkle of the wind chime which hung from the hinges. She smiled. That sound always made her feel like she was home.

"Come on, Jynx, let's go to the diner. I'll even spring for a burger for you. I don't feel like cooking tonight." Jynx bounded past Amy and headed for the driver's side door of the Wrangler. Owing to the warm July temperatures, and a weather report that said the monsoons were in abeyance, Amy had left the cover down on the Jeep. Jynx didn't wait for Amy to come around and open the door, but instead jumped up over the side and took her spot on the passenger side.

Amy smiled and shook her head at the same time. She swore that if Jynx was given a set of keys, she'd be the one driving, and Amy would be relegated to riding shotgun.

"Fine. I guess I'm too slow, huh? Well just too bad for you." Amy opened the door and slid in behind the wheel, pushed in the clutch and started the vehicle, then reversed out of the parking spot and headed down Route 66 to the Copper Springs Diner. One of their 'world famous' Route 66 burgers and their delicious home fries would totally hit the spot before she headed out to the empty house on the edge of town.

The parking lot in front of the Copper Springs Diner was half filled with a wide variety of license plates, attached to an even wider variety of vehicles. While Copper Springs boasted a couple of chain restaurants, many of the tourists were drawn by the 50s era diner. Still, it appeared as though there was plenty of room, and besides Gladys and Em would always find a seat for the daughter of their favorite rock purveyor.

Amy pulled into an empty spot several rows out from the front of the diner, and climbed out of the Jeep. "Jynx, you wait here, okay?" Amy shut the door and walked toward the front of the building, knowing that as soon as she was out of sight in the building the dog would curl up on the driver's seat and refuse to budge until Amy's return. Both Australian shepherds and border collies were considered to be at the top of the list intelligence wise, and Jynx right there with the best of them. Sometimes, Amy thought, she was almost too smart. Still, it was nice not having to worry about the dog when Amy wasn't there. If she could just teach Jynx to answer the phone, everything would be perfect.

The sign on the door said "Copper Springs Diner" in swirly gold and black type. Beneath that it boldly declared itself to be "Arizona's only Five Spur Establishment" with five little gold and silver spurs painted at the bottom. Amy always got a laugh out of that legend. She pushed open the door then stepped back, and held it for a young family on their way out, arms filled with sleeping children. Amy smiled and nodded at the couple, then released the door, and turned to survey the diner, taking in the eclectic mixture of 50s retro and old time mining and mineral specimens. It was a decorating style that shouldn't work... and didn't, but the diner was always busy, and no one seemed to mind that there was a ceramic Elvis statue sitting next to a large amethyst geode with a rusty pickaxe head resting behind.

Amy surveyed the diner, and finally decided on a stool at the end of the counter, versus sitting at one of the booths. As she walked across the black and white checked linoleum, she glanced around the room, trying to see if anyone she knew was there. No one that she noticed. *Oh well,* she thought, *I guess I'll be eating alone tonight.* Still, it gave her some time to think.

Amy had just slid into a spot at the end of the counter when she heard her name called out from across the room. She turned to look toward the voice, and saw a tall, thin woman, her black hair and dark rose brown skin speaking to her native heritage. A huge smile grew on Amy's face.

"Hey Maria! How are you?" Amy slipped off the stool

and walked across the room and gave her friend a huge hug.

"I'm doing great, Amy. I heard you were coming back into town for a while. Sorry about your dad. How's he feeling?" Maria Kissoon's face took on a concerned expression.

"He's doing really well from what I can see." Amy grinned at Maria. "You know him, he's having fun messing with the nurses' heads, and getting antsy to get out of there. They're hoping to get him into a rehab facility in Kingman in the next couple of days. So what have you been doing? Are you here visiting your folks?"

"No, I moved here, as a matter of fact. I've opened my own office."

Maria Kissoon and Amy had been close friends throughout school, and both had gone to Northern Arizona University in Flagstaff, but while Amy had been called by the Earth, Maria had been called by the law and transferred to the University of Arizona Law School her fourth year.

"There's enough business here for you?"

"There's enough. Besides, I wanted to be closer to my folks. Dad hasn't been doing well lately, and Mom's really struggling with his Alzheimer's. I'm closer here than I would be in any of the larger cities. Still it's a lot of work being in independent practice. Speaking of which, I've got an early meeting tomorrow morning. Give me a call and we'll get together." Maria pulled out her cell, and the two women went through the modern 'handshake' of exchanging numbers, then Maria hurried out the door, waving as she left.

Smiling to herself, Amy headed back toward her stool.

"Amethyst, dear, I'm so glad you stopped by! What can we get you?"

Amy looked up to see Gladys, a huge smile plastered to her face and a large white apron wrapped around her middle. "Hi Gladys, I decided that I wasn't up to cooking tonight. Can I get a Route 66 burger and fries for me, and two plain patties for my furry friend in the Jeep?"

"Certainly dear." Gladys scribbled something on the pad she pulled from her apron pocket, then turned and handed it through the pass-through into the kitchen, where Emily took it, glanced down, then waved out the window at Amy.

"I see the two of you haven't slowed down any. When are you going to turn the diner over to your employees?"

Gladys looked offended. "We're no older than your father, you know. Besides, working keeps us young. Right, Em?" Gladys looked back over her shoulder to the pass-through. Emily poked her head through the small gap and waved at Amy, another big smile on her face.

"Besides, we're short handed today. Mike had to go home early to deal with a sick child, and two of our waitresses are out, so we're filling in. We'll probably close a bit early unless Mike comes back to man the kitchen after his wife gets home."

"Ah, that explains it," Amy nodded. Mike Tilousi was the diner's main cook. When the women had first bought the diner, after their retirement from the Copper Springs Unified School District, Emily did all the cooking and baking. The Copper Springs Diner quickly became known for its amazing pies, good food, huge portions, and reasonable prices; in that order. However, after several years of success they hired Mike to take over most of the kitchen duties, except for the pies. Emily had a lock on those and never let anyone help. A series of high school students rotated through the diner as waitresses, but Gladys maintained a firm hold on the reins. Still, as the women got older, they tended to embrace a slightly looser work schedule. As well as the embracing the proximity to Laughlin and Las Vegas.

Amy looked around the room. "I see you've added some new specimens to the collection. That's a pretty amazing piece of turquoise over there." Amy gestured at a glass case where an exceptionally large piece of robin's egg blue stone with a spider web matrix of brown rock sat next to a model Studebaker of approximately the same color.

"Isn't it beautiful. It's Skystone Mine," Gladys said, her voice clearly displaying her love for the mineral. "Look at this one here." She gestured toward another piece, nearly as large, but this time the blue ran through a golden brown matrix, the type of turquoise Amy always preferred.

"Gorgeous. Dad didn't tell me he'd gotten anything like this into the shop. Where on earth did you find any old

Skystone turquoise? You're not two timing him with another rock dealer are you?" She laughed at the sly expression on Gladys' face.

"A lady should never disclose her sources." Gladys winked at her, and hustled off to fill the water glasses of several other customers, and clean the table from another family who had left.

While waiting for her food, Amy pulled out her cell and checked some of her messages. There wasn't much. Most of her life in Phoenix had been centered around Jeff, and with him gone, so were all the friends that came with him. There was an email from her sister, Opal, who lived with her husband and two kids in Quartzsite, down off I-10 not far from the California border. Typical Opie stuff, asking how Nick was doing, saying they might make it up that weekend to Kingman, if he was in the rehab facility by then. Nothing from Jas, her brother Jasper, but then he was pretty busy this time of year, and never was the most reliable communicator at the best of times.

"Here you are, honey. Enjoy." Gladys slipped the plate under Amy's nose, and the delicious aroma attacked her senses.

"Thank you Gladys, it smells wonderful. I haven't had anything but a granola bar since breakfast, and I hadn't realized how hungry I was." Amy shoved the phone into her pocket, and reached for the burger.

"The ketchup and mustard are right here, as well as salt if you need it." Gladys slid a couple of squeeze containers of condiments down the counter closer to Amy.

"You know I don't need anything when you've got your special Route 66 Sauce on it. When are you going to tell me the recipe? Those of us not lucky enough to live in Copper Springs are dying to have it at home, you know."

"Em won't tell anyone the recipe for the sauce, right Em?" Gladys looked back toward the pass-through, where Emily was smiling at Amy. She nodded, and then disappeared from view.

"Well, then I'll just have to keep coming in frequently while I'm here, and try and soak up as much as I can."

"You just do that, honey. We love seeing you." With that Gladys bustled off on another round of water replenishment and table bussing. Amy chuckled to herself. She didn't know where Emily and Gladys came from, but she guessed there weren't too many more like them anywhere on the planet. Amy's stomach growled, reminding her how hungry she was, and she tucked into her burger and fries, sure that there wasn't anything, anywhere on the planet as good as this meal, not even Nick's hospital Jell-O.

About forty-five minutes later, stomach filled to bursting, Amy emerged from the diner, carrying two Styrofoam boxes, one with Jynx's hamburger patties, and the other with an obscenely large slice of homemade strawberry rhubarb pie, forced on her by Emily. At least Amy liked to pretend it was forced on her. It made her feel slightly more virtuous know-ing that she hadn't ordered it, even if she'd been sitting star-ing at it for fifteen minutes, trying to convince herself that she truly had room after her meal. She didn't, but that didn't stop Emily from popping it into a takeout box and pushing it into Amy's hands. Emily knew her a little too well.

Amy opened the Jeep's door and slid behind the wheel. Jynx pushed in, nose sniffing double-time, knowing that there was something in one of those boxes with her name on it.

"Jynx, get back. You get yours when we get home. No eat-ing in the car. You know that." Amy reached up and scratched the dog's ears. "No grease on the expensive upholstery, you know." Amy laughed at the joke, since the Wrangler's up-holstery, while clean, was certainly not new, and frequently covered in dog hair.

Amy started the Wrangler and pulled out of the park-ing spot, then turned right onto the highway, heading for her parent's house outside town. Traffic was light, even though there was still plenty of light left to the day. About a mile down the road, she saw Stone's Gem's and Minerals squat-ting like a toad between the two newer and shinier buildings on either side. To her surprise, Carl's sports car was parked out in front again, and she could dimly see the lights on in the shop itself. For a moment she thought about stopping to check on him, then decided that he'd probably just forgotten something when he left. He'd said that there were a couple of auctions that would be running late. Besides, she didn't want her feelings about Carl to curdle her burger and fries. She'd find out what he was doing in the morning.

Monsoon storms hit late that night, waking Amy from sleep. For a little while it seemed as though the entire world was being torn apart. Lightning and thunder were nearly continuous, and the wind, rain and hail lashed the side of the house. The noise made sleep impossible, and Amy finally got up and went to do some storm watching through the large living room windows.

When Nick and Crystal moved to the sixty acres outside Copper Springs, there were no buildings. The family of five lived for a while in an ancient motor home, giving togetherness a whole new meaning. Gradually over time they had built the various portions of what was now the house. First came the basement, and the family was able to move from the motor home to the subterranean structure. Then, as they could afford it, they built upwards, their efforts eventually resulting in the large granite and log house where Amy currently sat.

It was nearly an hour before the storm burned itself out, and as the thunder rumbled off into the distance, Amy felt herself drift off to sleep.

Amy opened her eyes to a silver gray dawn. *Crap,* she groaned, *I'm getting too old to sleep in a recliner!* She sat up gingerly, stretching muscles that were cramped from her unaccustomed sleeping position. She heard a quick shuffle of sound and glanced over toward the hallway that led back toward the kitchen and lower bedrooms. Jynx had taken refuge in the basement during the storm itself, but now she was back above ground and interested in the world.

"So, back up here to protect me, huh, you big weenie?"

No response, just the border collie gaze which occasionally made Amy itch with discomfort.

"Okay, I'm sorry. I shouldn't have called you names. It was loud last night." Amy stretched and got out of the chair, at which point Jynx bounded to her feet and ran to the side door.

Hearing a commotion, Bess, her parents' corgi who had been sleeping somewhere in the back of the house, came running down the hall, and cannoned into Amy's legs, knocking her off balance momentarily.

"Hey Bessie, I don't suppose *you* snuck off down to the basement did you. Come on." Amy went to the door and let both dogs out into the fenced yard. Her folks may have built out in the country, but the yard was to protect the dogs as much as to keep them confined. Coyotes had been well known to lure domestic dogs out, away from the protection of their owners, where the pack would then kill them. Nick and Crystal didn't believe in losing one of their dogs due to carelessness.

Amy glanced at the clock, and figured she had about two hours before she should be at the shop. Plenty of time for a shower and breakfast, then off for another day of fun and games with Carl. She was really going to have to talk with her dad about him, especially if Nick was going to be laid up for very long.

Amy pulled up in front of Stone's Gems and Minerals shortly after seven o'clock with both Jynx and Bess in tow, and was surprised to see Carl's yellow sports car back in the parking lot again. She frowned, *Huh? Burning the candle at both ends, Carl? I guess those auctions were something.*

She opened the door to the Wrangler, and held it so that both dogs could jump out, then whistled to them as she headed for the front door. She glanced over at the convertible as she was walking, then paused, an alarm going off in her head. Yesterday Carl had the top down, but it rained last night, and looked like more rain today. Surely he hadn't left it down.

Changing direction, she walked over to the car, and looked in. Water pooled on the seats and floor mats. A lot of water. Amy felt a knot of concern growing in her chest. She looked behind the car. There were no tire marks in the gravel and dirt parking lot. She looked over toward her own vehicle to confirm her suspicions, and sure enough, evidence of her arrival was pressed into the wet ground. Carl's car had been here all night. But why? Surely if he fell asleep at his computer, the storm would have woken him and he would have come out to put up the convertible's top. Maybe he had car trouble, and left it here, but didn't put the top up because he didn't think it was going to rain. Not too likely, considering it was monsoon season in Arizona.

Suddenly the sound of barking interrupted her train of thought, and she turned to look toward the front of the building. Both Jynx and Bess were barking at the front door, the small corgi throwing herself at the glass as if trying to break through. The knot in Amy's chest expanded exponentially, nearly causing her to choke.

She took a step, then hesitated. Should she call 911? Copper Springs didn't have its own police force, but they contracted with the Mohave County Sheriff's Department. Amy started to fish in her pocket for her phone, the stopped again. What would she tell them? That her dogs were barking at the front door of the business and her employee had been careless and left the top down on his convertible. *Well,* she thought, *the damage done to that beautiful car is a crime, but not one that will interest the sheriff's department.*

She shoved the phone back into her pocket, and walked to the door. The dogs quieted at her approach, but Jynx continued to whine quietly, eyes fixed on something inside that Amy couldn't see. She reached out and pulled the door handle.

Locked.

"Well it should be, shouldn't it?" Amy said to herself. She set down her backpack and pulled out her keys. She went through the ones on the ring, and separated the big brass key that went to the front door. She started to fit the key into the lock, then noticed that her hands were shaking.

"Stop it!" Amy muttered to herself. "Just stop it. There's nothing to be so freaked out about." She took a deep breath, shoved the key into the lock, turned it and pulled the door open. Jynx and Bess pushed past her and ran into the dark interior of the store. Amy paused, but couldn't hear anything but the jangling of the tags on the dogs' collars.

"Carl? Carl, are you there?" Nothing.

Amy walked the few steps down the hall, and reached around the corner for the bank of light switches. This time she found them immediately, and flipped them up, illuminating the shop. Amy froze, hand on the switches. Even the soft lighting couldn't hide the disarray... or the body lying in the middle of the room.

Jynx and Bess were sniffing around it, stepping in the blood that had puddled on the carpeted floor, turning it dark. Amy felt the rock in her stomach grip even tighter. "Jynx, Bess, come." Amy could hear her voice squeaking, higher than normal. The dogs looked up at her and then left the body and ran to Amy. She ushered them both behind the counter and closed the gate, telling them not to pass.

Dogs secured, she approached the body. No signs of life, but she squatted and reached for the neck to be sure. No pulse and the skin was cold. Carl was dead. It had to be Carl, although it was hard to tell. Still, the bleached yellow fuzzy caterpillar that was his soul patch, was now a red fuzzy caterpillar. Amy felt her stomach make a leap for her throat and she stood and backed away quickly, groping for her phone.

She punched in 911, and was connected with the sheriff's office in Kingman. The dispatcher promised that a deputy was on the way, and to please wait outside the building for his arrival. Amy looked at the dogs waiting behind the counter. They'd been next to the body... almost on top of it. Could they have evidence on them. If so, she should leave them here? She really didn't want to leave them alone in the shop with the body, however.

Finally she decided it couldn't matter, she wasn't going anywhere, and she opened the gate, and called the dogs. Even though they wanted to go back into the shop, toward Carl, she hustled them out the door and to the Jeep. Amy knew Jynx would stay in the vehicle unless told she could get out. She just hoped that Nick had trained Bess the same way. Looking at the blonde and white face and pricked ears of the corgi peeping over the door of the Jeep, she had her doubts, but maybe at least the dog had enough survival instinct not to launch herself from such a high vantage point. She had doubts about that as well, but decided she really didn't have a choice right now. She couldn't really take Bess back out to the house at the moment.

Amy was sitting in the Jeep, trying to keep her mind off the body in the shop when the refrain from Queen's *We Will Rock You* blared out of her cell phone. It was Nick. What was she going to tell him? Amy thought for a moment before answering. Maybe she should just let it go to voice mail. He might think she was with a customer. She glanced at the time on the phone. Nope, the shop still had five minutes before it opened.

Gritting her teeth, she punched the green phone icon on the screen.

"Uh, Hi Dad. How are you doing?" Amy cringed at her words. She sounded so lame she knew that Nick would figure there was something going on.

There was a pause at the other end of the call, then Nick's deep voice came booming through, causing Amy to hold the phone out away from her ear. She didn't know why, but Nick always sounded as though he were yelling into the receiver, and she usually forgot to turn down the volume when she first answered the phone.

"Amethyst? What's wrong? And don't tell me nothing. I can hear it in your voice."

"I don't want you to worry Dad, but something happened at the shop last night. Something pretty bad, but I've got it handled. How are you doing? Any word on the move?"

"Yes, that's why I was calling. They're shipping me out to the Canyon View Rehab Facility in Kingman later this morning. Now what's going on? Has there been a break-in?"

"Opie will be glad to hear it. She said she, Bob and the

kids would come up and visit once you got settled. I'll let her know what's happening and..."

"Amethyst, what's going on!" From the sound of Nick's voice, she knew she couldn't delay any longer.

"There's been an..." Amy started to say accident, but then stopped herself. There was no way that the damage to Carl's head and face could be anything but deliberate. "Something happened last night, Dad, and Carl's dead."

Silence.

Amy began to wonder if the cell phone had dropped the call. She pulled it away from her ear and looked at the screen, but the indicator showed the call was still active and there were plenty of bars.

"Dad, are you there? Did you hear me? Carl's..."

"I heard you, Amethyst. Carl's dead. You said it was at the shop, so it can't be a car accident. Was it a break in? You've called the sheriff, correct?"

"I'm waiting for a deputy right now. I don't know if it was a break in. The door was locked this morning, but I didn't check the back door. Carl came back last night after he left at five. I saw his car in front of the shop as I was heading home about six-thirty. Maybe he left the door unlocked while he ran in to get something and someone followed him, but that wouldn't explain how it got locked again. The main part of the store is a wreck, with trays and shelves overturned. I didn't check out the rest of the shop, I just came out and called 911."

"Alright, kiddo. You call me back as soon as you've talked with the sheriff's deputies, okay?"

"I will Dad." Amy hesitated then asked, "Do you know if Carl had anyone who hated him?" *Except for me* Amy thought as she said the words. *But I didn't hate him enough to kill him... just enough to vomit. Profusely.*

"I don't know, Amethyst. I never met any of Carl's friends. He never mentioned anyone. At least I don't think he did. He seemed to live on the computer most of the time."

"Okay, Dad. I'm guessing an investigator will be calling you, but I have to go now. I hear sirens."

"Take care of yourself, Amethyst. I don't like it that Carl

was found in our shop, behind closed, locked doors."

"It will be fine, Dad. I didn't do anything. There's got to be a logical answer. Say hi to Mom, okay? Tell her I'll call in a little bit, but the deputies are here now, and I have to go."

Amy pushed the end icon, shoved her phone back into her pocket and got out of the Jeep. She suddenly realized that she'd been so upset that she hadn't corrected Nick on her name even once. She was sure he wouldn't have missed that, either. The name battle had been ongoing since she was in her early teens, and neither had ever given ground... until now.

She shrugged. Nothing she could do about it at this point.

Unsure exactly what she was supposed to do, Amy stood at the right front corner of the Jeep, looking at the white SUV with "Mohave County Sheriff" emblazoned in gold across the side. She shifted from foot to foot, the nervous tension increasing. Finally the door opened, and the deputy stepped out. Amy's gut contracted yet again.

Tommy Kissoon. Maria's brother, and Amy's high school crush. Not that it went anywhere. Tommy was the star of the school football team, as small as it was. Besides, because the school was so tiny, it almost seemed like all the other students were your brothers or sisters, and dating just seemed weird.

Tommy and Maria were some of the kids from Supi who came out during the school year. Most went to Seligman, since it was in Yavapai County, but Tommy and Maria's grandparents lived outside Copper Springs, so the kids were able to live with them from the months of August through May. Coming from Cataract Canyon probably increased Tommy's attraction in Amy's adolescent eyes.

Tommy had always said he intended to go into the military. She didn't realize he'd come back to the area. Nick hadn't mentioned seeing him, but maybe he hadn't had the opportunity to run into the young man.

"Hi, Tommy."

"Hey, Amy." A bright smile flashed. "It's been a long time. I got a call that you have a body? Who is it?"

"It's Carl... uh..." *Oh crap! What the heck is Carl's last name?* Amy wracked her brain, trying to pull up the memory of a time when her dad had called Carl something other than just Carl. *It starts with an 's'...*

"Schrader. Carl Schrader. He is... was Nick's assistant. He handled all the computer stuff, as well as helping out in the shop in general."

"What happened? Where is he?" A frown crossed Tommy's face as he looked around.

"He's inside. Last night he left about five, but must have come back since I saw his car in front of the shop on my way home from having dinner at the Copper Springs Diner. It's that yellow one there. It's been here all night. We had a huge storm and the interior is soaked." Amy gestured at the convertible. Tommy walked over and took a look, then jotted a few notes down on a pad of paper he pulled from his breast pocket.

"I know it was here all night because there are no tire tracks in the mud. See," Amy said, then kicked herself. She knew she was babbling, and that Tommy would be good at his job and didn't need her help.

"I see. You said it was about six-thirty when you were heading home?"

"Yes. Around then. I figured he'd come back to pick something up. He said we had a few auctions that were going to end later that night, so he'd taken the laptop with him."

"So you got here this morning, and then what?"

"Well, I noticed that Carl's car was here, and the top was down, which was strange because we had that storm. I thought maybe he'd fallen asleep or had car trouble or something. But the dogs were upset." Amy gestured back at her Jeep, where Jynx and Bess were watching intently from the passenger side of the vehicle.

"I went to the door, but it was locked, so I used the key and let myself in." Amy looked down, feeling a little guilty about the next part. "The dogs went in ahead of me. I'm sorry, but I don't know if they contaminated anything. I know they walked through the blood."

"It's not great, but you couldn't know what you'd find. It's just as well that you allowed the dogs to go in first. It might have been dangerous. Let's go see what you've got." He made a move toward the door.

"Do I have to go? I don't really want to see it again."

"No, you can wait here." Tommy looked at her, sympathy evident in his eyes.

He walked to the front door, and disappeared inside. It seemed to Amy like he was gone for a century, but it was actually only a few minutes. Just when Amy thought she was going to explode, Tommy appeared back at the door.

"You said that this is Carl Schrader. You're sure?"

"Yes, I know the face is a bit messed up, but it's him. Now what?"

"Now what is that I've called additional support in, they'll remove the body for examination and process the scene. We'll have to ask you some more questions, and go over your statement. You're going to be closed for a few days, obviously. Did it seem to you as though anything was missing?"

"It's hard to say. I just got here yesterday. I'm filling in while Nick is recovering from breaking his leg."

"Yeah, Maria mentioned he'd had an accident. Sorry to hear about that." Tommy smiled at her surprised look. "Small town grapevine, remember. We know everything around here."

"I forgot about that." Amy said ruefully, thinking about the times as a kid when tales of her wrongdoings had gotten back to Nick and Crystal well before she got home.

"Well, first things first. We'll get the body moved and the scene processed. We..." Tommy stopped talking as a large gold SUV pulled into the parking lot next to Amy's Wrangler. A frown crossed his face as the door opened and Gladys climbed out.

"Amy, Tommy, what's happening, is everything okay?"

"Hi Gladys. I, uh..." Amy stopped and looked at Tommy, not sure what she should say.

"Hello Ms. Sanchez. I'm afraid that there's been an incident. May I ask you when was the last time you saw Mr. Carl Schrader?" Tommy looked at Gladys curiously, knowing that Gladys made it her business to know nearly everything going on in Copper Springs. In fact, in the small town grapevine, Gladys was one of the principle strands.

"Oh," Gladys looked horrified. "Has something happened to Carl? I just saw him yesterday morning when Em and I stopped by to see Amy, and... and..." Gladys stuttered to a stop, wide eyes on Amy.

Tommy frowned. "And what, Ms. Sanchez?"

Gladys looked at Amy, misery in her eyes. "Well, Amy and Carl were fighting, she stopped when Em and I came in, but she was awfully angry. Still, I'm sure she wouldn't have done anything, right Em?" Gladys looked around, and realized she was alone, then looked back at Amy.

Tommy's gaze shifted over to Amy. "You didn't mention arguing with Mr. Schrader yesterday, Amy."

"It was nothing, something stupid. He made a slimy comment, and I lost my temper." Amy held her hands up. "It was just... just stress. Everything that's happened with Nick and my job, and... just stress and I lost it. I didn't do anything."

"I think it would be best if you stopped there, Ms. Stone," Tommy said, the formal term freezing Amy's heart. "We'll be getting your statement shortly. I believe we'll also want to get a statement from both you and Ms. James," He said looking at Gladys. He made some notes on his pad, then lifted his head. "Ah, here comes the backup. Amy, please have a seat over there." Tommy gestured over toward Amy's Jeep. "Gladys, you can go sit in your vehicle. We'll be with you shortly."

5

A my stood looking at the disaster that was the front room of Stone's Gems and Minerals. If she thought it looked bad before, it was nothing compared to what was left when the sheriff's department and the biohazard remediation team vacated the premises.

It was hard to believe that only a week and a half ago the shop had been open, and business thriving. Nick was behind the counter, and Carl was working in the computer room. Two days ago, although Nick wasn't behind the counter, Carl was still in his computer room, and Amy was trying to figure out a good way to fire him.

Now, Carl was gone, the store was a mess, and there was a huge hole in the indoor/outdoor carpeting that covered the floor. Oh, and it appeared Amy was suspect number one on the "who killed Carl" list.

"Okay, first things first. Don't worry about the investigation, just start getting this mess cleaned up so that I can reopen the shop," Amy muttered to herself.

Amy was gathering together an upended tray of agate cabs, or cabochons, and starting to sort them out when she heard the wind chime on the front door jingle. She looked around the edge of the partition that ran down the center of the room, a frown on her face, but she couldn't see the doorway. She was sure that she'd left the "closed" sign visible in the window, but apparently she hadn't locked the door. It was probably one of the local grapevine members, wanting some first hand experience to relate to others in town.

"Hello, I'm sorry, we're closed right now," Amy called out.

No one answered, but the door didn't chime again, so she was sure whoever had come in hadn't left yet. Amy pushed herself to her feet and started for the front of the shop, feeling a growing sense of annoyance. Somebody died here. It shouldn't be used as entertainment for those people without a life.

"Hello. We're closed. If you want to come back tomorrow, we should be open by then. We..." Amy came to a stop when she saw the man standing next to the counter, scratching Jynx's ears. Jynx never let strangers touch her. Heck, she hardly let Jeff touch her and they'd lived in the same apartment.

"Excuse me. I'm sorry, but we're closed right now."

The man looked up at Amy, a smile on his face as he continued to rub Jynx's head. The dog had an absolutely imbecilic look of pleasure on her face which made Amy grit her teeth. So much for being a guard dog.

"Hi there. I didn't mean to disturb you, but a woman down at the Copper Springs Diner said that you might have a job opening, so I thought I'd come down and check it out. I'm Jackson Wolf, by the way." The man stopped scratching Jynx's ears, much to the dog's apparent disappointment, and put out his hand to shake Amy's. "Oh, and you might want to close your mouth, since I'm guessing this fine establishment has its fair share of spiders." The smile broadened into a grin as he looked around the disheveled room.

Amy took his hand, and deliberately shut her mouth which she realized had been hanging half open in surprise.

"Uh, I.. um.. Who was it that told you I had a job opening? You said down at the diner?"

"Yes, I was in at the diner this morning for breakfast, and mentioned to the owner that I was considering staying in the area, and asked if she knew of anyone with a job opening. She mentioned that there'd been an accident here a couple days ago, and you might be looking for someone."

"Did she also mention that I found the body, and that I was now probably the chief suspect in the murder?" Amy felt a rising current of frustration, although she wasn't sure whether it was aimed toward Gladys or this man.

"She might have brought up something like that, yes."

Jackson's smile was undimmed, and his blue eyes sparkled as though he found the idea of Amy being a suspect a huge joke.

Amy took a step back and examined the man. He appeared to be about her age, early to mid-thirties or thereabout. He wasn't tall, about her own five six or so, but he carried himself with such assurance that it seemed like he was much larger; stocky, but not fat by any means, just muscular. She looked back at his face, and found his eyes fixed on her with a quizzical expression.

"Do I pass muster?"

Amy could feel herself flushing with embarrassment that he'd noticed her scrutiny, and felt the urge to tell him there was no job opening, so sorry, don't call us, we'll call you, and don't let the door hit you on the way out. But she needed help. At least until she was arrested for murder, but then Nick would need help after that. Still, it wouldn't do to be too eager.

"I guess Gladys already told you that Carl, my father's assistant, was killed two days ago, so yes, we need someone to take over for him. I think I need to get to know you a little first. Let me lock the door, and we can go sit in the office and discuss things. At least the office is in one piece." Amy's face twisted, remembering her father's organizational skills. "Well, sort of in one piece. But there are chairs, and coffee, so we should be fine."

"Sounds good to me. Lead the way." The man stood back out of her path.

Amy went to the front door and turned the lock with determination, then headed back out into the main room and walked toward Nick's office, past the closed computer room door. She hit the light switch, and entered the narrow, cluttered space. She scooped an armful of papers off the spare chair as she walked by and deposited them on the corner of the desk, then turned back toward her visitor

"Here, have a seat. Do you want some coffee?"

"I'm good. Thanks though." The man sat where Amy indicated, then looked at her expectantly. "I'm guessing that you have a lot of questions, so fire away." His smile flashed out of his deeply tanned face.

Amy sat in Nick's chair and turned to look at her visitor. "You said your name is Jackson Wolf?"

He nodded. "It is, although I shortened my original last name to Wolf. You don't even want to know what it was to start with." He shook his head with a wry smile.

"Of course, now I *do* want to know, but I'm guessing you won't tell, correct?"

"You've got that right." His ever present grin was turned on her again.

"Okay, Mr. Wolf..."

"Jackson, please. I'd say that only my father is called 'Mr. Wolf,' but he never shortened his name, so I can't even say that."

"Okay, Jackson. When did you move to Copper Springs? I haven't ever met you before, have I?"

"No, I moved here about a month ago to help my sister, Merri Thompson. Her husband just passed away, and she's struggling to make it with two small children."

"She's one of the waitresses at the Copper Springs Diner, isn't she? The one with the short blonde hair?"

"That's her. She likes it here, and wants so stay, but with Lou dying she needs support." A look passed over Jackson's face, quickly there and gone. "Our parents are dead, and I'm all she's got left, so I said I'd come up and help her out."

Amy nodded, impressed that the man would alter his life to help out his sister.

"You're living with her, then?"

"No, actually I've got a small RV I've been living in for a few years now. I'm a landscape and wildlife photographer, and a mobile place of residence is handy in my line of work. Right now it's parked in her driveway, although if I like the area, I may buy some land and making it my permanent home base."

Amy nodded. She got the RV lifestyle, considering how she was raised. She was a little concerned that Jackson wouldn't be a long term employee, but maybe he'd do to get them through this rough patch.

"The job involves a lot of computer work. You'd have to maintain the website, as well as handling any online auctions through sites like eBay and Facebook. Do you have any experience with that type of work?"

"Yes, I have my own website as a photographer, and I've worked with several different online auctions, so that's no problem at all," Jackson said, nodding. "I'm also able to take any photos necessary for your online store if you have one."

"That's great." Amy felt a little shiver of hope. Then she remembered one of Carl's greatest downfalls. "I don't suppose you know anything about rock and mineral specimens, do you?"

"Probably not as much as you, of course." Jackson shrugged, then stood and picked a large chunk of geode off the shelf over Amy's head. He fingered the dark orange and yellow crystals. "I can tell you that this used to be a purple amethyst, before it was heated to the point it turned yellow and is now called citrine." He grinned at the look of shock on Amy's face. "It's the same chemical formula, but the addition of heat changes the color. Of course, if you then add radiation, you can change the color back again. There are a number of stones out there that are changed in color either due to heat or radiation."

"How do you know that?" Amy looked at Jackson in amazement. Many people had no idea that the stones in their favorite jewelry had been altered, either died, heated or irradiated. Citrine was one of the best known, and the majority of the citrine on the market was heat treated amethyst, unless it was advertised as "natural" by a reputable dealer. Of course, natural citrine was much rarer than the heat treated form, so brought a much heftier price. For that matter, much of the southwest's turquoise jewelry was dyed howlite or magnesite, or if it was actual turquoise, it might be stabilized and dyed to make it a brighter blue. In recent years block turquoise had come on the market, and was either reconstituted turquoise, or outright synthetic. Not all of the turquoise jewelry was made this way, of course, but as Nick said, if the price was too good to be true, you should be suspicious.

"An old girlfriend was a jewelry maker and made her own cabs and beads. She got me interested in it, although I was always more fascinated in the natural specimens."

Jackson put the citrine geode back on the shelf, and smiled down at Amy.

"So what do you say, boss? Do I have the job?"

Amy looked at the man standing in front of her, completely at ease. His cheerful presence was as far from that of Carl's slimy one as the Earth was from the moon.

"Ultimately, it's got to be my Dad's choice, but I'd say for now, you're hired." Amy grinned back at Jackson. "So, now will you tell me what Wolf is short for?"

"Not a chance," Jackson laughed.

"If I guess it will you tell me?" Amy's voice held a teasing note that surprised her.

"I'll tell you what," Jackson sat back down in the spare chair. "You guess my name, and you can claim a favor from me."

"Good grief, I just hired Rumpelstiltskin!" Amy laughed.

"Nope, that's not it. I suppose we ought to get out and clean up the shop. Do you want to repair that snazzy hole in the carpet, or do you want all the carpet pulled up and go with bare concrete?"

6

Amy and Jackson worked for most of the morning, gathering all the items scattered around and across the floor. Several delicate crystals had been broken, although Amy couldn't tell if it happened when Carl was killed, or when the deputies and investigators swarmed the shop later on.

Amy was collecting a tray of quartz points together, when Jackson held up a small piece of geode that he'd pulled off a tray set well back on one of the shelves. "These are some interesting pieces here. They look like amethyst, but they've got a red cap on them. If I didn't know better, I'd say they were dipped in blood, and the deputies missed them. Did they say what the murder weapon was?"

"They said that he'd been hit in the head with something heavy, and with many pointed ends." Amy felt the anxiety that had loosened over the past few hours start to gain a grip on her chest again. "So, yeah, a geode would be perfect. The problem is that they couldn't find the geode in question. Those pieces are too small of course."

Amy walked over to where Jackson was studying the crystal clump in question. "I didn't know Nick had gotten any of those. They're amethyst from Thunder Bay, Canada. It's the hematite inclusions that gives them those red caps." Amy took the geode piece from Jackson's fingers and looked at it, turning it over in her hand. "A lot of people don't care for the look, but some of the avid collectors like it, as well as some of the crystal healers."

"Huh," Jackson picked up another piece from the tray and examined it. "Still looks like it was dipped in blood to me. Where do you want the tray? Back on the shelf?"

"Yeah, that's fine." Amy put the piece she was holding back into the display tray, which Jackson then slid up onto the shelf next to several others that had escaped the upheaval.

"We've been at it for a few hours now. Let's grab some lunch. I need a break." Amy wiped her hands on her jean shorts and headed for the door. "We can go to the diner if you want, or over to the deli in the gas station."

"Deli's good. I like their sandwiches." Jackson hurried to catch up with Amy, matching her step for step as they crossed the parking lot, heading for the gas station across the highway from the rock shop.

They decided to eat their meal on the small patio attached to the station's convenience store, and within a few minutes had gathered their sandwiches, chips and drinks, and found a good table in the shade. Amy studied Jackson as he dug into his roast beef sub, his attention momentarily consumed by the food. Suddenly he looked up, caught her eyes on him, and smiled.

"I'd like to ask you something, if I may,"

Amy nodded, "I guess. What is it?"

"You said you were the chief suspect in your man's murder? Why do you think that?" Jackson looked at her. For once the smile was replaced by a frown, which didn't sit well on his naturally cheerful features.

"Someone witnessed me lose my temper pretty badly with him the day before, then he's murdered in my family's shop, and all the doors are locked, meaning that whoever did it either had to have a key, or be some sort of magician to be able to get out of the shop without unlocking the door."

"I take it they found his keys with him, then."

"Yeah. Right in his pocket where they belonged. I'm the only other one with the keys. At least the only other one in town."

"What about fingerprints on the doors?" Jackson had a stubborn set to his chin.

"I opened the door that morning to get in, so my fingerprints were on it. No one else's."

"So someone wiped down the door before you got there. They're taking that into consideration, right?"

"Probably. Geez, Jackson. You've been watching too much TV." Amy couldn't help it, she had to laugh at the look on his face. "If I was a smart criminal, though, wouldn't I wipe down the door, then put my own prints there to make the authorities think that someone else was trying to hide his or her prints?"

"But you didn't do it. You called 911. If you'd killed him, wouldn't you have just hidden the body out in the desert?"

"I think I've been watching too many crime shows too. I would have had trouble moving Carl's body, so why not make it look like it was someone else?"

"Because of exactly what's happening now. They'll take the path of least resistance. If you're the most obvious person, then you're going to undergo most of the scrutiny."

"Tell me about it." Amy suddenly lost her appetite and put her turkey and avocado sandwich down on the paper plate.

"So, what are you going to do about it?" Jackson asked, a dangerous glint in his eyes.

"What do you mean? What can I do? I'm just going to have to hope that they realize I had nothing to do with Carl's murder, and start investigating other people."

"So why not be one step in front of them? Who else can you think of who might want to hurt Carl?"

"I don't know, Jackson. I really didn't know him very well. The investigator asked me the same thing. I don't know if he had a girlfriend, though heaven help any woman going out with him. Yuck! Maybe he hit on other women in town, and those women had something against him, or boyfriends of those women. It's a small town, though, and most of the time things like that are common knowledge." Amy put her chin on her fist and sat thinking for a few moments as Jackson studied her.

"He did say something about the town giving Nick a hard time about the business. He seemed to think it was a bit of a joke, but I don't know how that could have anything to do with his death."

"Are they investigating all these things, or just you?"

Amy sighed, and lifted her head. "I don't know, Jackson.

All I know is that I've got to get the shop opened back up, or Dad might not have a business to come home to." She pushed her chair back, and waited for Jackson to stand, then the two headed back across the highway to Stone's Gems and Minerals.

Once back in the shop, Amy stood for a moment in the newly cleared front showroom. The hole in the carpeting stood out like a sore thumb, but she wasn't really sure what to do about it. She'd called Nick at Canyon View the night before, and asked his opinion. Other than saying he wanted her to get the shop back up and open, he hadn't had a lot of suggestions. Finally they'd decided that they'd just pull a Navajo style rug over the hole for the time being, until Nick got home and decided on what direction he wanted to go.

As she was standing there, her phone rang... a real ring this time, not Queen's famous anthem. She glanced at the screen, but the caller was simply listed at Mohave County Sheriff's Department, with the number unavailable. She hit the green button, and held the device to her ear.

"Hello?"

"Hi Amy, it's Tommy Kissoon."

"Uh... hi, Tommy," Amy looked over at Jackson who was watching her with a curious expression on his face. She made the okay sign then walked over toward Nick's office. "What can I do for you?" She glanced back over at Jackson who was busy behind the counter, apparently sorting through the variety of trays stacked haphazardly over most of the surface.

"I was wondering if you'd gotten a chance to inventory the store yet... see if anything is missing." Amy's heart jumped. Maybe they were taking the possibility of a robbery gone wrong seriously, and Amy didn't have to worry about being arrested. Then she remembered the locked door. There was also the possibility that they were just doing their due diligence.

"I'm sorry, not yet. We've been trying to pick up everything that was dumped. I'll try to get to it this afternoon."

"We...?" Tommy let the word trail off.

"I hired a man to replace Carl. His name is Jackson Wolf. He's Merri Thompson's brother. You know, the blonde who works at the diner? Her husband Lou, died recently and he's come to Copper Springs to help her out."

"Merri Thompson..." Amy could hear a note of concentration in his voice, as though he was trying to remember. "Oh, yes. I remember. Dang shame about her husband. He was a cowboy on the Slash Z, and his horse went over backward on him. It was a young colt and it tried to jump a wash. Lost its footing and flipped, from what I heard."

"I didn't know that, Jackson just said he'd passed away suddenly, and he seems to have a mobile lifestyle, so he came up to give her a hand. Anyway he knows computers and rocks, so hopefully he'll be a good match for the shop. I'll get him to help me to go through everything, and try and come up with an inventory for you. Nick said that was Carl's job, so hopefully we can find something in his office. Should I give you a call when we're done?"

"No, either I, or Davis, the inspector assigned to the case will call you. Thanks, Amy."

"Tommy...?" Amy hesitated, unsure how to proceed.

"Yes?"

"Do I have to be worried?"

"I can't discuss this with you, Amy. You know that."

"Yeah, I was just hoping you'd at least tell me if I need a lawyer."

"Talk with my sister, Amy. Ask her. Thank you for your help, Amy. We'll be in touch." The phone call ended and Amy stood there looking at the phone. *Talk to my sister? Talk to Maria? Why.* Then it hit her. Maria was a lawyer. Tommy told her to talk to a lawyer.

"Is everything okay, Amy?" Jackson had come up behind her and was looking at her with concern.

"Maybe not." Amy said absently, her mind whirling, churning over what Tommy might have meant by his suggestion. Suddenly she shook herself and looked at Jackson with renewed focus. "I think you were right, Jackson. I think I need to look into who might have had something against Carl. I think I need to figure out who else might have killed him."

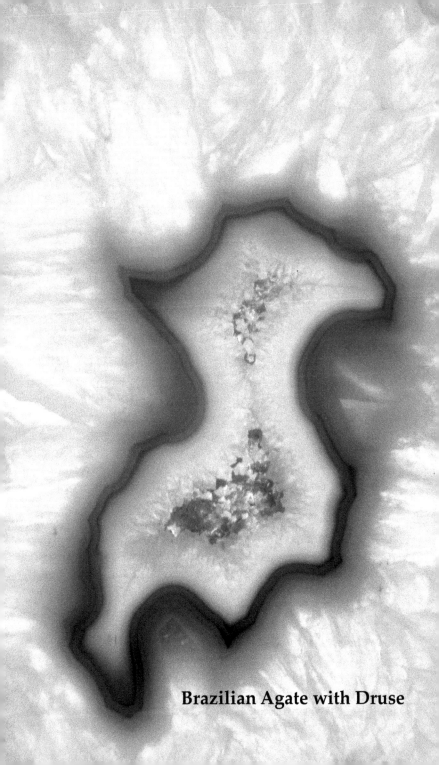

Brazilian Agate with Druse

7

Jackson looked at Amy and nodded. "So where do we start?"

"You just met me, Jackson. How do you know I'm not the murderer?"

"The way I see it is that the locked doors work as much for you, as against you. I figure the police see it the same way or they would have arrested you already. By Carl being behind locked doors, in other words a locked room mystery, it points the finger at you too easily. No murderer with any sense would do that. You'd have left the door open, maybe taken out some of the more valuable items to make it look like a robbery. You didn't do it, and if you didn't do it, there is someone else out there who did."

Amy looked at Jackson, and felt a rising flood of hope. Sitting here, waiting to be arrested would drive her insane. It would be much better to take action, even if there was nothing to be found, and having a friend backing her would be even better. Amy nodded to herself, decision made.

"Okay, I told Tommy that I'd get him an inventory as soon as possible, and see if I could compare it to an old inventory. Dad said that one was done every year for tax purposes." Amy looked around the cluttered room and shook her head. "Although it sure doesn't look that way. I found an old one, but Dad said that Carl computerized everything a few years ago, so maybe you could start going through the computer files and see what you can turn up."

"I can do that, no problem." Jackson nodded, and started to move toward the computer room. "Do you have your password?"

Amy groaned. "No, Oh no! Carl knew all the passwords. I don't even know if Nick knows them."

"Don't worry. If we need to, you can give your dad a call and see if he knows. Odds are, even if he doesn't remember them, Carl would have left it somewhere, just in case your dad needed to get into the computer when Carl was gone. Besides, even if Carl didn't, the odds are it's a simple password, and I should be able to get around it pretty easily. I might have to run home first, though." Jackson gave her a mischievous smile.

"Don't tell me, you're a computer hacker too?" Amy looked at him as though he'd grown two heads.

"Nah, not really. But I've locked myself out of a computer or two in my day, and an old girlfriend gave me the steps to unlock the password. I keep it written in a notebook at home in case I need it again."

"Same old girlfriend who was the jewelry maker?"

"Nope, this one was a computer programmer." Jackson laughed at the look on Amy's face. "Still, before we go to that extreme, let me check the computer and see what we have." He opened the door into the computer room, walked over to the desktop and pressed the power button, making the machine hum to life.

Amy stood in the door and watched Jackson as he studied the screen, waiting for the computer to finish starting. "We also have a laptop that Carl often used. He'd... He'd taken it with him the night he was killed. I don't remember seeing it in the shop. It must either be at his house, or somewhere here, unless whoever killed him took it." She frowned, trying to remember if she'd seen it anywhere while they were cleaning up. She looked around the small computer office, searching for the black case. Nothing.

She pulled her cell phone from her pocket and dialed the number of the Mohave County Sheriff's Office, and asked the dispatcher to connect her with Tommy Kissoon. After a couple of clicks, Tommy's voice mail came out of the speaker, assuring the listener that he would get back to him or her as soon as possible.

"Hi Tommy, this is Amy. Give me a call when you get a chance. I've just realized that the shop's laptop computer is missing. Carl had it with him when he left that night, so I was wondering if it was left at his house, assuming that you guys have searched it already. Anyway, let me know. Thanks."

Hanging up the cell, she returned it to her pocket. "Hopefully it's safe at Carl's house, or we'll find it in the shop somewhere." Amy looked at Jackson who was busy looking through the drawers of the desk where the computer sat. "Are you finding anything important?"

Jackson pulled out a small notebook and started thumbing through the pages. He stopped on a page and tapped a few keys on the keyboard, frowned, then flipped through a few more pages. He glanced up at Amy a look of concentration creating a line between his eyebrows. "I think I found a password book, but there are several in here, and I haven't found the one for the computer itself yet." He turned another page, and his face lightened. "I bet this is it. Amethyst only spelled 8m3thyst and with an exclamation point afterward." He typed in the code, and the computer's desktop picture, a large amethyst geode against a black background, appeared.

"Dad used my name as his password?" Amy wasn't sure how she felt about that. After all, she was only one of three children. It seemed like Nick was playing favorites.

"Well, he used your name for the computer. It appears that for most of the accounts he used your name, then a code for the business, such as FB for Facebook, or EB for eBay. It makes it easy to remember."

"You're saying all this is written in that notebook? That doesn't seem very safe."

"No, not too smart, although to give Carl and your dad credit, the notebook actually doesn't say which passwords and user names go where, and they did have the notebook hidden in the back of this drawer, so it could have been worse. There are a lot of people who used the default password on all their devices, or the same password on everything."

"Okay, I'll take your word for it. Why don't you check out the computer. I'll start the inventory, counting everything in the shop to see what's actually here and..." Her cell phone's ring interrupted her. She pulled it out and looked at the caller ID. Mohave County Sheriff's Department.

"Hello."

"Hi Amy, this is Tommy." Tommy's voice was garbled slightly with periodic breaks.

"Hey Tommy, you got my message? Did you search Carl's house, and if you did, did you happen to see a laptop case?"

The connection was terrible, but Amy managed to pick out the words, "search," and "no laptop" but then the call was dropped. She waited for a few moments, looking at the phone, hoping that it would ring again, but nothing happened to disturb the picture of the lavender and citrine cactus quartz that she had set as her wallpaper.

Finally Amy shoved the phone back into her pocket and looked at Jackson. "I think I'm going to run down to the Copper Springs Diner for a few minutes."

Jackson jerked his head up and looked at Amy. "What for? You just ate."

"Gladys and Em know everything that's going on in this town, even when they don't know they know, if you get my meaning. I'd really like to find that laptop, and since it doesn't appear to be here." Amy looked around the small office. "I'm thinking it must be at his home. Gladys will know where that is, I'm sure of it."

Jackson nodded. "It makes sense. I'll stay here and see what I can find on this computer, but if Carl had anything he was trying to keep secret, it would probably be on the laptop, or an external hard drive or flash drive, unless he has his own computer." He fixed Amy with a stern look. "However, don't go over to Carl's home by yourself. Come back and get me once you find out where it is, okay? Don't forget there's a murderer out there."

Amy smiled at Jackson. It was nice to have someone watching her back. That thought brought up another, and she pulled out her phone and dialed Maria's number and left a message for her to call when she got the chance. Maybe she was overreacting, but if Tommy said to talk to his sister, then she should probably follow the suggestion.

The diner was having a busy afternoon when Amy arrived. She pulled the Wrangler in to one of only a few empty

spots left, and made her way to the front door of the establishment hoping that Gladys and Emily had a full staff today
if the number of vehicles was anything to go by.

As Amy entered the restaurant, she was met by the hum
of the happy crowd of diners. She paused just inside the door
and looked around, trying to find Gladys or Em. Several
waitresses were either taking orders or talking to customers,
but the two older women weren't to be seen. Finally Amy
made her way over to the end of the counter where a single
unoccupied seat remained. It didn't take long until a young
woman Amy couldn't identify appeared in front of her, carrying a glass of ice water and a double-sided lunch menu
covered in plastic.

"Hello, my name is Larissa, can I get you something else
to drink while you're checking out the menu?"

Amy smiled at the girl. "Just a glass of ice tea for now,
Larissa. I'm looking for Gladys. Is she or Emily around."

"Certainly. Both Gladys and Emily are in the office right
now taking a break. It's been a pretty hectic afternoon so far.
I'll go get them for you."

The girl headed for the door to the kitchen, and disappeared inside. Amy sat looking around the diner, noting the
number of tourists from different countries filling the seats.
Amy had frequently traveled up and down I-40, the inter-
state that bypassed Route 66 years ago, making it nearly
obsolete. In that case, pulling in to a truck stop or restaurant you frequently heard numerous languages spoken by
the tourists who came to northern Arizona to see the Grand
Canyon. However, it was only recently that the small ranching and mining town of Copper Springs started receiving its
share of visitors. Still, it was good for business, especially as
the mines in the area were becoming extinct.

In a couple of minutes Larissa pushed back through the
kitchen door, and nodded to Amy. "They'll be right out. Let
me get your iced tea." The girl bustled off to a large glass
doored cooler, pulled out a pitcher of iced tea and filled a
glass. She returned and set it in front of Amy, reassuring her
once again that Gladys and Emily would be with her momentarily.

Amy thanked her, and picked up the glass and took a sip and sat for another minute, trying not to focus on the events of the last several days. She was terrified that if she sat and thought too much about everything that had happened, she'd panic. She'd be frozen and unable to make a move to save herself.

Just as she began to feel herself getting caught up into those scared little girl thoughts against her will, Gladys emerged from the kitchen, followed closely by Emily. A huge smile split Gladys' face when she saw Amy sitting at the at the counter.

"Amethyst! It's so good to see you. I was afraid that after... I mean, I know you didn't do anything to Carl, but I was scared you'd be angry that Em and I had to talk with the police. Everything's okay though, right? I mean, you're not arrested? They don't think you did it?" A look of such fear filled Gladys' eyes that Amy felt bad for her. Sometimes it sucked to be the town gossip.

"It's fine Gladys. No, I'm not arrested, although I'm not really sure that I won't be. After all, he was found in Dad's shop, and I had an argument with him the day before." Amy did her best to sooth the older woman's feelings. She needed Gladys and Emily on her side. "Actually, Gladys, I need your help."

"Anything child. Right Em?" Gladys looked over her shoulder to where Emily stood, looking at Amy sympathetically. Emily nodded.

How in the world did Emily ever control a class full of children when she was a teacher? I don't know if I've ever heard her talk more than three or four words at a time. That might have been an exaggeration, but it seemed that the older Emily James got, the quieter she became. Amy tried to remember back to when Emily's husband, Skeeter James was alive. Even then Skeeter did all the talking for the family. When he died, Emily's best friend, Gladys, just seemed to slide into that role.

"It's nothing big, really. I just have a couple of questions. First, where was Carl living? Surely he didn't buy a house in the area, so he must have been renting somewhere."

Gladys frowned for a moment, as if trying to remember.

"I think he was staying with Moria Larson... you know old lady Larson, out on Bullock Road west of town? She's got that bunkhouse behind her home from when it was part of the Diamond V Ranch, and I'm pretty sure she was renting to Carl. Occasionally he'd stop and collect some take-out for her on his way home. Why do you need to know dear?"

Amy nearly choked at Gladys' description of Moira Larson as an 'old lady' considering that both she and Emily had to be pushing sixty-five, and Ms. Larson was likely only in her early seventies. However, the description fit. If Gladys and Emily were young for their ages, Moira was old for hers.

"The night that Carl was murdered, he had the shop's laptop computer with him. I'm trying to find the inventory and any other records, since it might help the sheriff's department if we knew something had been stolen. Jackson's searching for files on the desktop right now, but we haven't found the laptop yet. Jackson thinks that those records might have been kept either on it or on some type of external hard drive."

Too late Amy realized her mistake in mentioning Jackson. Gladys' eyes grew large behind her glasses, and she looked back at Emily who grinned at Amy. *Ah crap! Small town grapevine fodder for sure. The single daughter of Nick Stone hires a stranger who wanders into town.*

"Gladys. Emily, knock it off! You're the ones who sent him down for the job, after all," Amy grumbled, feeling her cheeks heating up with embarrassment.

"I'm so glad that it worked out." Gladys' smile was so big Amy was afraid her face was going to rip in two. "He seems like such a nice young man. Talented too. I've seen some of his pictures of the Grand Canyon, and have even ordered a couple for the diner. He's Merri's brother, you know."

"Yes, he told me he came to give her a hand after Lou died."

"Poor girl." Gladys looked over to where Merri Thompson, Jackson's sister, was taking an order from a family of Chinese tourists. She was a slight woman in her mid-twenties, and one of the few waitresses employed by the diner who wasn't a high school student. Her bright gold hair was tied up in a pony tail, making her look younger than she was, but Amy could see the resemblance between her and her brother.

"She's had a tough time of it this past couple of months until her brother came. First with Lou's accident, and then there was something else going on. She wouldn't talk to us about whatever it was. It had her very upset, however. She even called out sick several times, or had to go home in the middle of a shift. Fortunately that seems to have worked its way out." Gladys watched Merri for a moment.

Amy smiled to herself. Maybe it was a leftover from all her years of teaching, but she always took an almost motherly view of her employees; laughing with them, crying with them, offering them advice, and helping them out of tough situations.

"It's a good thing she had you, Gladys. Anyway, I'll run out to Ms. Larson's. I'm sure the sheriff's department has been out there and searched, but they might not have realized that the computer was ours. I was also wondering if you knew anything about Carl's social life."

"That man tended to hit on a lot of girls." Gladys sniffed as though she smelled something rather nasty, and Emily's sunny face took on a frown. "I finally had to give him a stern talking to about leaving the waitresses alone."

"There was no one in particular he was dating, though? I mean, no girlfriend who might be angry with him, or whose ex-boyfriend might want to hurt him?"

"No, not that I know of, dear. Most of the girls just seemed to brush him off."

"Dad said he'd been here about four years. Do you remember when he came? Did he ever say why he moved here. Dad said Carl was pretty close-lipped when it came to his past." Amy looked at the women, fingers crossed that the small town grapevine would have wormed something out of Carl that no one else knew.

"No, he talked a lot about himself, but it was mostly about how good he was at different things. He could be charming, at least at first, but he didn't fit here very well." Gladys pursed her lips as she thought about Carl.

Amy rolled her eyes at the thought of the man. His dyed

black hair and bleached yellow soul patch, his slimy way of looking at women. None of those fit very well into a small western ranching town, but she imagined that they tried to include him.

Amy finished off her iced tea and slid off the stool, sliding a five dollar bill across the counter.

"Thank you so much Gladys. Emily. I appreciate the information on Moira Larson's place. I think I'll run out there right now and see if by any chance the computer is in the bunkhouse. I really need to find the inventory to see if anything is missing."

"Amy?" Emily spoke up softly. "Nick said he'd gotten a beautiful large chunk of red capped amethyst plate that he'd save for me. Have you found that?"

Amy looked at Emily in surprise. "I'm sorry Emily. I haven't found that yet, but we've just started inventorying the shop. I did find some nice chunks of Thunder Bay amethyst with a very pronounced red hematite cap, but they were small. Beautiful points, though. Bigger than I would have expected. Maybe Nick got them at the same time as the large plate. I'll ask."

"Please do. From what your dad said this one was very large, several pounds in size. It was very expensive, but I've wanted one for a long time, and you seldom see them this large."

Amy smiled at Emily. "I'll be sure to look. If it was that expensive it's probably in the back room with the valuable specimens. It didn't look like that room had been touched at all, so it's probably just on a shelf and I haven't seen it. I'll let you know."

"Thank you, Amy. I appreciate it." Emily gave Amy a bright smile.

With a wave, Amy headed back out of the diner. She glanced at the sky. Huge monsoon clouds were building up and it looked like they might get another evening of rain. Bullock Road, where Moira Larson lived, was five miles outside town, and dirt the whole way. The Jeep was four-wheel drive, but if she wanted to get out and back without going mud bogging, it would probably be best to go sooner rather than later.

She climbed into the Wrangler and headed back up Route 66 to the rock shop to pick up Jackson. If she was going to have to face Old Lady Larson, she wasn't going to do it alone.

Calcite Geode

The monsoon rains of the night before had left parts of Bullock Road muddy, and it was easy to see where other four-wheel drive vehicles had traversed some of the bigger dips. The arroyos had run the night before, and in several places the road had washed out severely, but the Wrangler handled the rough terrain easily.

Jackson sat in the passenger seat, occasionally reaching for the grab handle as Amy navigated the rough surface, throwing the vehicle back and forth. The dogs sitting in the short bed of the Jeep seemed to do better at keeping their balance.

Amy had considered the wisdom of taking the dogs with her. Moira Larson was bound to have at least one dog. Most of the people living out in the country did, and while Jynx would stay in the Jeep, she wasn't sure about Bess. She really didn't want to have to tell Nick that she'd fed his beloved corgi to a vicious guard dog.

Still, she finally decided that having a few guard dogs... well, okay one guard dog... of her own couldn't hurt. She remembered Old Lady Larson from when she was a child. Not that she ever came into the shop. She certainly wasn't the type of person to waste good money on rocks. However, when she was younger she ran a small dry goods store near where the Copper Springs Diner was now.

The children would often go in with what little money they had to buy candy or toys. The rumor was that Old Lady Larson occasionally took small children and cooked them for dinner. At least that was the explanation that went around whenever a family with children left the area unexpectedly. It was like she was the older sister of the witch in the story

Hansel and Gretel. Not that Amy ever believed those stories. Although if she had to admit it, she did use the tale to scare her younger brother and sister on occasion, telling them that if they didn't do what she wanted, Old Lady Larson would come and get them. Of course it eventually got back to Nick and Crystal, and Amy's punishment was creative. Nick asked Moira if Amy could help clean the store for two weeks as a "community service" project.

It took nearly twenty minutes for Amy and Jackson to navigate the five mile stretch of road, but finally they pulled into the large open area behind the old clapboard ranch house where Moira Larson lived since she was a child. As Amy pulled to a stop, she examined the structure, noting that it looked exactly the same as the last time she'd seen it... at least fifteen years ago.

"You sure someone lives here?" Jackson started to open the door.

Before Amy could answer, a large black and tan dog came around the corner of the house and started barking viciously. Jackson slammed the door shut and looked at Amy. Jynx pushed her head between the two front seats, eyes fixed on the strange dog, and growled low her in throat.

"Jynx, no. Quiet." A sudden sharp bark in her ear caused her to jump. "Bess! Quiet now." She could hear scuffling in the back of the Jeep, as the dogs pushed each other for the best position in which to watch the newcomer.

"Yeah, Jackson. Someone lives here, and we're just going to sit for a moment until she comes to the door and calls off the hound."

It seemed like it took forever, but finally the back door of the house opened, and Moira Larson herself appeared, leaning on her cane and moving slowly. She studied the Jeep, and Amy pulled down the window and waved, hoping that the older woman would recognize her from when she was younger.

"Hi, Ms. Larson. It's Amy Stone. Remember me? I worked for you for a few weeks? I'd like to speak with you if I could."

Moira Larson didn't move, and Amy began to think that either she hadn't heard Amy's call, or that she wasn't going to let them out of the Jeep, when suddenly the woman uttered a loud whistle. The huge mixed breed, who had given up barking, but was still sniffing around the tires of the Jeep, whipped around, ran to the back door of the house and sat at the woman's feet. Old Lady Larson opened the door and ushered the dog inside, then closed both the solid inner door and the screen door, ensuring the dog remained within the home.

Amy released a breath she hadn't realized she'd been holding, and looked over at Jackson. "I guess it's safe for us to get out now." She opened the door of the Wrangler, and slid to the ground as Jackson did the same on the other side. Moira Larson stood and watched, a sour expression on her face.

"Hi, Ms. Larson." Amy started to walk forward. She glanced to her side and noticed Jackson walking next to her, his best welcoming smile plastered on his face. "Do you remember me? I'm Nick Stone's daughter, Amy. And, this is Jackson Wolf. He works for the shop now. I was hoping you'd have time to talk with us?"

Ms. Larson nodded. "I remember you, girl. You were that cheeky one that was always running off with the Kissoon kids and digging up rocks."

Amy felt her face redden a little at the description of her as a kid. "Uh, Yeah... I mean yes, that was me. It's sort of embarrassing to think of those things now. I'm sorry if I was ever rude to you." Amy tried her best apologetic smile.

"And who is this one?" Ms. Larson twitched her cane toward Jackson, making him flinch slightly, although Amy noticed that the smile was unfazed.

"Hi Ms. Larson. I'm Jackson Wolf. I just moved to this area about a month ago, and I just started working for Stone's Gems and Minerals. Today as a matter of fact."

Amy nodded. She felt like she was trying to walk through a sand desert and kept sinking in. "We were hoping that you could help us. Gladys Sanchez said that Carl Schrader was renting your bunkhouse?" She made the statement a question.

The older woman looked at Amy and nodded. "Yes, he's

been living here for the past four years. Good tenant, even if he looked like a..." Ms. Larson dragged to a stop, as though she realized what she was about to say wasn't appropriate. "Well, I don't honestly know what he looked like. But he always paid his rent on time, kept to himself, didn't play any loud music. I didn't even know what had happened until the sheriff's deputies showed up here wanting to search his place." There was an almost sad note to Moira's voice at the end, which surprised Amy. She looked around again. It must be lonely out here by herself. Even Carl might have been better than no one at all.

Jackson spoke up. Apparently he'd picked up the same sorrow in the older woman's voice that Amy had. "I'm so sorry, Ms. Larson. It must have been such a huge shock to find out that way."

"Yes, well, the boy was a help, there's no denying that. He'd pick up my groceries and the mail or other things in town. It's not so easy getting around these days, or keeping up with the place. He did little jobs around here as part of the rent. Worked out for both of us."

Amy found herself feeling sorry for Ms. Larson, which surprised her greatly. Never in a million years did she think she could feel sorry for The Witch of her childhood.

"Ms. Larson, you said the sheriff's deputies had already been here and searched Carl's place. We were hoping that we'd be able to go in." Amy saw a frown take over Moira's face, deepening the lines that already seemed eroded by time, and she hurried on before the older woman just said no outright. "The night that he was killed he left work with the shop's laptop computer. We don't know if he had it with him when the shop was broken into, or if he left it here in his apartment. It may have some important records on it."

"I don't know nothing about any laptop. I didn't see the sheriff's deputies take anything with them when they left. They said everything was clear and I could empty the place of all his belongings, but how am I going to get that done, I ask you?" The grumpy old woman was back, and Amy gritted her teeth, trying to channel that feeling of sympathy she'd had only a few moments before.

Jackson came to the rescue with his unflappable good nature. "I'll tell you what, Ms. Larson... Moira if I may?" He hesitated for a moment watching the woman's face. There was a barely perceptible nod and his smile grew larger as he continued. "Go ahead and let us take a look right now. Tomorrow's Saturday, and I have to work, right?" He looked at Amy who nodded affirmative. "But on Sunday I'll come back out and help you pack everything up. Do you know Carl's next of kin?"

Moira shook her head. "Nah, he said he didn't have any family left. He didn't fill in that blank on his lease."

"Well then, we can pack everything up and... and..." Jackson looked around the compound, trying to come up with a good solution. "And, we'll stash it in a corner of the barn over there until you decide what to do with it. How's that sound?"

"I guess that might work." Moira said grudgingly.

"Great," Amy said with forced cheerfulness. She glanced at the clouds which had built even taller, and tried to calculate how long they had until the storms hit. "If it's okay, Ms. Larson, I'd like to look for the laptop and head home before the washes start running again."

"Okay, let me get the key." Moira turned slowly and hobbled back inside the house, emerging momentarily with a set of keys and headed across the parking area. "Need to get another set of these. Police didn't bring back Carl's set and I only had two." She looked out of the corner of her eyes toward Jackson, and Amy nearly started giggling.

Jackson looked at Amy behind Moira's back and she could see the laughter in his eyes as well. He knew exactly what the older woman was doing. "If you want, Ms. Moira, I can take your keys and get some copies made tomorrow, then bring them back out with me on Sunday."

Moira glanced at him again. "That would work. You be careful you don't lose them, okay?" she grumbled, but Amy could see a small smile twitch her lips. Amy bit her cheek to keep from laughing.

When they reached the bunkhouse, Moira fit the key into the lock, pushed the door open and froze. Amy looked over Moira's shoulder into the spacious room and gasped.

Everything was overturned and scattered around the room. Jackson stepped through the doorway and looked all around the space, his smile transformed to a frown.

"Did the sheriff's deputies leave it this way?" he asked, anger obvious in his voice.

"They did not. Someone's been here, dammit. Look at this mess!"

Amy looked around feeling helpless. How on earth could they find anything here. Surely if the laptop was in the apartment, then it would have been stolen. She walked farther into the apartment and looked around.

"Jackson, I don't know what..." A sparkle caught her attention, and she made her way to the far side of the room. She moved a torn pillow, and on the floor in front of her was a large zoned yellow and green fluorite cluster. A fluorite cluster that Nick bought at a rock show several years ago, and which should be sitting nice and safe in the back room of Stone's Gems and Minerals. Amy stooped, picked up the piece and stood examining it.

"What did you find, Amy?" Jackson walked over to where she stood.

"It's a large zoned fluorite crystal cluster."

"Beautiful." Jackson took the piece out of Amy's hand and turned it over. "I thought you said Carl had no interest in the rocks or minerals."

"He didn't. This isn't his. I'm sure of it. Nick paid two hundred for it about three years ago, and it was one of the ones he really didn't want to sell. Carl had to have taken this from the shop without Nick's knowledge."

Amy looked around the room and saw a few other pieces: A large kyanite sphere, an exceptional specimen of malachite and azurite and a rutilated quartz free form. Each piece worth several hundred dollars.

Amy felt anger bubbling up inside. "I think Carl has been stealing from Nick. He's got things that aren't cheap, but not the most expensive either. With everything in the back room, it would be easy to sneak things out."

"What's the point? You said he wasn't interested in rocks himself, so why bother?"

Moira banged her cane on the floor several times. "What's going on? What are you two talking about? That isn't a laptop computer."

"I'm sorry, Ms. Larson, but it looks like Carl may have been stealing items from the shop. Do you mind if I take these?" *Not that I intend to leave any of them,* Amy thought.

Moira waved her hand in the air, as if dismissing the question. "If they're yours, then take them. I've got no use for them. Besides, this young man here is going to pack everything up on Sunday anyway." She shuffled her way over to a threadbare couch and lowered herself down, as if to watch a show.

Amy looked at Jackson, chewing on her lower lip in concentration. "Okay, what about this? Say Carl wants to make a little extra money. He knows that the odds are that Nick wouldn't miss smaller items. I don't know how my dad finds everything anyway. So Carl opens a second auction account, and posts the things he steals there, and keeps that money."

Jackson scratched his chin, a distant look in his eyes. "You know, he probably wouldn't even have had to bring things home and taken a chance of being caught. Would your dad have noticed that things which were shipped out were maybe not appearing on his accounts?"

"Probably not. He'd turned more and more of the paperwork over to Carl in the last few years. But if he could do it so easily from the shop, then why bring these pieces home with him?"

"I'd say it's possible that he did that when your dad got hurt and there was no risk that anyone would find out. For all he knew, your father would sell the shop, or you wouldn't be as lackadaisical about checking the shipments against the auction records, and he wanted a little cushion."

Amy thought for a second, rolling a beautiful pink and green Willow Creek jasper sphere between her fingers. "That makes sense. But how could we find out for sure? Besides how is it relevant? A few hundred dollars in rock specimens isn't worth murdering for, is it?"

"It may not be, but it shows that Carl's moral fiber was about as strong as cotton candy. If he was cheating the shop, then who knows what else he'd be into." A brief look of intense anger surprised Amy. She didn't know Jackson's face was capable of such an expression.

"We need to find that laptop," he continued. "Maybe we'll be able to find a record of his second auction account, or his banking records, or something. I don't see any computer here. Was it stolen?"

Jackson turned to Moira who was listening to this exchange with interest. "Did Carl have a computer of his own in here?"

"Not that I know of. He always seemed to be fiddling around with one of those huge... what do they call them... smart phones. Dang thing was the size of a book."

Amy groaned, "That's it. He could do anything he needed to do on his phone. No one ever mentioned seeing his phone when he was killed. I suppose we need to find that as well."

"He could have done everything, from taking pictures to posting auctions using a phone like that, although it's not as convenient as a computer. I've been thinking, though," Jackson said. "It took us twenty minutes to get out here from town. That sports car may have been modified, but I can't imagine it covering that road any quicker. You said he left at five, so yeah, he could have likely made it all the way out here, unloaded his stuff, and then driven back into town so that his car was in front of the store by six-fifteen or six-thirty. Isn't it more likely that he didn't come out here, and instead went back to the shop as soon as you left?"

"I guess," Amy said, trying to grasp where Jackson was going with this train of thought.

"And if he did that, then it's more likely that the computer is somewhere at the shop, or was stolen by the murderer."

"If it's stolen, we might never find it." Amy said frustrated. Carl was up to something more than stealing rocks... something that had gotten him killed, but she felt like they were as far away from the answer as ever.

"That's true, but I think the first thing we need to do is a top to bottom search of the shop. We have to do an inventory anyway, so we kill two birds with one stone, so to speak."

The rumble of thunder crept its way into the bunkhouse. She could smell rain in the distance. "Okay, I agree. We do a thorough search. Right now, however, we'd better gather these specimens, and head for town before the rain keeps us here several more hours."

A flash of lightning was visible through the open door, and the long, drawn out growl of thunder that followed shook the windows. A howl sounded from the Jeep. Jynx was telling the world that the storm was approaching, and she didn't approve.

An unknown stone with Quartz

9

Amy and Jackson made it halfway back to town before the rain started in earnest. It was one of those monsoon storms where the lightning seemed so close overhead that Amy could feel the electricity prickling the hair on her head, and the thunder made her feel like she was driving through a battle field. Still she was able to get by the major washes before they flooded, and while the remainder of the road was slick, and the going slow, the four-wheel drive Jeep made its way through undaunted. Amy just hoped that they'd get enough rain to wash some of the thick mud from its sides once they got into town.

It was nearly six when Amy and Jackson pulled up in front of Stone's Gems and Minerals. The rain was starting to abate, and the thunder was moving off to the east, much to Jynx's relief. Amy turned the key and sat in silence for a moment, trying to collect her thoughts. Jackson sat beside her, staring at the front of the store.

After a few moments where neither of them spoke, Amy finally turned to Jackson. "I guess we'd better take the pieces we got from Carl's place into the shop. Let me go open the door, and you grab the specimens, okay?"

"Sounds good to me," Jackson said, nodding.

Once inside the building, Jackson set the box of minerals they'd rescued from Carl's apartment down on the counter. He looked around the shop, and rubbed his hands through his sandy brown hair, his face focused in concentration. "What now? Do we start looking for the laptop?"

Amy looked around the room, feeling weariness pushing her shoulders down.

"No, I think we'll let it go until tomorrow. I'm beat, and I need to feed the animals out at my parents' place. Maybe we should put off reopening until Monday, and use tomorrow to search the building. That laptop has to be here. Unless it was stolen."

"That's right, keep up the positive thinking." Jackson's smile reemerged, although it had a tinge of exhaustion around the edges.

"Yeah, well I'm a lot more positive when I'm not so tired." Amy smiled back at him. "Do you need a ride home? You didn't drive here this morning... Good grief, was it only this morning that you started to work here?"

"I believe it was this morning. Seems like a long time, huh? But no, I don't need a ride. Merri is working at the diner, and I'll just walk down and catch a ride home with her. She should be getting off about now. I'll call her and tell her to wait."

As the two headed for the front door of the shop, Amy noticed a yellow piece of paper lying flat on the floor, having apparently been slid under the door while they'd been out at Moira Larson's bunkhouse. She bent and picked it up. In the dim illumination, she examined the writing, then moved closer to the door where the light was brighter. All of a sudden her exhaustion was gone, and she felt a jolt of adrenaline.

"Of all the..."

"What is it?" Jackson tried to look over Amy's shoulder at the paper.

Amy turned and faced Jackson, anger and frustration warring on her face and in her guts. "It's a letter of warning from the town council saying that the shop isn't meeting the town building code. It give us ten days to bring everything up to snuff."

"Does it say where it doesn't meet code?"

"It mentions a vermin infestation and the disorganized state of the store. They're calling it a health and safety hazard." Amy looked at Jackson with desperation in her eyes. "Nick said that he might have seen a bat and that several have gotten in lately, but how the heck would the town council know that, and it's only a couple of bats, not an infestation."

"How does the town find out about things that don't meet code?" Jackson asked. "I haven't been here long enough, and from looking around the town, I wouldn't have thought the building codes were very stringent. It's just an old mining town, for pete's sake."

"They say it's a 'complaint based' system, meaning that if someone complains, then the town investigates."

"So easy, go down to the town offices and find out who complained."

"Not easy. The town allows anonymous complaints. Nick hasn't dealt with it too much in the past, since he's had a pretty good relationship with the rest of the residents. It is a small town after all. But in the past neighbors who disliked each other could file numerous complaints against one another, or even someone five miles away from them, and never have to disclose their names to anyone but the town. Everyone knew who likely filed the complaints, and usually they were baseless, but they were a pain nevertheless. On top of that, there's no consequence for the person abusing the system to attack a neighbor; no frivolous complaint procedures." Amy felt disgusted by the entire system which encouraged arguments rather than communication.

Jackson looked toward the ceiling, as if studying the holes in the acoustic tile. Then he brought his focus back to Amy. "Has your dad gotten sideways with anyone? I mean someone who might file a complaint?"

"Not that I know of. Carl did mention that the town was..." Amy stopped as the memory of the conversation with Carl surfaced. Her eyes widened in shock. "That the town was getting after Nick about the condition of the store. He said that he'd heard that someone wanted to put in a restaurant."

"So Carl knew about this situation at least four days ago, before the warning was issued? Doesn't that seem strange to you? Especially when you're just getting the ten day notice today?" Jackson flicked the paper with his finger. "Your dad would have probably told you if he'd been given a time deadline."

"Yeah... Yeah it does seem suspicious, but it's too late to do anything about it now." She glanced at the time on the screen of her phone. It was six-fifteen, and the town's offices closed at five, and it was a Friday. That meant that she couldn't do anything about the complaint until Monday morning, two days from now, and two days into her ten day notice.

"What do I do, Jackson? I can't tell Nick about this. He's got enough on his mind. This shop is his life." Amy felt tears start to build in her eyes and was afraid that she would break apart at any moment.

"When you get home, call your dad. See how he's doing. Figure out some way to ask him about Carl's statement without letting him know that the letter has been delivered. That should tell us whether or not Carl knew in advance."

"Do you think Carl would have filed a complaint about my dad? He seemed to like Nick. What would Carl have gotten out of that? If the shop were closed, he would have been out of a job. It doesn't make sense."

Jackson gave her a quick hug. "We'll get it figured out. Just make that call. Tomorrow we'll inventory, organize and clean."

"I wanted to reopen tomorrow," Amy said plaintively.

"Monday is soon enough. We need to have the weekend to go through the shop with a fine toothed comb." Jackson shook her shoulder slightly.

"Okay. But you promised to see your girlfriend on Sunday?" Amy gave Jackson a tremulous smile.

He looked at her with confusion. "My girlfriend?"

"Yup, Ms. Moira." The smile became stronger and more genuine at the look of shock on Jackson's face.

"You think I laid it on a bit thick?"

"I think she's planning on your taking the bunkhouse in place of Carl." Amy laughed.

Jackson's mobile features took on a considering look. "You know, might not be bad. My sister would probably like having the RV out of the driveway."

"You wouldn't." Amy started laughing.

"You never know," Jackson said, nodding. "Still, I'll give her a call this evening when I get home and let her know I'll have to put things off until next week sometime. I'll talk her around." He grinned, sure of his effect on the older woman.

"Just wait, Jackson. You know what they say about a woman scorned."

Jackson started laughing, and ushered Amy out of the shop and to her Jeep. Amy slid in behind the wheel and shoved the key into the ignition.

"Drive carefully, Amethyst. Don't worry. We'll get it figured out tomorrow." Jackson rested his hand on her shoulder for a moment, then turned to walk down the road toward the diner.

"Thank you, Mr. Wolfram!" Amy called out after him.

Jackson didn't turn around, but he waved his arm in the air and called out, "Not even close!"

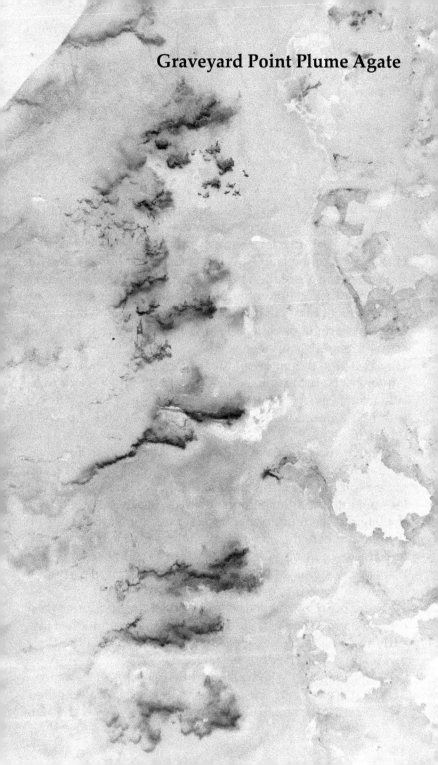

Graveyard Point Plume Agate

10

An old teal green GMC Jimmy was sitting in front of Stone's Gems and Minerals when Amy pulled in to the parking lot the next morning at seven. As she climbed out of the Jeep Amy saw Jackson walking across the road from the gas station holding two large cups, and with a paper bag tucked under his arm. She walked across the gravel lot to meet him. He held out one of the cups, which Amy took. The aroma of coffee reached her nose and she inhaled with pleasure.

"You are the man of my dreams, Mr. Jackson Wolf. Anyone who brings me coffee in the morning has got to be sent from heaven." Amy took a tentative sip. Strong with just the right amount of coconut creamer. "How did you know what I like?"

"Judy, the cashier at the station, knew, or at least was willing to take a chance. She said if she got it wrong, I could get a replacement at no charge. I got apple fritters, too, but let's get into the shop before we break into them." He pulled the bag out from under his arm and examined the stains on the paper where the oil had leaked through. He frowned and looked down at his side, but apparently didn't see any corresponding stains on his shirt because his expression immediately lightened.

Amy hurried back to the Jeep and let the dogs out, whistling to them to come as she headed for the front door. "How early did you get here?" She asked as she shooed the dogs inside, then held the door for Jackson.

"Not long ago. Maybe about fifteen minutes, but since I don't have a key yet." He gave her a pointed look, "I figured I'd run across the street and get something to give us strength for the day ahead. We'll need it if it's anything like yesterday." Jackson laughed lightheartedly, as though the day before had been just an average day.

Amy ushered the dogs into the space behind the counter, and stood looking at the shop. Admittedly it was in much better condition than it had been the day before. That didn't change the fact however, that there was still a lot to be done. Especially if the town council, or someone on the town council was determined to shut them down or move them out.

"So, where do we start?" Jackson asked, setting the bag with the fritters down on the counter.

"I say we start at the front, and work toward the back, leaving no stone unturned."

Jackson groaned at the pun, turned and headed toward the computer room, cup of coffee and a fritter in his hands.

Several hours later, the front of the shop was perfectly organized. They were stuck with the threadbare indoor/outdoor carpeting, the dull walls and stained ceiling for the time being, but everything was hung neatly on hooks mounted on the pegboard paneling, or stacked in labeled trays on the shelving. Nothing protruded into the aisles any longer.

Jackson had turned the computer office upside down, and right side up again, but didn't find a black computer case, laptop computer or flash drive anywhere in the room. Amy did the same to Nick's office and the behind the counter work area with the same results.

Finally at eleven Jackson volunteered to run back across the highway to replenish the coffee, and the two took a break before tackling the back storage room. Amy was surprised at how quickly things had come together. The shop still had a dim, subdued air, which in a strange way allowed the rocks and mineral specimens to shine even more brightly. She supposed that was why Nick had kept the store the way he had... that and the fact that he just liked old, worn things. Amy smiled to herself as she stood looking around the room.

"What did your dad say when you called him last night?" Jackson asked. He was leaning against the glass counter, absently scratching Jynx and Bess who were vying for his attention.

"We talked about getting the shop back open, and I mentioned Carl saying that the town had been after him to pack up and move the shop out of town so that someone could put in a restaurant. He did say that he'd been approached by a developer interested in buying the shop a few months ago, but that he wasn't interested, so he just sent the man away."

"Well, that certainly makes it sound like Carl had more information than Nick."

"Maybe. It could also be that Nick was downplaying everything. Not taking it seriously. He did mention a couple of minor complaints to the town... potholes in the parking lot. A front light that was too bright. The Dumpster left out after the trash was picked up. That type of thing. It was annoying, but it didn't worry him too much. He wasn't sure who was complaining, but none of them went anywhere." Amy chewed her lip in concentration.

"You didn't tell him about the ten day notice?" Jackson looked at her intently.

"No, how could I? He's stuck there in the rehab facility. It's not as if he can do anything about it, and he'd just worry. Mom's got enough on her plate dealing with him. I'll figure things out, I have to." Amy saw Jackson's smile turn broaden, and she realized that she'd taken on a combative stance, chin lifted, as though about to get into an actual fight.

"At least the pest control people are due here on Monday to check things out. It's so strange. As we've been cleaning and organizing I haven't seen any sign of bats or any other vermin. You'd think we'd find droppings or something if the situation was as bad as the town makes it out to be."

"Yeah," Jackson said. He nodded and took another sip of his coffee. "It's another thing that is making me a bit suspicious."

"Let me get this right. We have to: One, find out who killed Carl and why. Two, find out exactly what Carl was up to, and how much he's stolen from the shop. Three, find out who's sabotaging the shop and why. And four, get the town off our backs about the condition of the shop. Is that it?"

"I guess that about sums it up." Jackson took another sip from his cup, a bland expression on his face.

"I think I'm going to need a lot more coffee." She stared at her empty cup morosely.

"Or something stronger?" He laughed. "We'd better get back to work. I hear the boss is a slave driver." Jackson headed toward the back storage room, ducking a small piece of quartz which Amy tossed at him.

Jackson reached the narrow passage between the main part of the shop and the storage area in the back, and pushed the warped wooden door open.

"The deputies searched back here as well, didn't they?"

"I'm sure they did. After all, they haven't found the murder weapon. They would have searched every area where it could have been hidden."

"Looks like this room didn't get torn up as badly as the rest of the store." He looked around the room which was filled with shelves, each covered with various specimens, boxes and bins. Several small barrels stood at the end of the shelves filled with small geodes or tumbled stones.

"I don't know why. Maybe because it's a bit more organized than the main shop."

Jackson walked to the first shelf, and started pulling the items, several polished petrified wood bookends, off and setting them on the floor. "We definitely need a little bit of dusting back here, but there's nothing dangerous that I can see. No laptop case though. This could take a while." Jackson stepped back and turned to Amy. "I guess I'd better go get some towels and we'll get started. We..."

A loud knocking came from the front of the building causing Amy to jump. She heard the dogs bark in response. Amy looked back toward Jackson. "We locked the front door right?"

"I'm sure we did. Otherwise whoever is knocking would have probably walked right on in. People do, you know." Jackson looked at Amy and quirked an eyebrow, causing her to start laughing at his sly reference to his own entrance the morning before.

The knocking sounded again, even louder this time. "I

guess I'd better see who it is. Who knows, it might be Ms. Moira, hunting you down because she didn't like being stood up," Amy said, and headed out of the storeroom for the front of the shop.

"Yeah, well these new relationships are always difficult," Jackson called after her. "Bring back some towels and cleaner when you come."

As Amy entered the short hallway leading to the front door, she could see a silver gray Trailblazer parked next to Amy's Wrangler. An older man was standing impatiently in front of the building, a scowl on his face. Just as Amy reached the front door, the man raised his fist to bang on the glass again. Frowning, she pushed the door open before he had the chance.

"Can I help you?" Her voice had cactus spines.

"Hello. I presume you're Nick Stone's daughter, Amethyst? I am Jon Hazelton, and this is my wife, Bea." Hazelton nodded toward a tall, rawboned woman standing a few feet away with a sour expression on her face.

"It's nice to meet you. I guess you know my dad? I'm sorry, but I don't think he's mentioned you."

"My wife and I just moved here five years ago. Wonderful little town, and only going to get better." Hazelton gave a determined nod, but there was something in his eyes that made Amy uncomfortable. Besides, she thought his wife was just down right creepy with her pale blue eyes, and straw-like bleached blonde hair piled tall on her head.

"Well, it's been nice meeting you, Jon. I'm sorry, though. We're not open right now." Amy smiled at Hazelton, unwilling to alienate a customer, regardless of how distasteful.

"Actually, Amethyst, my wife and I need to talk with you. May we come in?"

Amy frowned. "I'm sorry, Jon, but as I said, we're not open right now. You may have heard but there was a situation here a few days ago, and I'm trying to get the shop cleaned up and ready to open again."

"I can appreciate that, Amethyst. I know about your situation, but I really do need to talk with you." He fixed Amy with a stare that made her cringe. "I think I wasn't clear. I'm one of the town council members for Copper Springs. The town council which just sent you a ten day warning."

It felt like Amy had just been slapped in the face and she took a step back. Apparently seeing that as an invitation, Hazelton took the door from Amy, and ushered his wife through. Amy backed into the main room of the shop and stood looking at her visitors.

"I see that you've gotten a little organization and cleaning done here. I emphasize the word 'little' unfortunately. I hear that you've had two major accidents in the shop recently, one resulting in someone's death?" Hazelton made the statement sound like a question, even though it seemed he was perfectly aware of both Nick's fall, and Carl's death.

Jackson's voice sounded from over Amy's shoulder before she could reply, "Carl Schrader's death was hardly an accident. It was a pretty sloppy attempt to frame Ms. Stone here for murder." Jackson sounded calm and in control. Amy's heart rate started to drop back down to normal, and a cold fury began to build.

"Is it appropriate for the town council members to be barging onto private property? I didn't know that code enforcement was part of the job. Even if we've been given a ten day warning, we still have nine of those days to deal with that bunch of trumped up complaints." Amy faced the man, hands fisted at her sides, chin in its characteristic defiant tilt.

Hazelton met her stare without flinching. The image of a lizard flashed into her mind. That was what Hazelton and his wife reminded her of, lizards. Gangly, rawboned, skin looking dry and stretched tight over the skeleton. Both had cold eyes, his the color of mud, and hers an icy, pale blue.

"Let's get down to it, Amethyst. The town is changing. People are moving in, and those people want something different. This little old building was cute in its day, but these days it's an eyesore for the tourists driving past."

"And what do you propose, Mr. Hazelton. This building has been here since the 1920s. It's part of the history of this town."

"It may be part of the history, Ms. Stone, but it's not part of the future. Face it, your father has been seriously injured and it may be quite a while before he's back at work, if ever. I suggest you talk him into selling the building to me, and moving the shop. Scott Branson, our code enforcement officer, informs me that there are multiple violations... too many to make it worth addressing. Besides, I'm sure the majority of your business is online these days," Hazelton sneered.

Amy frowned. Carl had said something similar to her when he mentioned that the town was harassing her dad. Still, most businesses like her dad's had resorted to online auctions and sites to market their wares. It wouldn't have been too much of a stretch for Hazelton to guess that a large portion of their business was online.

Suddenly Hazelton's wife spoke up, her voice as crinkly and dry as her hair. "Ms. Stone, I suggest that you convince your father to sell just as my husband has said. We'll be getting the store eventually. It's just a matter of time and circumstance. Mr. Branson assures us of this. We can have a nice, civilized real estate transaction, or the town will condemn this building and take the property through eminent domain. You seem to be an intelligent, educated young woman. I'm sure you know what *eminent domain* means. It's your choice." Bea Hazelton stepped back and looked around the room, the perpetual scowl on her face. "I intend to build the most beautiful restaurant here. We'll make that poky little dinner curl up its toes, I'll tell you."

"Bea, hush!" Hazelton looked at his wife, his scowl outdistancing hers by a mile in Amy's opinion.

"I thought eminent domain was to be used by towns to do things like put in roads and the like, not just to take property from one owner, and transfer it to another private party, just because the town likes them better." Jackson managed to keep all trace of anger out of his voice, but Amy could feel the tension in his body, even from the distance of several inches.

"Educate yourself, young man. This is our town now."

"Bea!" Hazelton sounded as though he were being strangled and his yellowish face was turning a fascinating shade of orange.

"I think we're done here, Mr. Hazelton." Amy said. "Neither I nor my father are at all interested in selling the shop. When the town's *code enforcement officer* comes, I'm sure that he will see that we've addressed the areas of concern. If we continue to be harassed, then I'm equally sure my father's lawyer will be interested in talking with you."

The shade of orange deepened, and Amy briefly wondered if there was going to be another death at Stone's Gems and Minerals. However, instead of keeling over, Hazelton turned to his wife, placed his hand under her arm and guided her to the door, muttering in her ear the whole way, just low enough that Amy couldn't make out the words.

As the Hazeltons pushed the outer door open, Jackson piped up from Amy's side. "Thank you for coming. Please come again... *not!*" the final word uttered in a low growl, so that only Amy could hear. A laugh burst out of her, and she punched Jackson in the arm as the door closed behind Hazelton and his wife.

"See, I've got this retail gig down pat. You're going to bless the day you hired me, Amethyst Stone, although I am thinking that maybe we could make some room for a few framed photographs... maybe make it a rock shop slash photo gallery? Whatdaya think?"

He looked at her with such huge, innocent blue eyes that Amy started laughing again. "I think I already bless the day I hired you, Jackson Wolverson, and I think the photos sound fantastic. We will have to get the idea okayed by Nick of course."

"Naturally," He grinned at her, "Although as far as the name Wolverson goes... you're so cold you need snowshoes. What was all that crap about anyway?"

"I don't really know." Laughter gone, Amy stood looking out the door, even though the Hazeltons had already pulled out of the parking lot. "Nick said that there were new people moving in, and they want to make changes, but I guess I didn't take it very seriously."

"It looks like it might be time to take things seriously. At the moment, however, I have a very important question."

Pulled out of her reflection on the changes happening in Copper Spring, Amy looked at Jackson, "What now?"

"Where are the towels and cleaner I sent you for?"

Amy rolled her eyes and start to laugh again. "What do you mean 'sent me for'? You said that when I came back to bring them. Have I come back yet?"

"Yeah, yeah, yeah. Excuses, excuses." Jackson snagged the pile of rags and the bottle of cleaner off the counter and headed back toward the storage room. "Hey, by the way, I noticed a door back there. Where does it lead that your dad keeps it hidden?"

"There's one that leads outside to a small vestibule and the basement stairs, and from there to a yard where we store some of the rough rock we've collected, but that hasn't been cut. It's our emergency exit."

"No, I checked that one out. There's another one, a hidden one, that leads to a stairwell going up to the second floor. Why is it hidden? What's up there?"

Amy frowned. "Up to the second floor apartment? That door is locked. Dad locked it to keep my brother, sister and I from playing in the apartment when we were kids."

"It's not locked, actually. It's not easy to see, but it's not locked."

Jackson entered the storeroom first, and strode over to where a panel of the wall was standing ajar, revealing the two narrow, steep staircases he had referred to. Amy walked over and looked upward toward the upstairs apartment.

"I haven't been up there in years," she said marveling. "When Dad bought the building to start the rock shop, he'd originally intended to use that space, as well as the basement, as additional storage. Then my sister, Opie, slipped and fell running down the stairs. She broke her ankle and wrist, so Nick decided that these stairs were too dangerous, and he didn't need the extra storage space anyway."

Jackson gave her a skeptical look, then pointedly looked around the storeroom, which was stacked to the ceiling with specimens and boxes, probably containing more specimens.

"Do you know if the sheriff's deputies searched up there, or down in the basement?" He asked.

"They didn't mention it. I would guess they'd have gone down into the basement when they looked out the back door. I'm not sure they saw the door to this stairwell, especially since that rug is hung in front of it. How did you find it anyway?" Amy looked at Jackson, a question on her face.

"It's a nice rug, and I thought it would fit well over that hole in the front room. When I pulled it down, I saw that there was a door behind it, so... well, curiosity may have killed the cat, but it seems to be my downfall as well." Jackson laughed.

"I just don't get it. My dad always kept the door locked. The key is in his office. The only reason he would have gone in would be to check periodically for mice and things like that."

"Maybe he unlocked the door when the pest control people were here last. They would have needed to check up there to see if they could find where the bats were getting in."

"I guess maybe that's it, although I can't believe he would have forgotten to go back and lock it afterward." Amy shook her head. "I suppose I should go get the key and lock it again." She started to turn to go to the front office to get the door key when Jackson reached out and grabbed her arm.

"Wait. It may have been locked as long as you can remember, but it's unlocked now, and who knows for how long. Besides, you can see someone has been both up and down these stairs. Look at the dust." Jackson indicated where footprints stood out on the dark, worn wood. It was obvious that someone had used the stairs, and recently.

Amy's head dropped as she admitted the inevitable to herself. She and Jackson would have to inspect the stairwells. Remembering the last time she'd been in the basement, she felt a sinking in her chest. *Ah crap!*

A note of resignation in her voice, Amy turned to head out of the storage room. "I'll go get the lantern and flashlight from the Jeep. I'll be right back."

"I'll be waiting right here. That is, unless some monster creeps out of that basement and drags me down to its lair, of course. Then I'll be in the basement."

Amy had a hard time forgiving the jovial tone in Jackson's voice this time.

11

Go toward the light, Amy thought, as she and Jackson deliberated and finally chose to head toward the second floor instead of the basement as the first stage of exploration. The upstairs apartment had a ceiling that slanted in all four directions, due to the low hipped roof. However, each end had a dormer window, while the sides had two, giving the upstairs room a soft light, in spite of the blinds that Nick had installed years ago.

A narrow door stood ajar at the top of the staircase, allowing a little of this light to sift down toward the first floor landing. Jackson took the flashlight Amy offered him, and slowly walked up the steps, casting the beam onto the ceiling, and around the walls. Nothing out of place. No bats, rats, and certainly no black laptop case. The walls were close to the stairs, providing no hiding spots to the side of the steps. The way the building had been constructed, the stairs were virtually installed in a slanted tube or shaft that ran from one floor to the next. In fact, it was possible to see the outline of the stairwell in the room where all the best display pieces were kept. It made an interesting little nook with a sloping top that Nick had turned into a lighted set of cases.

Pipes for the plumbing and electrical conduits to the top floor also ran under the stairs, keeping them nice and warm during the cold winter months on the edge of the Colorado Plateau. Years ago Nick had installed shut off valves in a small closet near the bottom of the stairs, and generally kept the water for the upstairs apartment turned off, but when Amy was a child, she could remember hearing the water running over her head when someone turned on a tap or flushed the toilet upstairs.

Jackson stepped out on the landing at the top of the stairwell and walked into the middle of the U-shaped room, giving Amy a chance to come in behind him. She hadn't been in this space since she was a young girl, and she found that over the years her memory had been liberally enhanced by her imagination. Amy looked around, noting the dirty walls and floor, but instead of the haunted house of her childhood, she saw a pleasant space which simply needed some TLC, although the temperature was already well within the uncomfortable range.

"I can't believe your dad never used this space," Jackson said, looking around the room and nodding in admiration. "When was the last time someone lived in the apartment?"

"I have no idea. I know that when Nick bought the property, it had been vacant for about ten years. We were told that the place was used as a bar back in the 1920s when it was built, and that the top room was used by the owner. After that I'm told that the building was used at different times as the main office for a mining company, a feed store, and a small, private museum."

"Well, it shouldn't take too long to search since it's pretty much empty, so let's get to it." Jackson moved toward the corner that housed a small kitchenette and started pulling open the few cupboards that were still there, shining the flashlight into the furthest reaches of the compartments..

Amy walked over to the dormer that looked out above the front door. This one, like the others, included a built in window seat, although the cushion was beginning to fall apart and it was apparent that at some point mice had gotten in and chewed holes and pulled out stuffing to make a nest. However, there were no fresh signs of infestation, and it was impossible to tell how long ago the damage had occurred.

She pulled off the upholstered seat, and used the lantern to illuminate the space inside. Nothing but dust. Replacing the seat, she moved on to the other five windows, pulling off the seats at each one, and in every case finding nothing but dust in the compartments below.

"Any luck over there?" Amy called out to Jackson who was investigating the small bathroom.

"Other than I'm a little concerned that some guy dressed as an old lady is going to show up with a knife, I'm good."

Amy peeked in the door and saw Jackson standing in the tub, the tattered shower curtain pulled most of the way around on an oval track. He saw her and let out a falsetto scream, grabbed the curtain and held it in front of his chest.

"Jackson, there is something seriously wrong with you," Amy laughed, as he continued to play it up, peeking at Amy over the curtain and acting the frightened ingenue.

"Yeah, that's what my sister always says." Jackson dropped the shower curtain and stepped out of the tub. "You know, this place has some real potential. A little paint, some rust remover, maybe an exorcist, and you'd have a great apartment here."

The two of them walked back out into the main room. Laughter gone, Amy sighed. "Is there anywhere we didn't look?"

"I don't know. There's something, but I can't put my finger on it." Jackson looked around at the open space, a serious expression on his face. He started to walk over toward the far dormer window then stopped and turned back to face Amy.

"From the outside the roof drops down to the first story, correct?"

Amy nodded. "Yes, the eves are at the same level that they would have been on a single story house. Why?"

"That means that the walls of the apartment should be slanting all the way down to the floor, but they're not. They've put up these short paneled walls in a few feet from the actual edge where the sloping roof meets the floor. That means that there's got to be a space behind them."

"You're right. There must be doors. We just have to find them."

Amy walked over to the wall closest to the front of the building and began examining the paneling while Jackson did the same for the wall opposite. Amy examined each of the seams in the rough pinewood board and batten paneling. Nothing stood out, and she felt her newfound hope falter.

Just as she was ready to move on to another wall, she saw it. A narrow crack near the top of the wall. She looked down, and could see where something had scraped an arc in the floor, as though a door opened, but hadn't fully cleared the surface.

"Jackson, over here. I think I found something." Amy could hear the excitement in her voice. She ran her fingers along the crack at the top, tracing it from side to side. Then she saw them. Two small hinges, tucked into a niche carved into a batten board, the antique brass blending in with the yellowed pine. It was definitely a door.

"What have you got?" Jackson looked over her shoulder.

"There's a crack here, and there are hinges tucked into that board, but I haven't figured out how to open it yet." Amy traced the crack the opposite direction from the hinges. It traversed several boards and then the battens, until it suddenly stopped at the far edge of a batten. She ran her fingers down the exposed edge of the framing board, trying to find a spot to get a grip, but the thin wood eluded her grasp.

Jackson moved around so that he could get a better look at the edge of the board, holding up his lantern so that the light fell on the wood.

"Look," He indicated two notches cut into the underside of the batten where it met the board it was apparently holding. "See if you can fit your fingers in this spot."

Amy slid the tips of her fingers into the notches, and was able to move the panel door about a half inch. She got a better grip, and this time was able to pull the door several more inches, the bottom scraping across the floor.

"Yes!"

"Now you can get a good grip!" Jackson said, the excitement building in his voice.

Amy grabbed the edge of the paneling and pulled the door all the way open, exposing a dim triangular space. The rough planking of the floor extended all the way to where the exposed rafters met them at a sharp angle. It was obvious that the dust had been disturbed recently, but nothing was in view.

"Jackson give me your lantern. That might work better than the flashlight." Amy took the small LED lantern from him and pushed it in through the opening, where it illuminated the space. Nothing was visible from the outside. Amy took a deep breath, and inched forward on her hands and knees, sticking her head and shoulders into the hidden compartment.

Amy looked right then left. The lantern illuminated several feet in either direction, but the far ends were shrouded in gloom. It was bright enough, however, to see several bait stations, still filled with mouse poison, set up to the left of the door. Amy's heart fell. The pest control people had been in here. That's why the dust was disturbed.

Amy crawled out and sat back on her heels. Her eyes met Jackson's, and she shook her head.

"Nothing in there?"

"No," Amy sighed with discouragement. "There's nothing in there but rat poison. The pest control people must have been up here and found the compartments back when Nick called them the first time for the bats."

"Well, that's a little like following a treasure map and finding a little kid's sand bucket and shovel buried where X marks the spot." Jackson said. He reached out and brushed Amy's short hair, surprising her. "Cobwebs. You must have hit a bumper crop in there." He smiled and showed her his hand coated with the fine strands.

"Thanks. Now what?"

"Hey, no giving up yet. For one thing, I'm guessing there's a compartment like this in every section of wall. They can't go past the window seats in the dormers, so they'd just have to put in a new door in every section. We've got to check all of them."

"But surely the pest people will have been in all of them," Amy said, exasperation clear in her voice.

"Yes, you're right." Jackson looked at her and smiled. "But when were the pest people here last?"

"I don't know. Dad said it had been awhile ago."

"Right. Think about it. Your dad would have unlocked the door to let them up here, because you can't treat just part of a building, especially not an old one like this."

"Okay," Amy said, a note of uncertainty in her voice.

"Don't you see? If Carl was working here when the pest

people came, and it sounds like he was, then he would have learned that there was a door behind the rug, and that the key was kept in your dad's office. Heck, if he came upstairs while they were inspecting and setting out the bait stations, he even would have learned about the hidden compartments, and may have decided to use them for his own purposes."

Amy blew out a breath. "You're so right. I didn't even think of that. Nick would have had no reason to keep the upstairs floor secret from Carl, and he seemed to want to keep his nose in everything."

"Okay, so you said nothing but bait stations in that compartment. You saw all the way to the end walls easily?"

"No, not well, but well enough to tell there wasn't a laptop case."

"Then let's move on to the next compartment."

Now that they knew what they were looking for, it didn't take long for the two of them to find the next door, and then the next and the next. Jackson moved along the east wall, Amy along the west. After backing out of the third compartment, covered with more cobwebs, but with nothing else to show for her effort, she started to wonder if they were heading in the right direction. After inspecting the fourth compartment, she was sure they were heading down the wrong trail.

Jackson had been moving along the far wall, checking the compartments that corresponded to Amy's on the west wall. Apparently he'd been having as much luck as Amy, as all she'd heard for the past few minutes were muffled exclamations and not so muffled sneezes. Amy was just feeling for the door edges on her fifth and last compartment when she heard a change in Jackson's tone.

"Amy!" She could hear the excitement in his voice and she stopped trying to open her door and whipped around.

"What is it? What did you find?" Amy looked down the wall to where Jackson knelt outside of the his fourth compartment, the one in the front right corner of the house.

"Come on, you've got to see this."

"I swear, Jackson, you'd better be serious, or I'm going to lock you in up here and let the ghosts have you." Amy hurried over to where Jackson was waiting, then stopped and stared. In front of him was a large cardboard box with several large crystals and mineral specimens, similar in size and quality to those they'd found in Carl's apartment.

"There's more. Let me have the lantern for a moment."

Amy handed it over and Jackson crawled back into the opening. She heard some more shuffling, and Jackson scooted back out dragging two more boxes, each containing more specimens.

"One last trip." Jackson said, breathing heavily. He sneezed several times, and tried to wipe the cobwebs from his face. Amy couldn't help snickering at his expression as the filaments stuck to his sweaty skin. The upstairs apartment didn't have much along the lines of insulation, and in this July afternoon, it was sweltering.

"Laugh, spider woman, laugh all you want." Jackson retorted, although the smile on his face belayed the words. "You've collected a comprehensive collection of the things yourself." He tried to toss the newly removed cobwebs toward Amy, but they refused to come loose from his fingers. Finally he gave up, and plunged once more into the compartment, only to return a moment later with another large cardboard box filled with rocks, and sitting on top of the rocks was a black laptop bag.

"You found it. Oh good heavens above, you actually found it!" Amy could hardly breath.

"I can't imagine that there would be two of them, so yes, we've got it, and I checked, the laptop is inside."

Jackson sat for a moment, then slowly rose to his feet. "It looks as though Carl has been skimming from the top for quite a while here. I wonder if he had them hidden elsewhere, and only had the idea to stash them up here after the pest control people visited, or if he just ramped up his activities when he found he had a perfect spot."

"I don't know, but I remember Nick saying that he often had Carl unpack the shipments, as well as pack the ones to go out. In fact, Carl was unpacking crystals at the time my dad fell. What if a shipment came in with multiple pieces, and he would just take one or two specimens out and stash them somewhere. Nick just wasn't paying close enough attention to the business. I don't know if we'll ever figure out exactly what Carl stole."

Jackson didn't answer her and seemed uncharacteristically serious, as though something was weighing on his mind.

"What's going on?" Amy studied Jackson. "Did you hear what I said about Carl?"

"Yeah, I heard you." Jackson paused, then continued, "You know that finding out that Carl has been stealing from your dad could be seen as a motive by the sheriff's department."

"What?" Amy said, shocked to the core. "You aren't starting to believe that I killed Carl are you?"

"No. I know you didn't kill him, but think about it the way the inspectors will, and the way they would present it to a jury. Carl may have been stealing from your dad for years. Who knows how much he's taken." Jackson paused and looked at Amy who nodded her understanding.

"Recently he finds out that there's a room upstairs, with hidden compartments, allowing him to increase his pilfering. He starts taking things that haven't even been placed out into the store yet, just slipping them upstairs when your dad wasn't watching. I'd say a lot of the stuff in these boxes was actually taken in the last two weeks since your dad's injury. There's not enough dust on most of these." He picked up a beautiful piece of tourmaline, glowing pink and green in the dim light.

"Okay. I think I see where you're going." Amy said, feeling her heart sink.

"Yeah. The prosecutors could argue that Carl had come back after you left that night in order to clear out the apartment. After all, he knows you called and made an appointment with the pest control company for Monday, and he needs to get the compartments emptied out before then."

"That makes sense. Obviously his stash would have been found on Monday when the extermination guys come."

"Right, but then the prosecutors are going to argue that you didn't go right home that night as you said, but instead stopped to see why he'd come back and caught him in the act. You fought, and ended up killing Carl."

Amy looked at Jackson, dark violet eyes huge. "Oh good grief, Jackson. I'm in trouble aren't I? They already believe that I did it, and then just walked off and locked the door. The authorities are going to see Carl stealing as even more motivation for me to kill him, aren't they? Jackson, what do I do?"

Jackson stood, gazing off into the distance, apparently thinking. After a moment he turned to look at Amy. "Did you ever call Maria Kissoon, as your friend Tommy suggested?"

"I did, but just got a message. I haven't heard back from her yet, but she may be down in the canyon visiting her folks," Amy said, referring to Cataract Canyon where Supi, the town Maria and Tommy's parents lived in on the Havasupi Reservation, was located. "She doesn't get very good reception down there."

"Okay, I think this is what we do. We take the laptop, because we need to find out what exactly is going on. However, for now, let's leave these specimens up here until you have a chance to talk with her and explain what's going on."

Amy nodded, unhappy about the turn in events. Jackson bent down, picked up the laptop case and headed for the stairwell.

At the bottom of the stairs, Jackson paused and looked back at Amy. "We got a bit interrupted on our cleaning."

"I suppose we shouldn't clean upstairs until we hear from Maria, but what do we do when the code enforcement officer comes?"

"We've got nine more days for that, at least. So by then you should have heard from Maria, and we will have done whatever she recommends as far as the apartment goes. I'm a little torn on the pest control people. It's obvious seeing the bait traps that nothing is up there, and I'd like to keep everyone out for a little while, but the town's going to want to see that the exterminator has been here, considering one of their *anonymous* complaints has been in regards to a serious infestation."

Amy pulled out her phone and looked at the screen. "It's three o'clock. Why don't I work back here in the storage room. You've got the cleaning petty well started, though the inventory will probably take days. Right now, I'd just like to get it put back together before we leave. You can go see what you can find from the laptop. Tomorrow we can tackle the basement." Amy gave a little shiver at the thought of the space below the shop.

"Okay, that works for me, except I need to go down to the hardware store and get a second key made for Ms. Moira before they close. I don't want her to be without her only means of entrance to the apartment for too long, so I thought I'd run her key and the spare back out tonight before I head home."

"Alright, why don't you go now? Gleason's closes at four on Saturdays, and isn't open at all on Sundays. On top of that they're not quick on the best of days."

Jackson laughed. "I think that is the general condition of most of the establishments in this town from what I've seen."

"Then you'd better get moving," Amy said with a chuckle, She looked around the storage room and sighed. "And I'd better get cleaning. I sure as heck hope Nick gets better soon."

"So he can do the cleaning? It won't happen if it hasn't already," Jackson said in a matter of fact voice.

"No, so I can beat him with this cleaning rag."

"Really, you're a suspect in a murder investigation and you're still talking about violence. Tsk, tsk, tsk." Jackson wagged a finger at Amy. She felt torn between being insulted by the comment, and finding it funny. Fortunately, she was able to settle on funny, and she laughed. Jackson continued, "It's really not that bad. It's cluttered, but I'm guessing that it's always been cluttered."

Amy nodded her head in agreement.

"The part about it being so dirty and rodent infested that it's a health hazard is just a made up bunch of crap. You're just scared right now, so everything is looking like it's in worse condition than it actually is."

Amy felt her shoulders relax. Jackson was right. Sure the storage room was a bit dusty, as was the apartment upstairs, but it was equally obvious that it wasn't years of accumulation. More like months, if that. This was a dusty part of the world.

"Yeah, you're right, Jackson. I'll try not to magnify my problems. I'm sure there are a lot worse ones out there."

"You betcha. Just try juggling two women at once."

Amy looked at Jackson appalled. "You've done that?"

"Yep, Ms. Moira and you. It's one heck of a balancing act." Jackson laughed and turned to head out of the room as Amy threw her rag at him.

Amy set the last polished bookend back on the shelf, a beautiful piece of green and pink imperial jasper, and stood back to survey her work. The storage room was completely swept and, if not organized, at least stacked neatly. She'd also started to look into a few boxes, to make sure that they were what the labels said they were, but a complete inventory back here would have to wait. Besides, they still had to find a prior inventory to compare any new ones to.

Jackson had made it back by four o'clock, grumbling about how a key cost a buck fifty and three stories. Amy smiled at the memory. He was right. Gus Gleason loved to talk about the "old times" and Jackson would have been fresh meat. She didn't have the heart to tell him that after he'd left she remembered that she hadn't gotten him a key to the shop yet. The smile widened to a grin. She'd let him do that on Monday. Gus had plenty of tales to tell.

She wandered out of the store room, and back toward the front of the shop, admiring the newly organized stock. There wasn't really anything that could be done about the paint, the worn carpet, or the stained ceiling, but those things shouldn't be considered to be a health or safety hazard.

The light was on in the computer room, and Amy headed in that direction, calling out as she walked, "Hey Jackson, are you ready to call it quits for the night." She stuck her head in the door. "It's about six, and... What do you have there? What the hell!"

Jackson was sitting at the desk staring at the screen of the laptop, a picture of a woman staring back at him, a woman dressed in much less than would normally be expected in a picture. Looking back at Amy, he quickly minimized the window. Amy could see a mixture of misery and fury in his eyes. The woman in the picture was Merri Thompson, Jackson's sister.

Calcite

12

"Jackson, what's going on? What is Merri's picture doing on the shop's computer?" Amy felt like the wind had been knocked out of her.

"It's hard to explain, Amy." Jackson put his head in his hands for a moment, then lifted it again and looked at her. "Please, have a seat. There are some things I need to tell you. Things I should have told you from the beginning."

Amy moved over to the spare chair and looked at the computer screen in front of Jackson. The explorer window was open, showing a list of files.

"I take it you found out how to get into Carl's data?"

"Yeah, it wasn't really that hard. Actually, I found an inventory of the shop set up on a spreadsheet. The problem is that if your dad was having Carl handle the inventory, he'll be sure that nothing he took is on that list."

"I'd thought about that. I asked Nick last night if he'd done one on paper, like he used to, but he said that when he hired Carl four years ago, he persuaded Nick to set up the inventory on a spreadsheet. Nick is okay with computers, but he figured why hire a computer guy and not use him."

"Yeah, well it turns out that Carl also had a second inventory, one containing all of the things he took, what he sold them for, when, where and how much."

"On the same computer? On my dad's computer? What was he thinking?" Amy looked at Jackson in amazement, the picture of Jackson's sister banished from her mind.

"He didn't expect your dad, or anyone else, to see it. He created a hidden partition on the hard drive."

"A what?" Amy ran her hand through her short, curly hair, making a fist. "I don't get it."

"A hidden partition. He did it the easy way, fortunately. He went into disk management, and set up a section of the hard drive as separate drive."

Amy looked at Jackson as though he'd grown a few extra heads and was talking Martian. "You want to put that in English?"

Jackson took a deep breath and rolled his eyes toward the ceiling for a moment. Then he fixed his gaze back on Amy. "Say you have a long couch. No pillows, just a clear area to sit."

"Following you so far, although I must say I don't get how my furniture has anything to do with a computer's hard drive."

"Imagine you want to break up that space. You run a pillow or a rolled-up blanket across the seat. Now you've got two places to sit, both smaller than the original, but when you add them together, it's the same space. That's creating a partition. Hide it from the person sitting on the main part of the couch by a curtain or something, and you've got a hidden partition. The person in the main seat can't see what's in the other seat, or even that the other seat exists.

"That's essentially what he did with the hard drive. He used disk management to section off a portion of the drive, then marked it as hidden. Then the average person looking at the files on the computer wouldn't have had any idea that this other partition was there." A glimmer of the normal Jackson appeared as he watched Amy's face. A slight smile played on his lips, although his blue eyes still appeared haunted.

"So Carl created one of these 'hidden partitions' and kept all his records there?"

"Yup. It's not a big partition, but it's there. I'd guess he has a backup on a flashdrive somewhere as well. He could have just hidden a file or a folder, but he has quite a bit in this partition, and probably felt this was the best way. Either that or he just got a kick thinking about Nick working on the computer with all this evidence sitting right under his nose, and never even realizing it."

"How the heck do you know all of this... no let me guess? Another old girlfriend?" The merest wisp of a laugh escaped Amy.

A real grin surfaced this time. "The same old girlfriend, truth be told. The one who was a programmer. There were times she'd hide things on my computer just to see how long it would take me to find them. Fortunately for us, Carl was apparently satisfied that your dad wasn't computer savvy enough to find a hidden partition, or he would have also hidden and password protected his files."

"So what else is in there?" Amy leaned in toward the laptop. "Why was there a picture of Merri on the computer?" she said, suddenly remembering the photo she'd seen when she first walked into the office.

Jackson looked briefly at the list of computer file folders, and clicked on one labeled *Collections*. A spreadsheet popped onto the screen. Lists of dates, followed by numbers and letters. A lot of numbers, that looked a great deal like dollar amounts. Amy frowned as she studied the screen.

"What is this? It looks like a ledger, other than there are only deposits, and no withdrawals."

"I think that's exactly what it is. Look," Jackson indicated a line located in the middle of the page. "Isn't this the day your dad had his accident?"

Amy looked at the line. Sure enough, it was dated the day Nick had his fall. Following the date was the number 1,000.00. The column after the numbers had a series of letters. The letters following the thousand were BJH. In the final column was the memo "services."

"Does BJH mean anything to you?" Amy asked Jackson. She looked down the column and noticed that the BJH appeared several times, always following an even number, as low as five hundred, and as high as a thousand. The word "services" always appeared in the final column.

"No," Jackson's forehead creased in concentration. "I think it's probably whoever paid Carl, I just have no idea who it is or why Carl was being paid. This last column probably indicates that, but he's got it coded as well. Who knows what 'services' he provided." Jackson pointed at another line. "SBSM even more than the BJH, but the numbers are all over the place, as are final codes."

Amy looked at the list of numbers, then up at Jackson. "I

suppose there could be several legitimate reasons for these payments." She found herself hoping that Jackson was going to tell her that this wasn't any big deal.

"Probably. I mean you said he worked with the computers and maintained the website. Maybe he did that type of work for other people and they paid him. I'm just not sure why he'd bother to keep that information hidden, or why he'd be using the shop's computer, instead of owning one of own."

Amy reached out to the computer, and closed the spreadsheet. She looked at the various files, noting that Carl even had one labeled *passwords*. "That jerk was so confident that Nick would never be able to find this partition thingy that he even kept a file of all his passwords? Lord, I wish he was alive, so that I could kill him! No wonder he was so possessive of the computer when I asked him if he wanted me to cover the evening auctions. He probably wasn't sure how much I knew about computers."

Jackson nearly choked on a laugh. "Yeah, I'd say that lack of confidence was not one of our Carl's weaknesses, but you probably threw him for a loop."

Amy used the mouse to move the pointer over a file labeled *pictures*. Noticing where Amy had moved the cursor, Jackson reached quickly for her hand. Before he could take the mouse, however, she clicked the button twice. Amy looked at Jackson, her violet eyes meeting his bright blue ones, a serious look on her face.

"Now what about the pictures?" Amy gestured toward the screen where five small pictures of different women were lined up across the window. Amy clicked on the middle one, and Merri Thompson's face filled the screen.

Jackson reached forward and shut the lid of the computer, effectively shutting it down. He looked at Amy and she could see the pain in his eyes. His body was so tense she thought that it might snap like a spring at any moment. She sat silently, looking at him, waiting.

Finally Jackson took a deep breath. "It seems that there isn't a lot that our friend Carl wasn't willing to do to turn an extra buck. Sports cars don't come cheap, after all. Especially modified ones like his. That picture isn't what it looks like, though. Carl was good with photo editing."

"Give."

"Okay," Jackson sighed. "You know that Lou, Merri's husband, died in an accident several months ago."

Amy nodded, but didn't say anything.

"It was after Lou died that Merri went to work for Gladys at the Copper Springs Diner. She loves it up here, and she wants to stay in her house, wants to raise the kids in this area. So, she got the job, and her neighbor watches over the boys during the day.

"About a month after Lou passed away, Merri called to say there was a guy at the diner who was harassing her, and she wasn't sure what to do. She was afraid of him, but she was terrified of losing her job, too. Then one day he came in to the diner for lunch, and after he orders he slips Merri a piece of paper. She figured it was just going to be his phone number, or something corny like that, but before she throws it away, she glances at it, and it's a printout of that picture. That picture you saw on the computer." Jackson gestured at the silent machine in front of them.

"There was a note on the back of the picture saying that if she wanted the picture to stay a secret between the two of them, then there were some things she was going to have to do."

Amy looked at Jackson in horror. She remembered Gladys talking about how Merri had been struggling for a while, but that she wouldn't talk about the situation.

"She didn't know what to do. This is a small town, and something like that picture, even though it's a fake, could make it impossible for her to live here. So, she called me." Jackson smiled at the memory, although the smile held a hint of sadness.

"You see, I was eighteen when our parents died in a car wreck, and Merri was twelve. I wasn't about to let her get lost in the foster system, so she came to live with me and I supported the both of us."

Amy looked at Jackson with new admiration. That had to have been tough for an eighteen-year-old to raise a little sister. She looked back down at the silent computer. It also must have made the current situation doubly difficult.

"So you came up here to take care of her again." It was a statement, not a question. Obviously Jackson loved his sister deeply and would take care of her if at all possible. Suddenly a thought crossed Amy's mind and she felt her heart sinking.

"You knew Carl," she said, her voice flat, as she processed the information she'd just received. "Before I ever got here, you'd met Carl, and you must have threatened him or fought with him." Amy's eyes rose to Jackson's. "You had more of a reason to kill him than I did."

Jackson's eyes were filled with sorrow and regret. He looked away, apparently unable to maintain the contact. "Yes, I knew Carl. Like I said before, I've had a pretty mobile life-style so far, just traveling around and taking pictures, selling them at art shows, that type of thing. So, when Merri called, it was pretty easy to just pack up and move here. When I got to Copper Springs, I confronted Carl. I demanded he delete the picture. I told him that if that picture ever surfaced, I would kill him. I think he probably believed me. I know I did."

"He didn't delete the picture, though. It's right there." Amy pointed at the laptop.

Jackson's smile held no humor. "You're right. He deleted it from his phone in front of me, but I was pretty sure he'd still have another copy hanging around somewhere. It's one of the reasons I stayed. Apparently this isn't the first time he's pulled this trick, either. I don't know those other women, but I'm guessing he did something similar with them."

"The sheriff's department needs to see those pictures. There are other people with motive to kill Carl. I..." Amy looked at Jackson, and saw his jaw tighten. He put a hand protectively on the computer.

"I'm not letting Merri be pulled through all that. She doesn't deserve to be put through any more pain." Jackson glanced at Amy.

"Jackson, one of those women may have killed Carl. The sheriff's department needs to know about these pictures. This could clear me of suspicion." Amy reached out for the computer, but Jackson slid it away.

"Merri didn't kill Carl, Amy. I didn't kill Carl."

"What about some of those other women. Dammit Jackson, this could save me." Amy punched her leg with her fist. "We need to call the sheriff's department and give them the computer." She started to fumble for her phone.

"Stop, please."

Amy paused at the pleading note in Jackson's voice.

"Just give me a few days, Amy. Let me think about it. There's got to be some way to do this. To get the sheriff's department what they need without putting Merri through all that pain. She's been through so much lately. She's just starting to get her life back together."

Amy was silent for a moment. Emotions warred in her chest. She'd only known Jackson for two days, but she liked and trusted him more than anyone in a long time. But, did she really know him. Amy looked up to see Jackson watching her, his expression one of wariness.

"Why did you apply for the job here, Jackson? Was it just to find the computer and delete Merri's picture?"

A look of surprise replaced the cautious appraisal. "No, it had nothing to do with Merri. I dealt with the Carl issue a month ago. He backed off, and I figured that it was pretty much a done deal. I was genuinely looking for work, Amy. It was just coincidence that it was with you. I didn't even realize Carl had been killed until Gladys told me that morning."

Amy pushed her chair back and stood. It felt like every emotion was boiling in her, ready to explode at a moment's notice.

Jackson looked up at her. "She's my sister, Amy."

"What do you want me to do?" Amy felt a tear start to slide its way down her cheek. "What exactly do you want me to do? It's my life. It's my dad's shop."

"Give me a couple of days," he said again. "You keep the computer so you don't have any concerns that I'll delete all the women's pictures. We print off the spreadsheets and give them to the sheriff's department. We still haven't figured out the locked door mystery..."

In spite of herself, a snort of laughter exploded from her

at the phrase, so reminiscent of the old mysteries she used to read as a girl.

Jackson gave her a weak smile. "I promise, if things start looking worse. If it looks like they're going to arrest you, we'll turn over the laptop with the pictures immediately."

"Even the one of Merri?"

"Yes, even the one of Merri." His voice sounded as though the words were being ripped out of the deepest part of his soul.

Amy sat back down, and leaned her forehead on her fisted hands. Jackson was silent while she thought, a fact which Amy appreciated. Finally, after what seemed like eons, Amy lifted her head.

"Okay, Jackson. You've got your few days." Amy could see Jackson's shoulders sag in relief, and he smiled at her.

"But don't ever hide anything like that from me again. Do you understand?" Amy's sense of betrayal made her voice harsher than she intended, and she saw Jackson flinch. There was a brief flash of anger in his eyes, and she thought he might react to her tone. As quickly as it came, however, it was gone, and Jackson gave her an apologetic smile.

"Yes, ma'am. I should have told you up front that I'd had a conflict with Carl. It's just that I couldn't see how to do that without betraying Merri."

Amy sighed and rose to her feet again. "Alright. Let's call it a day. I feel like a dishrag that's been wrung out." She turned and headed for the door to the computer room.

"Wait."

Amy turned around. Jackson was packing the laptop into the black case. Closing the zipper, he held the bag out to her.

"I don't think it's a good idea to leave this here. With everything that Carl was up to, and considering that his apartment was searched for something, plus the fact that someone was able to get in and out of here without unlocking the doors, I'm not sure it's safe. On the other hand, I don't think you really want me to take it, all things considered."

Hesitantly, Amy reached out and took the handle to the bag. "You're right, it wouldn't be secure here, and it won't fit into the safe. Good thinking. Thanks." Jackson was really trying to re-instill some of the trust that had been lost.

"Let's go home, Jackson."

"Right behind you, boss."

Amy stopped in the front room to gather the dogs and headed out the door with Jackson close behind her. As she walked into the parking lot, she noticed a light gray SUV drive by slower than normal for the highway. Something tickled her memory, but she couldn't grab it. Where had she seen that particular vehicle recently?

Shaking her head, she gave up and walked to the Wrangler. Amy looked back toward Jackson where he stood next to the Jimmy.

"Are you still on for tomorrow?"

"Are you kidding? A spooky, potentially haunted basement? I wouldn't miss it for the world." Jackson's smile was back in place as he opened the door of the Jimmy.

"I never said anything about the basement being haunted," Amy said laughing. "Or inhabited by monsters, or anything other than mice."

"No ghosts?" Jackson said, a plaintive note in his voice. "Or monsters? What a shame. I was thinking we could potentially feed the code enforcement officer... what was his name? Scott Branson?... to a hungry monster and solve at least one problem."

"No such luck. The best I can offer you is the rumor that there are some old tunnels under the town. Mine adits and shafts more than likely. Supposedly this shop is connected to the network. It's possible there are some ghosts there who might be willing to accommodate us by taking out Mr. Branson, but my brother, sister and I were never able to find the opening, and believe me, we tried." Amy opened the Wrangler's door and stood back so the dogs could jump up, then make their way to the bed of the Jeep. She set the laptop case on the passenger seat and slipped in behind the wheel.

"I'll see you tomorrow morning, Jackson," Amy called out waving. Jackson returned the wave, then climbed into the Jimmy and started the engine. Amy turned her own key and started to back out of the parking lot, but had to hit the brakes as a vehicle appeared from around the curve. Another light gray SUV or the same one, who knew. Again a memory scratched at the back door of her mind, but she just couldn't place why it was important. She tried to sort through all the things that had happened since she'd returned to Copper Springs, but she just couldn't place that vehicle. Finally she gave up, released the brake and headed home, too tired to even consider going to the diner.

Unknown specimen

13

In spite of her exhaustion, Amy struggled to sleep that night. The monsoon storms hadn't materialized and the heat didn't abate overnight as it usually did. Nightmares plagued her. Nightmares of finding Carl's body. Nightmares where she was one of the women Carl was extorting. Nightmares where Jackson was arrested or where she herself was arrested. In between the nightmares her mind whirled, replaying the warning notice, the decision about the pictures, the decision to temporarily withhold evidence from the sheriff's department. She couldn't stop thinking about the next day and the basement.

When Nick bought the shop, it came with rumors that it was connected to a series of mining tunnels. The three children were determined to find the entrance to the tunnel network, and they spent a great deal of time in the basement, in spite of its creepy atmosphere.

It was dark and dusty, with a stained concrete floor and old whitewashed brick walls. Posts held up a series of beams which themselves supported the floor joists. An old dinosaur of a furnace sat in the middle of the floor, and the duct work, as well as all pipes and electric conduits were exposed. It was a great adventure as far as the kids were concerned.

Until that day...

It happened when Amy was thirteen. Usually all three kids came to the shop to help Nick after school. That afternoon, however, Jas was playing football, and Opie had gone to a friend's house. Nick didn't have anything for Amy to do, so she decided to search for the tunnels again, even though she'd looked hundreds of times before. Just as she was moving a pile of scrap wood so that she could inspect an off-colored series of bricks, she felt a cold draft, and a creaking moan seemed to surround her, coming from every direction.

Amy figured she set a new land speed record that day. Dropping the wood, she sprinted for the narrow door leading to the stairwell. She slammed the door behind her and pelted up the stairs, racing through the storeroom and out into the main showroom of the shop. She hadn't been down into the basement since.

Now she lay in her bed, telling herself that it was just a basement, and there was no reason for her nervousness. However, her mind was cannibalizing itself, making the childhood episode bigger and scarier.

Amy turned over again, and punched her pillow, flipping it to try and find a cooler spot. She forced her mind to think of other things; more pleasant things, and eventually she fell asleep again.

Amy woke at dawn, only slightly more refreshed than when she went to bed. Still, liberal quantities of coffee and a walk around the sixty acres with Jynx and Bess pumped some adrenaline back into her system, and she drove toward town with a renewed sense of purpose, if no more desire to venture into the basement than she'd had the night before.

Once again Jackson was waiting for her when she pulled into the parking area in front of the shop, cups of coffee and a paper bag sitting on the hood of the Jimmy.

Amy pulled into the lot, and got out of the Jeep, holding the door for the dogs. As she walked around the hood of the Wrangler, Jackson strolled over, holding out a cup.

"I got you a dose of liquid motivation." He studied her face with a half smile. "It looks like you may need it."

"You got that right," Amy said, grimacing. "I may need a five gallon bucket of motivation at this point. Or I'll take whatever is in bag number one over there." She pointed at the paper bag still sitting on the teal green hood. "Assuming that what's in bag number one has plenty of carbs and absolutely no redeeming nutritional value whatsoever." She grinned at Jackson.

"I guess you're out of luck, then. The little apple chunks have to count for something in the nutritional world."

"Not when covered in sugar and deep fried."

Jackson laughed as he walked back to his vehicle to grab his cup of coffee and the bag of apple fritters that he'd picked up at the gas station across the street. Meanwhile Amy unlocked the shop door and called to Jynx and Bess. The dogs made a quick tour of the store, then adjourned to their spot behind the front counter.

Jackson plopped the paper bag on the glass surface, and reached inside, withdrawing a gigantic fritter. He pushed the bag toward Amy, with a smile.

"The fritter is calling your name, Amy."

"And I am responding." Amy pulled out a second huge fritter. "You've got to love the Mini Mart. They make the best fritters. Still, I'd better knock off this type of eating or I won't be able to fit down the stairwell to the basement."

"Speaking of which, what is the plan for the day?"

"The basement is the only place we haven't hit so far. Well, technically we didn't clean up stairs, but I'm not sure how much I want to do up there, considering what we found." Amy chewed her lip in concentration. "I think we should hit the basement, do some basic cleaning, and making sure that there's not a bunch of junk that has built up down there."

"I'll grab the broom and rags."

"And vampire spray?" Amy added facetiously, since Jackson seemed fixated on ghosts and monsters.

"There are vampires? Here all I'd been hoping for were a few ghosts. Maybe a jackalope or two." Jackson laughed, enjoying the joke.

"No chupacabras?" Amy teased, referring to the mythical animal described in many southwestern, Central and South American tales.

"Nah, I didn't bring my goat with me today."

"Dork. You've got an answer for everything. I'm not going to try any more." Amy grumbled with a laugh.

"Yeah, my sister says that too. I'll get the broom." Jackson headed for the closet in the computer room.

The stairway to the basement was just as narrow and steep as the one that let to the upstairs apartment. However, instead of leading to a relatively pleasant room, which, if Jackson was to be believed may need an exorcist, the stairs to the basement led down between peeling whitewashed bricks. A narrow dark wood paneled door opened into a low ceilinged, dark room which almost certainly needed an exorcist in Amy's opinion.

Jackson stood just inside the door, looking around the inky black space. Amy walked in just behind him. The cool damp smell of the basement hit her in the face.

"Is there light, or should I have brought my flashlight?" Jackson asked peering into the murk.

"If you take a couple of steps forward, and wave your arm, you'll hit the cord for the light bulb."

Jackson sighed, and started forward, waving his arm. "We're riding the wave of modern technology here, aren't we? None of this 'light switch' crap for us."

"Yeah, well just pray that the light bulb hasn't burned out or the cord doesn't break." She heard a snort of laughter, but couldn't see much until Jackson suddenly came across the string and pulled it sharply. A bare light bulb flared to life, causing Amy to flinch.

It took a few moments for her eyes to adjust to the brighter light and she squeezed them shut, then slowly opened them again.

"Holy...," Jackson stood looking around the room in amazement. "Has it always looked this way? I may need to rethink my ghost jokes."

Amy stepped up to his side and viewed the room. It wasn't too much different than her memories, at least the ones she had before her imagination ran wild with them. Same spotty whitewashed bricks, only with even more of the brick showing through than she remembered. Same exposed floor joists and piping in the ceiling. The gigantic furnace still sat in the corner, although many years ago Nick had switched to a heat pump to provide both air cooling and heating, retrofitting the duct work. He decided that it would be too difficult to remove the old furnace, however, so the old oil burner sat there unused and collecting dust.

"Welcome to the underworld, Jackson," Amy laughed nervously. "The sooner we get started, the sooner we can return to the surface."

"I'm on it, Persephone." Jackson started forward, examining the different items that had made their way into the basement of the shop. A pile of cardboard boxes of every size lined the wall to the right of the door. These had come filled with rocks and other items, and were saved for future outgoing shipments. Amy sighed. Since Carl had been in charge of the shipments, he'd obviously had access to the basement, and been down here on more than one occasion.

Jackson started sweeping the cleared area of the floor, whistling and humming to himself quietly. He moved to the far side of the basement and pulled the cord for the second light bulb. It increased the brightness, even if it did nothing for the overall sense of gloom in the place.

He stopped briefly and looked over at Amy. "You know, I'm still not seeing much evidence of rodents. It's strange that the town would have gotten an infestation complaint, and we haven't seen a single mouse turd. Spiders, now... spiders you've got." He gestured toward the ceiling of the basement which held a bounty of cobwebs and spider webs.

Amy, who had started sweeping cobwebs from the walls near the door, looked upward, trying to see what lived in the joists.

"Do you think we have any black widows or brown recluses?" she asked, referring to two of the more dangerous spiders in Arizona.

"I don't see any. Just the little dinky spiders. Still it might be a good idea to pick up a spider bomb tomorrow, that is if the exterminators don't treat the place. Ask them."

"Good idea. I'll put it on the list. Invisible mice and very visible spiders. Do you think I'll be able to open tomorrow?"

"I see no reason why not. If it weren't for the code violation warning, you would have been open yesterday. I don't see any way on earth they can condemn the shop based on what we've found."

Jackson went back to his humming and sweeping, while

Amy continued to concentrate on the walls and ceiling, moving around the basement until she reached a lumber rack consisting of six two by fours that stretched from the floor to the exposed joists. Three shelves had been constructed and a large pile of scrap lumber had built up over the years as Nick built shelves and display cases for the shop. Apparently some plans had not gone as expected, and Nick wound up with several extra sheets of plywood, which he'd leaned against the rack.

Amy started to move the huge sheets, intending to organize everything behind it, but just as she started to shift the top piece, she remembered what had happened the last time, and in this same spot and hesitated.

"Uh, Jackson?"

"Yeah," he glanced up from the floor where he was scrubbing on a persistent spot of dirt. "You need something?"

"Could you give me a hand with this? I want to organize the lumber, but the plywood is awkward."

Jackson leaned his broom against the wall and headed over to where she stood, apparently unaware that Amy had an ulterior motive.

"Here, let me take that." Jackson placed a hand on either edge of the sheet of plywood and started to lift it, intending to move it to the opposite wall. As he did so, Amy saw him look down toward his feet.

"Uh oh."

Amy's heartbeat increased. "What's wrong? What do you see?"

"It looks like there's some crumbled mortar on the floor. That could be a big problem if the foundation of the building is starting to fail. The town definitely would consider that to be a safety and health hazard."

"What do I do?" Amy asked. *Crap! Another piece of bad news to give Dad.* She tried to look at the wall behind the shelf, peering under the leaning sheets of plywood, but there seemed to be another sheet behind the rack as well.

"First things first," Jackson carried the top plywood sheet over to the wall and set it down. "Let's get this wood out of the way."

Amy and Jackson worked together to move the next few sheets until the shelving was visible. Amy looked at it in confusion. While there were twenty to thirty two by fours, and other boards of various lengths and widths on the top two shelves of the rack, nothing was on the bottom shelf, its surface clear of everything but a few more chunks of mortar.

"What's going on? Why did Nick stack everything on top?"

"Better question." Jackson swept his hand across the bottom shelf of the lumber rack and held it up toward Amy. "Why isn't there as much dust on this shelf as there is in the rest of the basement?"

Amy looked at Jackson's hand, trying to comprehend what he was saying. "Nick hasn't done anything with this wood in a long time. There should be plenty of dust on that shelf, unless he recently pulled off whatever wood was covering it."

"Yeah, there should be dust and dirt, but there isn't."

Amy looked around the shelving, trying to determine if some wood had been removed recently. "Maybe Nick gave some lumber to a friend who needed to build something. He was like that."

"Maybe." Jackson had a skeptical tone to his voice. "Let's move the rest of this wood. I can't see the back wall to tell if the mortar is intact. He must have slipped a few pieces of plywood behind the shelves, but then ran out of space and started stacking them in front."

Amy started pulling boards off the shelving, and setting them over against the wall next to the plywood. Meanwhile, Jackson climbed on to the bottom shelf and started trying to work the sheet of plywood toward the left edge of the rack so that he could remove it. Amy heard some banging and muttering, and the rack shook slightly.

"Are you going to bring the entire thing down on our heads, Jackson? Give me some warning, okay," Amy said, as she bent over to see what he was doing.

"Blast it, this thing seems jammed. I can't seem to get it to slide past this point." He demonstrated by sliding the wood back an inch, and then forward. It moved easily, then suddenly stopped with a bang and wouldn't move any further.

"There must be a nail or a screw on the other side, and it's catching somehow. I don't get it?" Jackson slid the panel again, and again it slid a short distance and then jammed.

"Can you slide it the other way? Slide it to the right, not the left? It seems to move easily that way."

"It won't work. The north wall is too close, and the plywood would run into it before it was clear of the shelf. I need to get a good look at the brick wall back here. I see more mortar on the floor behind the shelving."

"Maybe if you slide it as far as it goes that way, you can see part of the wall, then slide it back and you can see the rest. We should be able to get a pretty good view."

Jackson tried one more time to slide the plywood to the left, and once again it jammed. "Okay, I'm not making any progress this direction," he grumbled. Switching his grip to the left edge of the board he started pushing it to the right. It slid easily, making a grinding sound on concrete.

"It looks like that will work," Amy said, nodding. "You only have to..." Amy's voice trailed off as she saw what the sheet of wood had been covering.

"Oh, holy cow crap," Jackson breathed, a sound of awe in his voice.

A huge hole was exposed, the tunnel beyond extending into darkness. One of the rumored mine tunnels under Copper Springs come to life.

"I don't understand, Jackson. This was never here before. Believe me, my brother, sister and I looked. There's no way that we would have missed this huge hole." Amy looked in amazement at the approximately three by three foot opening in the wall.

"I'm sure it was covered up when you were a kid. Look," Jackson fingered the black iron lintel that ran from one side to the other of the opening. Another wide piece of metal formed uprights facing the brick on either side.

"I bet that this opening was completely bricked up, and with the mortar covering it, you wouldn't have seen the metal framework." He gestured at a pile of bricks they could dimly see inside the tunnel, piled haphazardly out of the way. A half brick had tumbled out of the pile and was laying in the middle of the passageway itself. "You probably wouldn't even have noticed the slight abnormality with some of the bricks, since they were careful to marry half bricks to half bricks."

Amy backed her way out of the shelving and knelt on the floor, staring at Jackson, violet eyes wide. "Do you realize what this means, Jackson?

He pulled back and sat, meeting her stare. "It means that we've found a way that someone could have gotten in and out of the shop without locking or unlocking the door. Maybe it was just Carl's bad luck that he came back when someone broke in through the tunnels to rob the place."

"Or maybe he was meeting that someone, and that meeting went wrong. After all, from what we can tell nothing was missing. Besides, he had to have hidden the laptop for a reason. If it was just a chance meeting, then the computer would have probably still been in the car, or sitting on the counter or somewhere else easy to access. Instead he hid it in the storage compartment upstairs. He must have known someone was coming, and been worried that they would try to get the computer."

"You're right, that makes more sense. That has to be why he hid the laptop. Speaking of which, what have you done with it? You didn't bring it back with you this morning."

"No, it's out at the house. I figured it was safe out there. No one knows I have it, after all."

Jackson frowned. "I guess not, although we didn't really try to hide it when we left last night."

"This may be a small town, Jackson, but we really don't sit around watching each other." Amy paused for a second. Then added with a wry note, thinking about the small town grapevine. "Well, most of us don't."

Jackson nodded his head, although he still appeared undecided. "I guess you're right. Still it makes me a bit nervous."

Amy gave a dismissive shake of her head, and continued on her primary train of thought. "What do we do now? I suppose we'd better call the sheriff's department. This will clear me. Maybe there will be DNA or something that they can connect with whoever came through that opening."

A sudden thought flashed through Amy's mind, and she sat back on the floor and put her head in her hands. "What the heck is the code enforcement officer going to say about this? I mean secret tunnels can't be in the building code of the town, can they?"

"I wouldn't think so." Jackson said in considering tones. "I suppose, though, that if we pull the sheet of wood back over the opening, and stack the lumber on the rack, the code enforcement officer would have no idea that the opening was there."

Amy looked up at him, a wry expression on her face. "You think so? Anything else go as we've planned recently?"

"No," Jackson stretched the word out. "This is true."

The two sat for a moment in silence until Amy finally pushed herself back to her knees and rose to her feet. She fumbled in her pocket for her cell. "I guess I'd better put in a call to the sheriff's department. There's no way Davis or Tommy are going to be in, but I can't see this as an emergency call either."

She checked the screen. No bars. Naturally, the basement would be unlikely to get a signal. She started to head for the door to the stairwell.

"Amy?"

She turned around and saw Jackson was still seated next to the lumber rack.

"What?"

"Are you sure we shouldn't explore the tunnels a little? I mean to see what's there? We wouldn't want someone coming in while we're waiting for the sheriff's department and removing all the evidence, right?" There was a yearning note in Jackson's voice.

Amy couldn't help it. She started laughing. Jackson grinned and twitched his head toward the exposed tunnel several times.

"One of those curiosity things again?" Amy asked, eyebrows raised.

"You know it. So, what do you say?"

Amy considered for a moment, looking at the tunnel. No actual crime had been committed there as far as she knew, and Jackson was right, if whoever had been using it had left evidence, that person might remove the evidence before the deputies got there.

"I don't know, Jackson. I've been in abandoned mining tunnels before. They really aren't safe. Plus, we don't have the equipment we need. There's no way we should go in without helmets and headlamps. Your boots are okay, but not my shorts or sneakers." Amy stood for a moment. She had to admit the draw of the tunnel. It was obvious that the draft and the noise that scared her so badly as a child had to have come from this tunnel network. Maybe some machinery moving cased the draft and the vibration through the wall, making it seem like it came from the basement itself. Now that she knew there was a real, identifiable source, she found much of her fear had vanished, and in its place was a curiosity equal to Jackson's.

"Is there any place we could get the equipment on a Sunday? Jackson asked.

"There are helmets and headlamps out at my folks' place. I guess we could run out there and get them and I could change clothes." She watched as Jackson's grin grew even wider. He apparently knew he had her.

"But what about the fact that whoever has been using these tunnels is probably the one who killed Carl?"

"There will be two of us. Besides, it's not like whoever it was came prepared to kill Carl."

"We don't know that. They never found the murder weapon."

"That may be true, but I'll be honest, I doubt that the murderer brought his own geode to a rock shop with the intention of killing someone." Jackson spoke with a matter of fact tone, and Amy had to agree with him. Still, she'd feel better if they'd found the geode in question.

"I'll tell you what," Jackson said with a wheedling note in his voice. "Why don't we just take a peek in the entrance area, and you can see what you think about the safety. Then we'll decide."

"Fine, I'll go get my flashlight, and place that call to Tommy at the same time."

"You just do that. I'll wait here."

Amy started to laugh again. "Jackson, you look like you're about to drool, you're so excited."

He laughed back. "Don't you know it. This is the most fun I've had in a long time."

"You've got a weird idea of fun." Amy shook her head and headed for the stairs, checking her phone as she walked. When she reached the back entry way, the bars appeared, and she dialed Tommy's number. His voice mail came on the through the speaker.

"Hi Tommy, it's Amy Stone again. I wanted to let you know that I found a tunnel in the basement of the shop. I'm wondering if that could be the way that Carl's murderer got in and out of the building without having to lock or unlock the door." Amy paused, wondering if she should also say that they'd found the laptop. Finally she continued, "And we also found some, um... some financial records that makes it look like Carl was into some suspicious activities. If you'd give me a call, I'd appreciate it."

Hitting the end button, Amy headed to the front of the shop. She checked on the dogs, and took them outside to take care of their business while she dug out her flashlight and lantern again. Whistling to Jynx and Bess, she walked back inside, and once again ushered them behind the counter. Dogs cared for, she headed back down to the basement where Jackson was waiting impatiently.

"Hey, what took you so long? I tried to use the flashlight app on my phone, but it just doesn't cut it. Although that might have something to do with my battery being nearly dead."

"I wanted to let the dogs out. We shouldn't be long, since we're not going far," Amy gave Jackson a pointed look, "but just in case I thought it was best to be prepared. Here," Amy offered Jackson the lantern, and kept the bright LED flashlight for herself.

Jackson took the lantern, turned, and getting down on hands and knees, he crawled through the lower shelf of the lumber rack and into the dark opening beyond. Taking a deep breath, and shaking her head at their foolishness, she knelt and crawled after him.

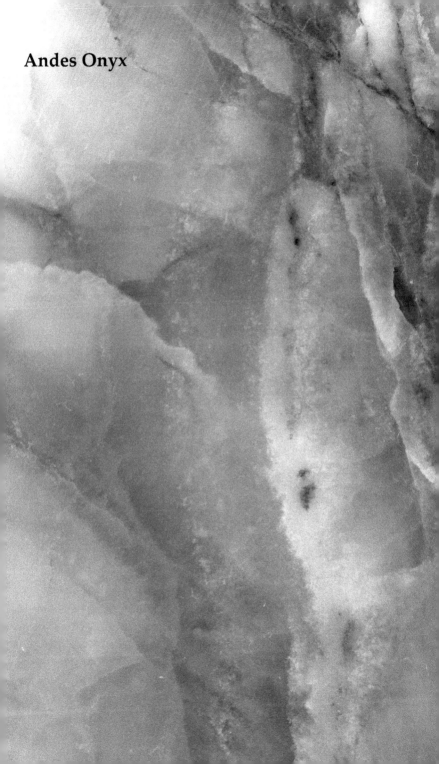

Andes Onyx

14

Rough rock walls greeted Amy's eyes as she held up her flashlight. Signs of whatever tools had been used to gouge out the space were still evident. A narrow tunnel, approximately five feet wide, butted up against the basement wall. Off to the left of the opening was the pile of bricks and mortar which had been removed from the doorway, and Amy found herself wondering about the construction of the hidden entrance. Because the metal framework for the door seemed to be included when the wall was originally built, it appeared that the builders always had the intention of having a secret exit. Why the builders felt the need was unknown. There were many tales of the tunnels running under cities like Flagstaff and Prescott, but those places were much larger, and even then there were debates on the purpose behind the tunnels. It was just as likely that this building had run up against old mining tunnels, and during prohibition the owner of the establishment decided to make use of them.

"Well, what do you think?" Jackson had walked about ten feet down the tunnel, looking at the walls and running his fingers over the rough surface. He looked upward and Amy followed his gaze. The roof seemed to be of solid rock, hovering only a few inches above their heads.

"It looks safe," Amy said, although with some hesitation. She walked toward the entrance to the basement, where several wooden supports stood, and examined them. The wood itself still seemed strong and solid. That didn't mean, however, that other places in the tunnel wouldn't have deteriorated with time. It also didn't mean the ceiling rock hadn't separated from the rock above. Still the floor was fairly clean from rock falls.

Amy turned back to look at the basement wall, roughly exposed where the rock had been chipped away. Her eye caught a glint from the corner formed by the brick wall meeting the rock, next to the pile of debris from where the door had been opened. She lost it and panned the flashlight back over the floor several times. Jackson, noticing her attention had shifted, looked the same direction.

"What is it? Is there a problem?" he asked.

"I don't know. I saw something." Amy cast the flashlight over the pile, trying to get the glint to show itself again. Just when she thought she'd been imagining things she caught the flash again. Amy carefully walked over, keeping her eyes glued on the spot where she'd seen the reflection. She bent down and picked up the object, then held it up in front of the flashlight.

"What is it?" Jackson asked, peering at it.

"It's an amethyst point." She turned the crystal over in her fingers, examining it from all directions.

"Are there amethyst mines in Arizona?"

"Not really, although Arizona is known for many of its minerals and amethyst can be found in pockets in a lot of old mines. Still, the only commercial amethyst mine I know of is Four Peaks down by Fountain Hills. Besides, this isn't a type of amethyst I've ever heard of being found in the state. I think this is a Thunder Bay amethyst, from Canada. Like the ones you found upstairs when we were cleaning. Look at the hematite cap on it." She held it out toward Jackson, showing him the red tip from the hematite inclusions at the end of the crystal.

"It's like those other small pieces up in the shop. It still looks like it's been dipped in blood to me."

"Maybe it has." Amy said, although she felt distracted, chasing down a thought.

"This piece isn't big enough to have killed Carl."

"No, you're right. But Emily James said that Nick had gotten a large plate of red capped amethyst for her. I could never find it, but I forgot to ask my dad, what with everything that was going on. What if whoever killed Carl, then rinsed off the geode in the sink and used a rock hammer from the equipment display to break it up into small pieces, so that no one would even suspect that it was used. The red cap is natural to this stone, so any blood still on it wouldn't be noticed."

"Wouldn't that take a lot of planning?"

"I don't know. Maybe it was just an accident and the killer recognized an opportunity to hide the murder weapon afterward. After all, there are a lot of small geode pieces in the shop, another tray of them wouldn't be surprising."

"And this crystal?" Jackson reached out and touched the single point.

"If he, or maybe she, was breaking the geode up with a hammer, then this one piece may have flown off and landed in his clothes, then fell out down here."

"That would make sense. That stuff is like glass. The killer probably didn't even realize that pieces flew everywhere considering that the light is a bit dim in the front room."

Jackson looked around the chamber again. "Is it safe to go farther into the tunnels?"

"I don't know, Jackson. I don't know. As I said, this area looks good." Amy walked a little farther back in the tunnel, inspecting the supports, and examining the floor. About twenty feet from the basement entrance she stopped and shown her flashlight down the passageway, directing the light at the walls, ceilings and floors that were visible, the beam of the flashlight creating streaks of light in the dusty air. The supports she could see looked solid, although it was hard to tell at a distance, and the floor was relatively clean, other than a small pile of rocks at the far end of the light.

Amy stood for a moment, looking at the floor and rubbing her forehead. Then she looked up at Jackson, "I'd say it's okay as long as we have the helmets and headlamps. I can run back out to the house to pick them up. Do you want to ride along?"

Jackson nodded. "There's not really much else to do around here," he said. "The shop is clean and ready to open, and I don't really want to go spend the rest of the day organizing Ms. Moira's bunkhouse, so let's go exploring." He grinned at her.

Ten minutes later, Amy and Jackson were heading for her parents' house outside town. Turning off on the dirt road that led nine miles out toward their property, Amy was surprised to see a cloud of dust in the distance.

"That's strange," She said to Jackson, talking loud to be heard over the sound of the Jeep rattling over the rough, road. "We don't often see other vehicles out this way since it doesn't lead to any good "TV trails and there aren't any houses out here other than my folks'."

"Probably someone lost, or just exploring. It seems like a nice area."

"Yeah, maybe."

Before long it was obvious that the cloud of dust was getting closer, and Amy slowed slightly. The road was narrow, with steep banks or deep ditches on either side, and seldom graded. They were approaching several sharp turns, and she knew from early experience that meeting something while traveling too fast around one of those curves could spell disaster. The first truck she owned when she was sixteen was a testament to that fact, and she'd often wondered if the cow she'd surprised in the middle of the road had ever recovered from its scare.

Amy just was navigating the second of the series of curves and entering into a short straight section of the road before the next turn when a large silver gray SUV came charging around the curve in front of her. It was traveling in the center of the road, and going well over the safe speed, causing dust to boil out from behind in spite of the recent rains.

"Hang on!" Amy hit the brakes, and steered for the far side of the road, expecting the driver of the SUV to do the same. Instead, the driver maintained his middle-of-the-road position, and if anything picked up speed. At the last moment Amy was forced to pull the wheel to the right to avoid collision. The Jeep rocketed off the road, jumping the mound of dirt on the verge, crashing through some brush and down the slope, coming to rest in the grassy, rock-strewn rangeland beyond. The engine stuttered to a stop and the sudden silence assaulted her ears.

Amy sat for a moment, staring straight ahead, feeling the

flush of adrenaline. She looked over to Jackson who was staring back at her.

"Nice driving, Walker Evans." His voice was shaking slightly and she knew he was struggling to make a joke by referring to the famous off-road racer.

"Are you okay?" She could hear a matching shake in her voice.

"I'm great, although I'm hoping I didn't soil the fancy upholstery."

The dogs! Amy whipped her head around, twisting her body to see into the bed of the Jeep. Both dogs were fine, although she was sure they'd been thrown around a bit in the rapid departure from the road. Bess had a slightly wild-eyed look on her face, while Jynx seemed to have a judgmental, accusing stare.

"What the heck was that, anyway?" Jackson said, anger taking place of the shock.

"I don't know. Everyone around here knows to be careful on the curves. Our dust had to have been as visible as his. Whoever that was, he had to have known another car was coming. Did you see the driver?"

"Not well. The sun was glinting off the windshield. Maybe he had the sun in his eyes and didn't see us. I think he had longish gray hair, maybe heavy set, but I'm not sure. I couldn't even say for certain whether it was a man or a woman."

"Same here." Amy said glumly. She unbuckled her seatbelt, climbed out of the Wrangler, and examined the sides. Jackson slid out the other side, and walked around to where she stood.

"Anything broken beyond repair?"

"I don't think so." She looked back up the slope, noting where the Jeep had broken over the pile of packed dirt on the edge of the road. She'd knocked the heck out of some oak brush and narrowly missed several small juniper trees, but it didn't look as though she'd hit anything large enough to cause major damage. Just some more "Arizona pin striping" the term given to the white scratches or brush marks found on most off road vehicles in Arizona.

"I guess we'd better see if we can get out of here." Amy started to climb back into the Wrangler.

"Aren't you going to call the sheriff's department? That guy... or gal... That person ran you off the road."

"I should, but what good would it do. I didn't get a license plate number, did you?"

Jackson shook his head, but still looked determined.

"I can't even say for sure what make or model the vehicle was, other than it was a silver..." Amy paused, thinking.

"A silver SUV?" Jackson said helpfully.

"Yeah, a silver gray SUV." Amy paused again, then hurried on. "Last night, when we were leaving, a light gray SUV drove past the shop twice. At least I think it was the same SUV. It was going by slowly when we came out, then a few minutes later came back from the other direction. It might have just been some lost tourist, but there was something about it that was familiar. I can't put my finger on it, though. It's suspicious, and now here's another silver gray SUV."

"You do know that every other vehicle in Arizona is either white, off white, silver or light gray. Okay, a few tans and desert golds, but those guys are the rebels."

Amy choked on a laugh. Jackson was right. The vast majority of vehicles in Arizona were exactly as he described, although there seemed to be a growing number of reds and some jewel tones during the last year.

"What are we going to do?"

Amy sobered quickly. "I don't want to wait for the authorities when I can't even tell them anything other than the color of the vehicle. You were right, and it was probably just someone who was exploring, and has no manners on the road. He didn't hit me, so there's no damage to identify the vehicle. I think we should just call ourselves lucky and get out of here. We need to pick up the helmets and get back if we're going to explore those tunnels."

"If you say so. Let's hit the road." Jackson walked back around to the passenger side of the Jeep and climbed in, making a big show of pulling the seat belt on and checking it to make sure it was secure. He gave Amy a grin and a thumbs up. "I'm ready."

Amy groaned and climbed in behind the wheel. The engine growled to life at the turn of the key. Amy listened for a moment, trying to hear if there were any unfamiliar knocks, pings or tings, or any other unwanted sounds. Nothing but the smooth rumble of the Jeep's engine met her ears.

Shifting the Wrangler into first, she pulled forward. Everything felt fine, so she turned the wheel, and headed back up the hill she'd just descended, swerving to avoid the oak brush, figuring it had enough of a beating on her way down. The vehicle pulled easily up and over the dirt edge of the road, and was soon pointing back toward Nick and Crystal's home.

The remainder of the trip was uneventful. No other vehicles met them, and the wildlife and the cattle stayed well away from the road. However, as Amy pulled into the driveway, her heart fell. The green pipe gates stood wide open. She was sure she'd shut and locked them when she left that morning. She brought the Jeep to a stop and examined the gravel drive, and the house beyond.

"What's the matter now?" Jackson asked, giving Amy a curious look.

"The gates are open."

"I take it they're not supposed to be." A frown creased Jackson's face as he assessed the meaning of her statement.

"No. Most of this land is open range, and the cattle will get in and ransack the hay barn if the gates aren't closed and locked. It's happened before." Amy chewed her lip and shook her head. "I know I was tired when I left this morning, but I'm sure I locked the gate behind me."

"Maybe you forgot. Does anyone else have a key? A housekeeper or something like that?"

"I didn't forget." In spite of her words, Amy's voice held a note of uncertainty. "Maybe the hay delivery people came. It's a combination lock, not a key, and they and the propane company both know the combination."

Amy opened the door to the Jeep and got out. She walked over to the gate where the chain hung loose. She picked up one end, then the other, then turned back to face Jackson who was sitting in the passenger seat watching her.

"They cut the chain. Whoever was here cut the chain." She held it up so that Jackson could see the two ends. "They couldn't even just cut the link nearest the lock. They had to cut all the way on the other side of the loop."

"Darned inconsiderate vandals," Jackson remarked. He looked up toward the house. "I don't see anything wrong. How about you?"

Amy studied the front of the house. Everything looked fine from a distance, but she couldn't see any of the doors from this angle.

"I don't know. The windows in the front aren't broken. I guess it still could have been someone looking for a way through to the public lands. Most people respect a locked gate, but there are a few who carry bolt cutters to take down fences or cut chains.

Amy shifted the Wrangler back into first and started down the driveway. As she drew closer, she felt relieved that all the windows she could see were in once piece, and the kitchen door was closed. She spared a glance for the hay barn and noted that it looked as though it had the same number of bales as it had that morning when she fed the animals. Back during the economic crash of 2008, while a drought was in full swing and hay prices soared, her parents experienced several hay thefts and started locking the gate instead of just closing it.

Amy pulled the Jeep to a stop at the side of the house and slid out from behind the wheel. The dogs scrambled out through the open driver's door, and jumped to the ground, nosing around to see what interesting things had happened while they were gone. Jackson climbed out on the passenger side and stood there, looking at the wall of the house.

"It looks okay from this side." He started to walk around the front of the house. Amy hurried to follow, looking at the ground as she went.

"There are tire tracks here I don't recognize. Someone was here, and I've got the suspicion that it was whoever was driving that silver SUV."

"I suppose you have all the tires of all the vehicles memorized do you?" He looked at her with a quizzical expression.

It appeared as though he was trying not to laugh, and it irritated Amy.

"No, I don't have all the tire tracks memorized, but I've been the only person here for a few days, unless Mom came home to pick some things up without telling me, and it's rained." She gestured toward some tracks that followed the drive around to the far side of the house. "I never drive over there. It ruins the view. None of the family park on that side of the house, so who would have left those tracks?" Her voice sounded harsher than she intended. Stress was causing her to react more sharply than she liked.

Jackson gave her a curious look, but decided to let it go for the moment. The dogs, intent on a trail, headed around the far side of the house, following the tire tracks that Amy had indicated. With a feeling of dread, Amy walked in that direction with Jackson close beside her.

Jackson examined the side of the house, then looked out toward the hills in the direction the large windows faced. "Amazing view your folks have here," he said with admiration. Looking back at the house he studied the side windows. Amy opened the gate to the yard and let the dogs through. They ran up on the porch and sat at the side door, waiting for the humans to follow.

Amy took a deep breath, and felt some tension leave her shoulders. Everything looked to be okay. Maybe it was just someone who was lost, or looking for access to the public lands, who'd cut the chain, and once they found out the driveway led nowhere but the house, they'd turned around and left. Maybe it was the gray SUV, maybe not, but the house looked fine. She started up the steps toward the front deck.

At that moment, Bess, apparently tired of waiting to be let into the house, turned and jumped up against the door leading to the living room. The door swung open, and Amy could see where the small window pane in lower right had been broken out completely. The previous feeling of relief was replaced by dread all over again.

Silver Lace Onyx

15

Amy looked at Jackson, who met her gaze with a worried one of his own. "I'm thinking that you don't usually leave that door hanging open, huh?"

"Definitely not." Amy started forward, but Jackson put a hand out and stopped her.

"It's time to call the authorities, Amy. This is a break in."

Amy stopped, "Yeah, you're right." She pulled out her cell phone and dialed 911, and waited for the dispatcher to answer.

"This is 911. What is your emergency?"

"I'm calling from Copper Springs, on Turquoise Hill Road. I'm Amy Stone, and my parents' house has been broken into."

"Are the people who broke in still there? Are you in imminent danger?"

"No, whoever did it is gone."

Amy went through the process of letting the dispatcher know where the house was located, and was told that the sheriff's department was notified, and that a deputy would call shortly. Amy hit the end icon, and put the phone away.

"I guess we wait a little." Amy looked at the door, standing open after Bess ran into the house. She turned to Jackson. "I'm going in. I'm not going to just stand here and do nothing." She started for the door, stopping only when Jackson grabbed her arm.

"Hey, I'm not going to talk you out of it, but don't touch anything, okay," Jackson said, stepping in front of her. "Let's go."

"You don't have to, Jackson."

"Yeah, I do." He gave her a crooked smile, and Amy

could see the man who would do anything, including go to jail, to protect his little sister.

Jackson stepped through the door, with Amy right behind him. She stopped and looked around the large front room, with its full length windows facing northeast. Everything looked as though it was in its place. Nothing torn up or over turned.

Amy looked over to Jackson. "I don't get it. There's nothing missing." She gestured to the TV in the corner, as well as a pair of high end binoculars sitting on a low table in front of the couch. Nearly every flat surface in the room was covered with different spheres and other items that Nick had made out in his workshop, some out of very rare and valuable minerals. All were untouched.

"I hate to ask this, but what about the shop's laptop." Jackson looked uncharacteristically serious, and Amy felt the thrill of panic. That laptop was the only thing that held evidence of Carl's actions. She strode to the stairwell, and ran up the stairs to her bedroom, throwing open the door. Jackson was right behind her. Bess, sure that something fun was going on and that she was missing out, ran behind, barking.

The room was unchanged from that morning when she headed off to the shop. She hurried over to the desk, and looked underneath. To her relief, the laptop case was sitting right where she left it. She unzipped the main compartment just to be sure. The computer was still snugly tucked inside.

"I just don't get it," Amy said, frowning. "Why break into the place if you're not going to take anything?" She turned and looked at Jackson who was standing at the door looking around the room.

"You're right, it doesn't make sense. We need to go through every room in the house." He gestured toward the laptop computer. "I think you also need to put that laptop somewhere where no one can find it. Maybe the break-in had nothing to do with the computer, but I'm having trouble buying that the two things are just coincidence."

"I can put it in Dad's gun safe. It's in the den downstairs."

"That's a good idea. Hopefully whoever broke in has accepted that the computer isn't here, but a locked gun safe might be the best plan." Jackson started to back out of the room.

"Of course, if the person who broke in was the guy driving the silver SUV, then he, or she knows that we've come back here. Do you think that he might believe we brought the computer back with us?"

"Anything is possible." Jackson shrugged. "That's why you need to lock the computer up. Of course, Mr. SUV will also likely be sure that you're calling the cops right now, having found that the house has been broken into. I don't think there's any way he'll come back. At least not right now."

"You're right. Speaking of which, I wonder when..." The phone's ringtone chimed out, startling Amy and making her jump. She glanced at the screen, "...the deputy will call." She hit the green icon.

"Hello?"

"This is Deputy Arlen with the Mohave County Sheriff's Department. Am I speaking with Amy Stone?" A male voice was on the other end of the phone call.

"Yes, this is Amy Stone."

"I'm told that you had a break in."

Amy described what she and Jackson had found when they reached her parents' house. She explained that they had entered the home, but hadn't yet found anything missing. Deputy Arlen wasn't exactly happy that they'd entered, but he understood the situation. She briefly mentioned the SUV, and her suspicions that the driver was the person who broke in, but Arlen didn't seem very impressed.

"I'm going to need to come up and get some information and take some pictures. Your parents will need that for their homeowner's insurance if they choose to put in a claim. The problem is that there's a situation on Route 66 at the moment, a potential road rage situation resulting in a shooting, and then a multi-car pileup. Everyone's going to be tied up for some time, and it will be awhile before I can get up there. I suggest that you take some pictures, and put something over the window. I'll call you when I'm on my way."

"Is it okay if I go back into town? I've got a shop that I'm reopening tomorrow, and I still have some things to do," Amy said, hesitant to tell the deputy the real reason she wanted to return to the shop.

"That should be fine. As I said, I'll call before I head in your direction, and you can meet me back out at the house."

With that, the deputy ended the call.

Amy shoved the phone back into her pocket and looked at Jackson. "I guess we should still go through the house and make sure nothing has been disturbed, but it looks as though we got lucky. Then we can grab the helmets and head back for the shop."

"You still want to go? That deputy will be calling back to meet you, and you're not going to get any signal underground." In spite of Jackson's cautionary words, his voice held a note of hope.

"Yes, we're going. I'm done just sitting back and letting things happen, then having to react. I feel like I'm always playing catch up. I don't believe that everything is coincidental, and I've got a feeling that all the answers are somewhere in that hole in the ground." Amy could hear the anger and frustration in her voice, and tried to get it under control. Going off like a hand grenade on Jackson wasn't going to help anything. She grabbed the laptop case and headed out of the room.

"Let's get this locked up just in case whoever was in that gray SUV comes back. We can grab a piece of plywood from the barn and patch the window. Then we pick up the helmets and headlamps. We probably should have some hydration packs as well. Oh, and I've got to grab a pair of jeans, a long sleeve shirt and some hiking boots. I'm not changing here. It's too danged hot outside."

The pair headed back downstairs, carrying the laptop case. At the bottom, Amy turned right, and walked to the large double doors that led to her father's office. One stood ajar, which wasn't unusual, and Amy pushed it the rest of the way open.

The custom gun safe sat in the back corner behind Nick's desk. Amy walked straight to it, and punched in the combination, then pulled the heavy door open. The laptop case fit without too much rearrangement, sliding in behind the

stocks of the rifles and shotguns. Once everything was secure, she shut the door, and spun the dial on the lock.

As Amy turned, her eyes swept over the desk, and she
froze. While Nick's old dinosaur of a computer sat untouched
on the corner of the desk, her own laptop was missing.

"Jackson," She called out to the living room where he
was waiting.

His head popped in through the door. "Yeah, what's up?"

"My computer is gone. It was sitting right here. I was using the office because he doesn't have a wi-fi router in the
house, so I have to plug in directly."

Jackson came the rest of the way into the room, and
looked over the desk, as if verifying to himself that there was
no laptop residing on its surface.

"Do you think Gray SUV Man took the computer thinking it was the one from the shop, and that's why he didn't go
anywhere else in the house?"

Amy nodded, "I think that's exactly what happened." She
looked under the desk. "The case is gone too, and it looked
a lot like the one Nick bought with his laptop. It must be the
guy in the SUV. He saw me in front of the shop with the computer case last night when we left, and came out here to get it
because he saw both our vehicles in front of the building this
morning, and knew no one was home."

"Okay, anything else missing here?"

Amy ran her hand over the papers on the desk, and
stopped again. "Yes. Dammit! I'd used Nick's printer to run
off those spreadsheets that Carl had hidden. I thought maybe
we could give those to Tommy and Detective Davis, instead of
the computer. I couldn't get the shop's computer to hook up
with Dad's printer, though, so I copied them to a flashdrive,
then used my computer to print. They were sitting right here.
Now they're missing and the flashdrive is missing as well."

"At least we have the original computer. When the sheriff's deputy arrives, we can tell him your computer is missing. Davis and Tommy already know the shop's laptop is
missing, right? They might put two and two together, but
they still don't know that we've found your dad's computer
or what it holds."

"We're going to have to show them, Jackson. I just don't see any way around it. They're going to wonder why that computer is so important that someone would come out to the house to look for it."

Jackson nodded, sadness filling his eyes. "You're right. I don't see any way around it now. I wish I could just erase Merri's picture, but if they find out, she and I would be in even worse trouble, and it would make us look even more guilty."

The two stood looking at each other in silence for a few moments, each lost in his or her own thoughts. Finally Amy shook herself out of her mental quagmire, "There's nothing we can do about it now. Aw, blast it! All my personal files are on that computer. I've got some backups, but not everything." A new weight fell onto her shoulders. Before long Nick would be up and moving again, and at that point she'd need to find a new job. Unfortunately, her resume and portfolio were all saved on the hard drive of the computer, or backed up on the external hard drive that was stored in the case, both of which were missing.

"Don't worry," Jackson patted her shoulder. "We'll find SUV Man and get it back for you."

Amy gave him a faint smile. Apparently the name SUV Man was going to stick, in spite of the fact that they didn't even know if it was a man driving the vehicle which ran them off the road.

"I'm going to trust you on that one, Jackson."

"I'm an eminently trustworthy person," he said puffing up his chest.

Amy coughed, and gave him a skeptical look.

"Yeah, yeah, I know. I did say I was sorry, remember? I'm a reformed person." He gave her an ingratiating smile.

Cheered by Jackson's silliness, Amy laughed and the tension in her body dissipated.

"Okay, reformed person of eminent trustworthiness, let's go get the equipment and head back to the shop to explore the underworld."

It didn't take long to patch the window, gather and load all the equipment they needed, collect the dogs and head back into town. This time no other vehicles met them on the curves, although Amy worriedly scanned the horizon for plumes of dust.

About twenty minutes later Amy pulled into the parking lot in front of the shop, and turned off the ignition. She looked at Jackson, "Are we ready to do this?"

"I know I am." He gave her his patented grin, and jumped out of the Jeep. He turned and reached in for the helmets and backpacks. Amy climbed out of the driver's side, and called to the dogs. Once they were out, she reached in the back for her jeans and boots, intending to change in the shop. Regardless of how hot it was outside in the mid-July Arizona sunshine, it was going to be cool in the tunnels. She'd been in enough of them over the years to know.

As she was stepping back, she happened to glance up and saw a silver gray SUV pulling up to the gas pumps across the highway from Stone's Gems and Minerals. She stopped dead. As she watched two people climbed out of the vehicle. The man in the driver's seat was Jon Hazelton, the Copper Springs Town Council member who had been to the shop the day before. The man who wanted to take the shop from her dad.

Brazilian Agate with Druse

16

"Jackson! Look over there." Amy jerked her chin in the direction of the gas station.

Jackson looked in the direction Amy indicated, narrowing his eyes against the bright afternoon sun. He glanced back at Amy.

"You're not thinking it was the Hazeltons are you?" Jackson had a frown of concentration on his face. "There was only one person in that SUV. I'm not even sure it was the same make and model as this one. I think this one is bigger. It was too fast. Besides, the Hazeltons' SUV is clean. Surely the one that ran us off the road would be covered in dust." Doubt was clear in his voice as he studied the council member.

"I don't know, but I'm darn sure going to find out." Amy slammed her jeans and boots on the hood of the Jeep and strode off across the tarmac, moving in quick and jerky steps as she fought to control her temper. She spared a glance for her side, and saw Jackson marching right along with her.

As she stepped up on the curb, she called out, "Mr. Hazelton. Excuse me, Mr. Hazelton?"

Hazelton looked up from where he was filling the gas tank of the vehicle as his wife went into the attached convenience store.

"Ms. Stone, can I help you?" Hazelton looked as though he'd rather do anything but help her, in spite of the question.

"Yes, I think maybe you can." Amy said as she and Jackson approached the SUV. She reached out and touched the back hatch. Water beaded in the seal around the window. The vehicle had just been washed.

"Were you just out on Turquoise Hill Road an hour or so ago? Maybe driving too fast around some curves?" Amy was so angry that she nearly spit the words at Hazelton, causing him to frown and pull his head back, as though a snake were striking at him.

"I was not out on Turquoise Hill Road, an hour ago or ever, if it's any of your business. Why do you ask?" Hazelton answered, barely keeping his own anger out of his voice.

"How about your wife?" Amy wasn't ready to give up yet.

"How about his wife what?" Amy heard a voice from over her shoulder, and saw Bea Hazelton walking across the parking lot from the store holding a cup of coffee and a newspaper.

"Were you anywhere near Turquoise Hill Road this afternoon?"

"Absolutely not!" The woman's sour face grew, if anything, even more sour. "I have no desire to wander off through the brush and dust."

"Now, Ms. Stone, may I ask again what this is all about?" Hazelton spoke with so much acid in his voice it nearly burned through Amy's last semblance of control.

"We were nearly run off the road by someone driving a silver gray SUV a little while ago. That same someone is suspected of cutting the chain on the gate to Mr. Stone's property and breaking into his house." Jackson spoke up, stepping quickly in front of Amy and putting out an arm to block her from moving forward as if not sure what she would do to Hazelton if she got any closer.

"It wasn't me, or my wife that's for sure. I find your accusations extremely disrespectful. Bea and I have been at home all day, and are just now heading down to Kingman for dinner."

"I noticed that your vehicle is pretty clean?" Jackson said, apparently having picked up on the same drops of water that Amy had seen. "Just wash it?"

"Yes I did, young man. I wash it every Sunday. This is a dusty country." Hazelton scowled at Jackson, at this point ignoring Amy completely. "Now if you're done..." Hazelton pulled the gas nozzle out of the SUV, and slammed it back on its hook, waited a moment for his receipt, and then opened the door and climbed in without another look at them. "Bea, get in the car. We're going."

Bea Hazelton glared at Jackson and Amy for a moment, and opened her mouth as though she were going to add something to her husband's final statement.

"Bea! Get in the car!" came Hazelton's voice from inside the vehicle.

Bea closed her mouth, got into the SUV as Hazelton turned the key and brought it to life. With an abrupt movement, he shifted the vehicle into drive and pulled out of the lot.

Jackson looked over toward Amy. "Well, that one's got a major case of RBF if there ever was one."

Amy felt confused. "RBF?"

"Yeah, RBF. You know, resting... uh, starts with a 'B' and ends with an 'itch'... face."

Amy puzzled it out for a moment, then realized what Jackson was trying to say, and started laughing. "You've got that one right, and I've heard the word, if not the term, before."

"Hey, I've got two young nephews who look up to me. Merri caught me swearing in front of them the other day and put me in time out for fifteen minutes. I don't want to take the chance again, so I'm trying to watch myself."

Amy chuckled at the thought of Jackson in time out. "Did you have to sit in a corner, go to your room or what?"

"She made me stand and face the wall. For fifteen minutes. Nothing but white paint. She said it should have been one minute for each year of my age, but she let me off early because she needed the laundry done."

"Oh, good heavens above, I wish I'd been there to see it!" Amy laughed again at the mental picture Jackson's description evoked. "Come on. Let's get back to the shop. It's already mid afternoon, and I don't know how long we'll be in the tunnels."

As the two started back across the highway Jackson suddenly punched her arm, and pointed down the road toward the Copper Springs Diner. Amy looked just in time to catch the rear end of a silver gray SUV turning on Miner Drive, heading back toward the old stone building used by the town government.

"See, there's another one. There are just too many gray SUVs out there. You can't chase them all down."

Amy watched as the vehicle's back bumper disappeared from view around the government building, then turned to look back at Jackson. She sighed.

"You're right. I wish it had been a florescent green or hot pink SUV that had run us off the road. Then we'd be able to pick it out in a crowd. I was just so sure that it was the Hazeltons when I saw them over there."

"It would have been nice if it were them, for sure. It would have not only solved the break in, and maybe the murder, but it would have gotten them off your dad's back as far as condemning the property."

"Think they might have another silver gray SUV? I mean they probably have two vehicles, one for each of them."

"You've got it in for them, don't you?" Jackson said grinning as he stepped out into the highway with Amy, and hurried across. "Can you really see Ms. Bea smashing Carl's face in with a geode?"

"I can see Ms. Bea doing just about anything. Can't you?"

"Maybe, but I'm having trouble picturing her wandering around in spider infested tunnels. They'd get into that rat's nest of a hairdo, and she'd never get them out." Jackson curled his fingers into "spiders" and wriggled them into Amy's hair, causing her to jump and dodge out of the way.

"Speaking of which, Mr. Wolfmeister, those same tunnels await us."

"Been holding that in a while, huh?" Jackson said in approving tones as he picked up the helmets and backpacks from where he'd left them at the side of the Jeep. "I like your creativity, but you're still as cold as a snowball on Everest." He whistled to the dogs who'd been waiting in the shade next to the Wrangler, and headed for the front door.

Once inside, Jackson carried the equipment down to the basement while Amy used Nick's office to change into jeans and hiking boots, and pulled her flannel shirt on over her t-shirt. If the tunnels were like other mines she'd been in, she figured it would be somewhere between the mid fifties and the mid sixties. Not freezing by any means, but cool enough that the heavier clothing would be welcome.

When she got to the basement, she saw that Jackson had already uncovered the tunnel entrance again. When they'd left for the house, Jackson had pulled the sheet of plywood back across the opening, then used a small piece of two by four wedged between the bottom of the lumber rack and the lower edge of the plywood to block it from being slid open from inside the tunnels.

He'd set out the backpacks which they'd supplied with water, granola bars, spare headlamps and batteries, as well as first aide packs and a small tool kit each. His helmet was swinging from one hand, the headlamp firmly attached.

Amy looked him over critically. She'd loaned him a warm shirt of Nick's, and his jeans and boots should keep him safe and unscraped. That was as long as the tunnel roof didn't cave in on them, or they didn't fall into a hidden shaft. In either of those cases a warm shirt probably wouldn't do either of them a lot of good.

Amy hadn't been exaggerating when she'd told Jackson how dangerous the old abandoned tunnels and mine shafts could be. The supports often rotted with age and pressure from the rocks they were holding back. Deep shafts might become hidden under dirt, broken wood and other debris, just waiting for someone to step in the wrong place. In addition, mines often became places of refuge for rattlesnakes or other wild animals that didn't appreciate humans trespassing into their sanctuary. As if all of those dangers weren't enough, various odorless and colorless poisonous gases such as carbon monoxide and methane could build up, suffocating someone before he even realized what had happened. Obviously whoever had been using these tunnels to get in and out of the shop hadn't run into any of the numerous abandoned mine hazards, but there was no guarantee that Amy and Jackson wouldn't take a different turn, and run into trouble.

Still, Amy thought, *I guess we're as prepared as we can be to*

head underground. At least we know that someone else has man-
aged this without dying. It's not like no one has been in this mine
for a hundred years. I hope.

"I guess you're ready to go?" Amy asked Jackson, in spite
of the fact that he was nearly vibrating with excitement.

"All set, boss. You lead, and I'll follow." He slapped the
beat up yellow hard hat on his head, and started to buckle
the straps.

"Alrighty then," Amy said, putting on her own scuffed
white helmet. When Amy was younger, Nick had taken
her and her siblings to several abandoned mines he knew
about through his work for the forest service, and which he
knew were relatively safe. It wasn't unusual to find abandoned mine shafts, open stopes, tunnels and pits, and the
forest service did little to secure them from explorers, beyond
warnings. Often the vertical shafts, or winzes, weren't even
marked, and someone hiking off a trail, or riding a horse
through the brush could easily fall into an unseen shaft or
open stope, the empty area where a mineral ore had been
removed, and be injured or killed.

Nick knew about most of the ones in his neck of the
woods from when he worked as a geologist for the Forest
Service, and often ignored his own recommendations to others by exploring some of the safer mines that he felt had the
greatest potential for producing unique mineral specimens.
Even so, he'd instilled in his children a healthy respect for
the mines and caves in the area, and while Amy had been
in a number of both working and none working mines, especially as a geologist, she never took anything for granted.

"Okay, Jackson, here are the rules." She picked up her
backpack and swung it over her shoulders, then buckled the
waist and sternum straps. "No going out in front of me, or
exploring on your own. You haven't ever been in any mines,
right?"

Jackson nodded his head, but Amy noticed the half smile.
He was getting a kick out of her taking command and she
worried that he'd disregard her orders if something caught
his attention.

"I'm serious about this. If you see debris on the floor, broken wood, that type of thing, don't step on it until we're sure that it's just that. Some of these old mines have winzes, or vertical shafts, and they can become covered up. Or if there's an elevator, it might have become rotted, and you could be dropped a long way down, and the landing might not be too pleasant if there's water or twisted metal down there."

"Yes ma'am!" Jackson saluted, making Amy roll her eyes.

"Okay then, let's get going." Amy switched on her head-lamp, then knelt and started to crawl through the lumber rack, past the opening in the brick wall and into the tunnel. Jackson shrugged on his own pack and followed close behind.

Once back inside the tunnel entrance, Amy looked around more closely, familiarizing herself with the walls and ceiling, the composition of the rock and the tool marks left behind by the drills and hammers used to create the passageway. She examined the walls closely, but couldn't see any signs of minerals that would have interested a miner. Still, that didn't mean that this wasn't a mining adit, but instead a tunnel allowing someone to move from one spot in the town to the other unseen.

Amy checked to see that Jackson was close behind her. He'd just finished crawling through, having caught his pack on the top of the entry, but now he was standing, headlamp switched on and looking interested in continuing. The head-lamps gave a great deal more light than had the lantern earlier, and he seemed fascinated by the structure of the tunnel.

"Are you ready?" Amy asked, giving him a crooked smile, her heart beating hard in her chest. The air was dry and dusty, with that smell that only the deep earth and old wood creates. However, she noticed a fairly good airflow, as the earth breathed around her. At least this portion of the tunnel was well ventilated, meaning there was less chance of running into any heavy, poisonous gases. A slight tension released.

"Lead on, I'm right behind you." Jackson gave her the thumbs up, and Amy turned and headed down the tunnel, watching the walls and floor, casting the beam of the headlamp all around as she walked. About fifty feet in, the tunnel narrowed to the point that if she held out her arms she could just touch each side in some places At the same point it turned gradually and started down a gentle incline deeper into the earth. Amy judged that she was heading roughly west or northwest, paralleling Route 66, aiming for the Copper Springs Diner. She glanced at the compass she'd clipped to the front of her chest. Sure enough, her estimation of direction was right on.

She glanced at the floor again, always checking for falls and loose rocks. The passageway was amazingly clean, with very few rocks scattered along the floor. There were no tracks for ore carts. If this had been an old mine, someone long ago pulled out the equipment. In fact, to Amy's surprise, there was very little remaining of the humans from before the mine was abandoned. No ventilation pipes, old tools, or any of the other things she commonly saw in the mines her father took her to as a child, or that she'd been in as a geologist.

They had gone about a thousand feet in Amy's estimation when they reached a two way intersection, with one adit wandering off to the right at approximately a sixty degree angle to the main tunnel, staying pretty much level, and the adit they'd been following heading straight ahead and also remaining level at this point. Amy paused and looked at the various choices. Jackson stepped up beside her in the widened space created by the intersection.

"Eeny, meeny, miney, moe?" Jackson said with a teasing note in his voice. He turned his head, causing the bright beam from his headlamp to shine down each of the tunnels.

"I take it that encompasses the totality of your decision making strategies?" Amy asked dryly. "Or do you flip coins as well?"

"You can't beat a good coin flip," Jackson said, nodding, causing the beam to bounce, making Amy slightly dizzy. "But if you want some logic, then the majority of the travel lately has been either straight ahead, and off to the north. There are very few footprints leading east toward the shop."

Amy looked at the floors of the tunnels in question and

realized that Jackson was right. Numerous footprints were visible in the dirt and sand that had gathered on the floor of the passageway, but mainly heading straight ahead or to the right.

Amy turned to look back down the tunnel to where she could dimly see the light from the opening to the basement glowing off the wall where the tunnel turned. Even though there were quite a few footprints heading in that direction, they still weren't as numerous as those heading to the east, or north.

"I guess it doesn't really matter which direction we go, although if these tunnels connect to another building, then straight ahead is our best bet." Amy walked a few feet down the adit on the right, and examined the walls, ceiling and floor, then returned and went a few feet down the main tunnel.

"So straight ahead, or to the right?" Jackson asked, as Amy walked back to where he was waiting in the intersection.

"I think we..."

A creaking moan filled the air, and a cool draft brushed across Amy's face, triggering a spurt of adrenaline giving her cold prickles all over her body.

"What the heck was that?" Jackson looked at Amy, his blue eyes wide with shock.

"I don't know. It's what I heard when I was a kid, and it scared me so badly I wouldn't come down to the basement again. I thought it was a ghost."

She heard a snort and a cough from Jackson's direction.

"Shut up, you. I was a kid," Amy said in mock severe tones. "Could you tell where the sound came from? Which tunnel?"

Jackson frowned. "No, it seemed like the sound came from every direction. It was like it came out of the walls. I've got no idea, but it could be either of these tunnels." He gestured toward the straight passage, and the one on the right. "However, if I were guessing, I'd say maybe the straight tunnel? It sounded like some type of machinery, and if these tunnels connect with some of the other old buildings, then it might be an elevator or door from one of them. This other tunnel seems like it leads out into the desert instead of along the highway."

"If it is an elevator, that could mean we're not alone any longer. That someone else is down here with us, and that someone might be the murderer."

"Yeah, or it might mean that someone just left, and now we are alone. You're a real 'glass half empty' type of person, aren't you?"

"I am not!" Amy protested. "It's just that my luck hasn't been very good lately. You've got to admit that."

"Hey, you met me, didn't you." Jackson's face in the light from the headlamp had weird shadows, making him look like someone else. "Your luck can't be too bad."

"That remains to be seen," Amy grumbled, although with a smile on her face. "Since I've met you, I've been in creepy empty apartments, been threatened by the town, run off a road, had my house broken into, and now I'm wandering down an abandoned mine."

"See, I told you I'm good luck. Let's go this way." Jackson pointed toward the straight tunnel, and Amy nodded and started in that direction.

The passageway snaked around, going through several gentle curves, but still moving roughly north by northwest, according to Amy's compass. She still wasn't positive about the purpose of the tunnels.

Approximately two thousand feet in, they came to another adit leading to the right and downward. Footprints headed in that direction, although not nearly as many as in the tunnel they were following, or the other tunnel that had branched off to the north farther back.

"It's not as well traveled. What do you think?" Amy asked, torn between wanting to check the passageway, and wanting to move on toward the end of the larger tunnel. Surely whatever caused the noise was down there.

"We could be here for days if this is an extensive system. I don't think anyone has been down this tunnel recently. Let's keep going straight."

Amy nodded, knowing that Jackson was right, but the

exploring bug had bitten and she was reluctant to pass up unknown spaces.

Only a few hundred feet further, Amy started to see some sparkle in the walls of the tunnel. She moved closer to examine the flash. Jackson noticed and stepped up beside her, also looking closely at the wall.

"Pyrite?"

"I think so. There's some mica too."

"I'm glad to see there's something down here. I was starting to feel sorry for whoever mined this area."

Amy laughed. "There are times miners had to sift through a lot of waste rock just to get to the good stuff. There must have been something here; A seam of gold or copper or something or they wouldn't have kept digging. That is assuming that this is a mine, and not just tunnels just to allow people to move around the town undetected. That's one of the reasons they say the tunnels were built under Flagstaff."

"Yeah, well. I just hope we're undetected. We've got to be getting close to being under the diner by now."

"Yeah, probably behind it if I'm judging the distance and the direction correctly. I'm amazed that all the construction in the area didn't cave in any of these tunnels. We must be farther down than I thought."

The two kept walking, Amy in front with Jackson following a few feet behind, staying in the main tunnel for another thousand feet. Suddenly the adit they were following dog-legged to the left, and ended in a rusty metal door embedded in the rock face. Amy looked at Jackson, eyebrows raised in question.

"So, what do you think this means?" Amy asked.

"I've got no idea. It must be one of the other old buildings in town. Judging from the door, it might be the building where the tunnel started, it certainly seems more planned than a hole in a brick wall in spite of the framework."

Amy traced the crack around the door with her finger. "It's strange. The door is old, but this mortar is new. Whoever has been using this passage must have found it, and did some repairs to make sure it would hold."

"Any idea which building it's under?" Jackson asked. He

reached out and took the curved, rusty U-shaped handle and gave the door a pull. Nothing.

"Jackson! What are you doing?" Amy hissed. "What if whoever is using these tunnels is on the other side."

"I suppose I'd like to introduce myself and ask him what the... uh, heck... he's up to."

"And 'would you mind turning yourself in for murdering Carl?', I suppose?"

Jackson gave her a cocky grin. "I'm not sure I'd put it quite so bluntly, no. So, do you know which building this is?"

Amy looked at her compass, and studied the rock walls as if they held a clue to what lay above.

"There aren't that many old buildings still in the town. I mean buildings from back in the 1920s. That's when the shop was built. I figure these tunnels had to have been dug around that time or slightly before. The rumor is that any tunnels under the town, especially one connected to the shop which began its career as a speakeasy, were used to smuggle alcohol, or hide it from raids. Most people think that's a myth, however, and that any tunnels, if they existed, are actually old mining adits and it is just a coincidence that the town was built over them."

"Let's get to the buildings, Professor History."

Amy gave him a sour look. "Okay. There are several houses back on Springs Road that might be old enough. I'm not sure if they have basements or not, but it's possible, I guess." Amy was silent for a moment. "You know where I think we are is under the town building. It's located in an old lodging house. You've seen it, I'm sure. Back behind the diner on Miner Road?"

"Oh, yeah. I've seen it. Right where that gray SUV was heading. The one we saw after you rattled Hazelton's chain."

Amy felt her chest clench. She'd forgotten about that.

"Yeah, right there. Still, I could be totally off base, and we could be under some totally different building." Amy looked toward the ceiling, as if the answer was written in the rough hewn rock above her head. Nothing was there except for rock, white and gray, with a little bit of green and blue. *Copper bearing* her mind said automatically.

Finally she looked at Jackson. "It doesn't make sense. There's no one I know of on the town council who wants Dad's shop except for the Hazeltons, and we were talking to them when we saw that other SUV turn down Miner toward the town offices. Besides it's Sunday and the offices aren't open."

"An office employee could get in if he or she had a key."

"But why? There's nothing down here other than empty tunnels. We haven't seen any minerals that would be worth killing someone to protect."

"We haven't explored all the tunnels, either," Jackson said.

Amy nodded. Jackson was right. They'd gotten on the main adit and followed it from one building to the other, skipping the tunnel back near the start, as well as the smaller inclined winze on the north side of the passageway.

"Alright. If we're going to do this, we're going all the way." Amy spoke with a determination that drew a grin from Jackson. She checked her phone. They'd only been in the mines for a little over a half hour. There was plenty of time left in the afternoon.

Amy headed back down the main tunnel toward Stone's Gems and Minerals. In much less time then it had taken to reach the metal door, they were once again in the wide inter-section, looking at the east branching tunnel. Even though Amy was certain she could remember how to get back to the shop, she shrugged off her backpack and pulled out a can of fluorescent orange mine marking paint. She shook it and walked to the wall, intending to mark the turn.

"What are you doing?" Jackson asked, as he reached out and took her arm.

"Marking the turn. So far this is a pretty easy complex, but I don't want to get lost down here."

"If you mark it, though, our mystery miner will know we've been here. It's like drawing a map straight to our door-step."

Amy hesitated. Jackson was right. Whoever was using the tunnels might miss their footsteps, but they sure wouldn't miss fluorescent orange paint. She felt a war inside. Nick had always impressed on his kids how easy it was to get lost in the mines. He used the story of a teenager who had gotten lost for five days in an old mine after becoming separated from his party as an example. She was sure she wouldn't get lost, but she didn't want to take any chances, especially if she and Jackson got split up somehow.

"Why don't you do this, put a spot on this support up here," Jackson pointed to the timber in the new tunnel, "and then another here, but just a spot." He pointed to a rough peak of rock that jutted down from the ceiling. "Maybe the spots will be small enough that MM won't see it, but we'll know where to look if we're lost."

"MM?" Amy asked, confused by this new name invention of Jackson's.

"Yeah, MM. Mystery Miner. Possibly Mystery Mole. Or, if you prefer, Mystery Murderer. It's up to you. It's a multipurpose acronym."

Amy just shook her head and rolled her eyes. She used the spray can to place spots where Jackson had suggested. Then she headed off down the tunnel, Jackson close behind.

17

This adit was much longer than the one that connected Stone's Gems and Minerals, and what Amy presumed was the town council chambers. It was also much rougher and tended to meander here and there, although it continued to maintain a roughly eastern trajectory.

After what Amy estimated to be a hundred feet or so there was a partial collapse of the roof on the left side of the tunnel, leaving a mound of rock piled nearly halfway to the ceiling. Amy paused for a moment, and looked back at Jackson.

"We go on, right?" Jackson pointed toward the pile. "You can see that ole' MM went right on over, and we're following him... uh, her?" Jackson was obviously eager to continue, but he followed Amy's instructions not to go on ahead, and to follow her lead.

"I guess it's relatively safe since someone else has gone on. But Jackson, if it starts looking like there are more collapses, or things are falling apart, we're turning around, okay?"

"I understand, Amy. But if we're going to find out who killed Carl, if we're going to find out who broke into the house and who's trying to frame you for murder, we need to continue."

"Or we need to let the sheriff's department handle the case and step back?"

"Where's the 'I'm not waiting anymore' gal I was talking to a few minutes ago?"

"She's picturing your head crushed by a rock, if you must know," Amy said dryly, gesturing toward the unstable roof of the mine, where broken wooden planking stuck out from behind the ribs like rotted teeth, allowing the rock to fall through.

"A little passive-aggressive there?" Jackson said, ignoring

Amy's reference to the ceiling. "Smashing people with rocks. Slightly reminiscent of how Carl was... well, you know?" He grinned at her, the shadows of the headlamp making his face into a caricature.

"You're getting entirely too much fun from this, Jackson." Amy grumbled as she turned and started to scramble over the pile of debris, looking overhead into the scar left by the fallen rock, and half expecting a boulder to drop on her shoulders. There actually was a fairly large rock wedged into the top of the scar, but it appeared to be relatively solid. If it fell, however, she wouldn't have a bruise to brag about later. She'd be squashed as flat as a bug.

Unlike the main tunnel, Amy and Jackson passed several areas in this new passageway where a vein of some type of mineral had been removed, leaving a timbered stope behind. At no point was the area large, and Amy couldn't tell from looking at the waste rock on the floor, what the miners had been after, whether gold or silver, or something else of value.

The tunnel was much rougher than the one they'd been in earlier, and Amy came to the conclusion that this was an older mine that at some point was connected with the newer mine up above, probably by accident. The construction was totally different, and it was obvious that these tunnels were mines, and not just a hidden way to move about the town.

In addition, there were more signs of those bygone miners themselves. The ones who spent much of their lives underground, looking for riches. In one spot an old lantern hung from a spike driven into a support. In another Amy and Jackson found several large, rusty gears. Several rusted cans were tossed haphazardly into a corner, and Amy couldn't tell if they were from some type of food, or something else. Air flow remained good, and Amy felt secure in continuing. As least as secure as she could, knowing that MM might pop up at any moment.

Approximately a fifteen hundred feet past the collapse, they came upon their first side tunnel, this one heading to the west, and the two paused again. Jackson looked at Amy, sticking to the "you lead and I'll follow" promise she'd extracted from him at the beginning.

"I say we keep going on the main adit. From what I can tell, this one hasn't been traveled much, and besides it looks a little dodgy to me." Amy pointed toward several piles of rocks which had spilled from the walls down to the floor. She walked a short distance into the tunnel, leaning slightly backward against the incline and digging her heels into the wooden slats which had been fixed to the floor of the winze, put there by the original miners to give traction. She cast her light over the wall and ceiling, noting the scar left behind when the rock fell. An old support stood to the side, and Amy put her hand out and ran her fingers over the wood, noting the rougher surface. This one hadn't held up as well as the others."

She came back out and joined Jackson, and they continued down their chosen tunnel. About five minutes farther on, Amy came to a stop so abruptly that Jackson ran into her back. She stumbled forward, and would have fallen if Jackson hadn't grabbed her arm.

"Hey want to warn me next time? Flick your brake lights or something?"

"Sorry. Did you hear something?"

"Like what. That door opening or closing?"

"Yeah, like that. It wasn't so much hearing, as feeling it in my feet and hands."

Jackson stood still, tilting his head as though trying to pick up a sound that was just out of reach. Finally he shook his head.

"I'm sorry. I don't hear anything."

"I don't hear it now, it was just a momentary impression of a sound."

"Do you want to go back?"

Amy thought for a moment, then shook her head. "No, I guess not. It was probably just my imagination. If that noise we heard earlier was our guy going out through that door, then there's no reason he'd be coming back so soon. If he entered then, we should have run into him."

"The good news is that if it's the Hazeltons, then they're in Kingman, having an early dinner."

"Oh, I wish." Amy laughed.

The mine was a dry for the most part, not unusual for Arizona. However, Amy noticed several places that showed evidence of flowstone, either from springs that ran in the past, or intermittently, and which left residue of dissolved minerals behind. Amy didn't expect to find any water in the mine, so was surprised when a half mile down the tunnel they came upon a seep with clear water trickling out of the wall. Someone in the long ago past had left a tin cup hanging on the rock, and Jackson picked it up and held it out to catch the stream.

"What are you doing?" Amy reached out to take the cup from him.

"I was going to get a drink. If there's a cup here, then the water should be fine shouldn't it?"

"Just use the water bottles you brought. You never know in a mine. Water leaches down through the different minerals, dissolving them, and you can wind up with a pretty toxic sludge."

"Like those small communities that keep finding arsenic in the water?"

"Yeah just like that. I don't want you glowing in the dark from uranium pollution."

Jackson hurriedly put the cup back on its rock, and looked at some dampness on his fingers. Then he grinned at Amy. "At least I wouldn't need a headlamp. I wouldn't have to worry about batteries running out either."

"Another plus is that if MM finds us down here, he won't have to use a flashlight to find you."

"There is that. Okay, bottled water it is."

The pair walked only a few hundred feet father when Amy noticed the first hints of blue in the rock lining the sides and top of the tunnel. At first she thought it was just a shadow from the headlamps, the light playing tricks on her eyes. Then they came around a sharp curve, and Amy saw a bright blue streak running down the side of the rock. Looking down, she saw several blue chunks.

Squatting, she picked up a piece of brown and yellow

rock, with streaks of bright sky blue. She rubbed her fingers across it, and looked at her fingers. A little red dirt, and maybe some blue. She turned and looked back at Jackson who was watching her curiously.

"What is it?" he asked.

"Copper of some sort. There might be some azurite or chrysocolla here, maybe chalcophyllite, although this is just surface material and thin veins. This can't be a copper mine, though. We've never had one up here, and I can't imagine this small mine producing enough copper to be worth the work."

Amy stood up and handed the piece she was looking at to Jackson. He studied it closely, rubbing his fingers over the blue veining, bright in the light of the headlamps. Jackson then looked back at Amy.

"Is there anything found around copper that could be worth the digging? I figured this would be a gold or silver mine. That's what you usually find in the small, old mines isn't it?"

"It could be anything that brings an income, but gold and silver are the best known."

Amy looked up and down the adit for a moment, absently wiping her hands on her jeans. "You know, I think there were two mines here, maybe three. This one, the one this one runs into, before that last intersection and fall, and then the top tunnel between the buildings. If you look at the workmanship in this mine, it's rougher. It seems older to me than the passage ways that connect Nick's shop and the other building, or the one that branches off. I'll bet that collapse is where the two mines were connected."

"Does it matter?"

"It might." Amy said, distracted. "I... did you hear something?"

Jackson looked around quickly and hesitated. "I think just some rock falling. Maybe some pieces we knocked loose. Maybe packrats." He fell silent again as they both listened to the sounds of the mine. Finally he shook his head. "I'm sorry. I think maybe I heard a few rocks falling, but that's got to be common down here. What were you going to say?"

"There's something. An old story about a mine that was lost, similar to the tales of the Lost Dutchman's mine, although not as valuable. I just can't remember." Amy tried to grab hold of the wisps of memory that hovered just out of reach. Finally she shrugged and looked at Jackson. "Let's go on. As soon as I stop trying so hard to remember it will come to me."

As the two continued to move forward, Amy noticed that the amount of blue and green copper ore was becoming more pronounced, the veining larger, and the reddish yellow background rock was becoming hidden from view. She saw several pieces of what appeared to be fair specimens of chrysocolla and malachite, and made a mental note to pick them up on the way back. They'd make good additions to the shop

Before long they arrived at an intersection of three other tunnels, all as narrow as the main tunnel they'd been following, but heading off at sixty-degree angles to the path they were following.

"Straight?" Amy asked, looking closely at the floor. There were more tracks here in all three of the tunnels, but it seemed to her that the straight tunnel was still the most traveled.

"Straight," Jackson agreed.

Straight turned out to be the magic direction. Before the two had walked another five hundred feet the tunnel began to widen out. Looking at the walls, Amy noticed a change in the nature of the blues that were showing. Several thicker veins of intense blue became evident in the rock. Amy stopped to examine the veining, but they were still so fine, she struggled to identify the mineral.

Then the tunnel took a sudden dogleg to the right, they entered a large stope with old timber supports, and Amy felt as though her breath had been knocked out of her.

18

Large veins of robin's egg blue and a brilliant blue green crisscrossed the walls and ceiling of the chamber dimly lit by the headlamps. Several large chunks were scattered across the floor. Amy's eyes were drawn by a particularly spectacular piece of white quartz with a large band of blue in the yellow brown matrix sitting at the edge of the lighted area.

"I don't believe this," Amy breathed. She felt like she was in a dream.

"Is this what I think it is?" Jackson said from where he stood behind her shoulder. Amy glanced to her side, and saw Jackson staring around the room with wonder. "It looks like turquoise, but I thought turquoise was surface mined."

"It's certainly turquoise." Amy said. "You're right. Most turquoise mines, at least in the United States, are surface mined, but occasionally you'll find an underground mine. They're usually pretty shallow, although sometimes the minerals can percolate down through cracks in the rock a fair distance." She walked slowly over to the fist-sized chunk of turquoise and quartz on a tawny matrix. She picked it up and examined it more closely in the light from her headlamp. It was spectacular, and she knew it would bring a hefty price from the right collector.

Suddenly the entire chamber was bathed in light, startling Amy. She spun, squinting and shading her eyes..

"What the heck, Jackson!"

"Sorry. I should have warned you. Whoever is working this mine leaves some of his equipment down here instead of carrying it back and forth." He gestured toward several small battery powered spot lights mounted on poles.

In the brighter light the turquoise was even more spectacular, and the missing memory Amy had been searching for flashed into her mind. She turned and looked at each of the walls, noting where the tunnel continued on the far side of the chamber, continuing its northeastern path from what she could tell.

"Jackson, have you ever heard of the Skystone Mine legend, or myth?"

Jackson frowned, searching his memory. "No. What is it? It sounds like it has something to do with turquoise." He bent over and picked up a large piece of rough turquoise and examined it with a critical expression. "I would say skystone certainly fits this rock. It certainly looks as though a piece of sky fell to the earth. So, where's the Skystone Mine?"

"That's the point. It's a lost mine. It's a legend and no one really knows anymore whether it's based in fact or not. The way I heard it back when I was a kid was that back in 1887, a miner named Jed Bucks came into town one day carrying a pack full of very high quality turquoise. Of course, that's not what he'd been looking for at the time. He was prospecting for gold, but the turquoise was all he'd found at that point. He brought some of it into town hoping to sell it in order to buy more supplies. He was able to trade the stones to the owner of the general store, and headed back out to his mine, determined to find the gold he was sure was there. No one ever heard from him again."

"So what does the legend say happened?"

"The stories range from being attacked by bandits, or Indians, to getting drunk and falling down a mine shaft. But there was an earthquake a few days after Jed was in town. The epicenter was down in Mexico, but it was felt well up into the Arizona and New Mexico Territories, as far up as Albuquerque. There were some reports of mines in the mountains experiencing collapses. There's always been speculation that he was caught in his mine at the time of the earthquake and never made it out."

"You think this is the mine?" Jackson asked. He bent and picked up another piece of turquoise and spit on it, rubbing the rock with his fingers to see what it looked like wet.

"It might be. This is certainly high quality turquoise, although I'm not an expert by any means. Nick has a piece that is reported to be from the Skystone Mine. He bought it years ago from one of the ranchers in the area. The guy said his grandfather bought it from the general store owner because his wife liked the color so much." Amy walked over to the wall where a vein of blue stood out in stark contrast to a deep red matrix.

"The thing that confuses me is that these days a lot of a piece of turquoise's value comes from it provenance, its history and where it was found. A stone from an old mine that didn't produce much, and has been abandoned is more valuable than a same quality stone from a mine still in operation, and that is producing well. I don't see how our Mystery Miner could be selling these stones, unless he's lying about the provenance, and claiming they're from a different mine."

"Maybe his plan is to sell a little at a time. After all, there is some out there from the Skystone Mine, mostly traded between collectors. If he were handling things slowly, and using the online auction sites carefully, he could..." Jackson's words came to a sudden stop, and he stared at Amy, eyes wide.

"What if that's the connection between MM and Carl. What if Carl found out about the hidden door when he was in the basement, storing boxes."

"Maybe he heard the same noise I heard when I was a kid, and went exploring."

"Instead of running and hiding?" Jackson asked, an innocent tone in his voice, blue eyes wide.

Amy gave him what she hoped was a withering look, and pointedly refused to respond to his question. "I think you're on to something. Maybe he found out about the mine, and he and MM went into business together selling the turquoise. We already know that Carl was stealing from Nick. What's to stop him from trying it with MM as well?"

"If our Mystery Miner found out that Carl was skimming from the top, and selling it on his own, maybe he lost it and attacked Carl, killing him. He'd want the laptop because it has the records of the turquoise sold." Suddenly Jackson stopped and looked at Amy, eyes wide. "Remember the lines on the spread sheet with "T" in the final column. That must have been the turquoise. It was labeled SBSM. Do you know anyone with an 'M' last name?"

Amy shook her head, a look of extreme concentration on her face. "Jackson, we need to get back to the shop." Amy swung off her backpack, and started filling it with some of the rough turquoise chunks that were sitting on the floor, including the quartz and turquoise on its matrix.

"What are you doing?" he asked, sounding confused.

"I want to compare these with the one in the shop, but I also want to look online to see if there are any pieces of Skystone Mine turquoise currently being offered." Amy finished filling her pack, and walked over to Jackson, reaching for his pack.

"Are you sure this is wise?" Jackson said, swinging the pack off and handing it to her. "MM may come back and realize that some of his pretty blue rocks are gone. I'm pretty sure he won't buy that the packrats did it, and he'll come looking for us."

"Like he hasn't already." Amy said in a matter of fact tone.

"Point taken." He helped her pick out a few more nice pieces.

Amy stopped and studied a particularly large specimen. "This vein rivals the best in the country. I'd say the hardness is up near a six, and the matrix is stunning. This is the type that doesn't need stabilization before it's cut and polished." She looked back up at Jackson and held out the pack. He took it and swung it over his shoulders.

"What I don't understand is why MM just didn't stake a claim." Jackson looked around the chamber again. "If there's not an active claim here already, he could just stake one, and not worry about the secrecy."

"Tribal lands."

"Tribal lands? You think we're on the Hualapai Reservation?"

"I don't know, but I'll bet our guy knows," Amy said with grim determination. "We're awfully close, though, if not actually there, and I'll bet the original entrance was on tribal lands. The reservation was created in 1883, so Jed would have been trespassing on tribal lands as well, but the boundaries were harder to determine and maintain back then."

Jackson nodded, a serious look on his face. "Okay, so you're saying our friend found these tunnels and started exploring. He came across the turquoise mine, and knowing the legend of Skystone Mine, realized he had to keep it secret if he wanted to cash in. Carl finds out, and the two go into business. However, Carl tries to rip off MM the same way that he's done to others. After all, who is MM going to complain to. If he discloses that he's found the mine and that Carl is stealing from him, the tribe finds out, and since the mineral actually belongs to them, MM loses it regardless. However, when Mystery Miner finds out that Carl has been stealing, he fights with Carl, kills him, and is now trying to find the laptop to make sure there are no records."

"It's a pretty good theory. Come on, let's head back out before MM decides to come back." Amy shouldered her pack and started back down the tunnel, heading back in the direction they'd come.

Jackson switched off the spot lights, and followed closely behind as the two made their way back toward the shop.

Scenic Brazilian Agate

19

As with most journeys, the trip back seemed to go much more quickly than the trip out, and before long Amy and Jackson were clambering back through the opening in the brick wall. Once he was all the way through, Jackson turned and slid the plywood back into place, blocking it with the chunk of two-by-four so that no one else could follow them, then climbed out of the lumber rack.

Amy had already turned off her headlamp, and pulled off her helmet. Jackson did the same, scratching his head where the straps of the helmet had matted down his sandy, light brown hair. He grinned at her, and she knew from seeing his dirty face, that she must look just as dilapidated.

"Geez, I wish we had a shower. It's amazing how dirty you can get down in one of those mines, without even doing anything," she groaned, rubbing her forehead and running her fingers through her own dark, curly brown hair.

"Whadaya mean you don't have a shower? There's the one in the penthouse suite two floors above." Jackson pointed upward.

"Be my guest, Mr. Wolf... ah..." She frowned for a moment.

"Hah! Ran out of guesses, princess?"

"No, I just forgot what I was going to say. Anyway, there's no water upstairs right now. Dad turned it off several years ago after he had a leak that went undetected for several days, causing a lot of damage. He got it fixed, and at the same time put in the shutoff valves. He said since no one was living in the attic apartment, there was no point in having water up there. I'm not turning them back on for darned sure."

"I guess the shop's restroom will have to do. Ladies first." Jackson gestured toward the door leading from the basement. She reshouldered her pack and headed for the main floor where she greeted the dogs. When they'd left, she'd decided not to put them behind the counter, but instead gave them run of the shop itself. What better way, she figured, to deter anyone from breaking in to look for the computer.

Face, hands and arms scrubbed, and head run under the tap to wash out the mine dust, Amy emerged from the small restroom a few minutes later, feeling a little more human. She could see the light outside beginning to turn yellow with the evening. Her stomach rumbled. It had been a busy day, and she hadn't eaten much. A visit to the diner might be in order as soon as they were done at the shop.

While Jackson was taking his turn at the sink, Amy started pulling the turquoise samples out of her and Jackson's backpacks and setting them in a row on the glass checkout counter. In the softer light of the shop they glowed, full of color. The matrix and color of some of the pieces reminded her strongly of turquoise she'd seen from the Kingman mine, but others seemed similar to the specimens brought out of the old abandoned mines in Nevada, particularly the Number 8 mine.

She walked around to the small work room behind the counter, and started searching through a series of small drawers.

"What are you looking for?"

Amy jumped and spun only to see Jackson standing in the doorway, looking surprised.

"Sorry, I didn't mean to scare you." He stood there, water dripping from his hair, and a wet stain spreading around the neck of his t-shirt from when he washed his face and neck.

Amy released a breath she hadn't realized she'd been holding. "No, it's okay. I guess I'm pretty tense about this whole situation."

"I don't blame you. I'm surprised you're still standing. I'd consider crawling under my bed leaving a wake up call for next year." He gave her a sympathetic smile. "Now, what were you looking for?"

"I was trying to find a set of hardness testing pens my dad keeps around here somewhere." She turned back to the cabinet and pulled open a few more drawers.

"Ah, there they are!" Amy pulled a small leather case out of the top drawer. As she walked out, Jackson stepped aside, watching her with curiosity. She pulled out one of the tools, a pen shaped item with a point at each end. She checked the numbers at the base of the tip, making sure that it was a six. She picked up one of the rough chunks, and tried to scratch the turquoise with the pick.

"Mohs hardness?" Jackson asked.

"Yeah. Did your girlfriend tell you about that?"

"Nah. High school geology class. I got an A." He grinned at her. "So, does it pass muster?"

"Yeah, it's a good six. I'm able to scratch it with the six pen, but it's not a deep scratch," Amy said, referring to the tools, each point a different level of hardness. If a pen was able to scratch a mineral sample, then that sample was the same harness or less than the pen being used. Turquoise was usually somewhere between three and six, with best quality being the six. That was the type that could easily be polished and made into jewelry without being stabilized.

"You said you had a sample from Skystone Mine?"

"Yes, it's in the back room." She walked to Nick's office where she'd left her keys, then headed for the display room where Jackson was waiting. Looking around at the series of glass fronted cases, she sighed. "This may take a little. You're looking for a chunk of turquoise about three inches by two by two."

The pair spent the next few minutes studying the specimens on the various shelves. The piece they were looking for wasn't in the cabinet where Nick was displaying it the last time she'd been home, naturally, and Amy started to wonder if he'd sold it. However, Jackson finally spotted it on the top shelf of the back cabinet, between a large piece of black tourmaline, and a stunning specimen of epidote included quartz, a cluster of clear quartz points which had developed around sprays of green epidote crystals. Amy admired that one for a moment before moving on to the turquoise. Epidote was one of her favorites, and Nick must have gotten it recently, but forgotten to tell her about it. Probably because he knew she'd try to talk him out of it.

Amy unlocked the cabinet, and pulled out the piece of turquoise. There was a card underneath with the provenance, which Amy read out loud so that Jackson could hear.

"Turquoise in matrix from Skystone Mine, 1887. The price is over two thousand, but that's not surprising, as it's so big. It gives a short history of the Skystone Mine, or the legend at any rate. It says the stone was sold to the rancher I told you, James Martin, and passed down eventually to his grandson, who sold it to Dad two years ago."

"So, is it the same as the stuff we picked up downstairs?"

"Downstairs? Really?" Amy laughed at the term, and Jackson's smile flashed out.

"Well, we went down the stairs to get there, didn't we?"

"And then walked about a mile or so."

"We still went downstairs. Stop changing the subject. Is this piece the same as the stuff we brought back?"

"I'm not sure. I'm no turquoise expert and there's so much to know about turquoise. It's a complicated mineral." She carried the Skystone Mine specimen back out into the front showroom and sat it on the glass counter next to the rough turquoise that she and Jackson had brought back from the mine.

"The color is pretty close, and the matrix is the same from what I can tell. I don't know, Jackson. Even in the same mine you can see a lot of variation in quality and color. What was so amazing about the stuff down in the mine was that it seemed so consistent and the pieces were exceptionally large. It's predominantly vein turquoise, formed when water percolates down through the cracks and fissures in the hard rock, dissolving other minerals. It's actually a hydrated phosphate of copper and aluminum."

"Huh? You speaking English?"

The tension broke and Amy laughed. "Sorry Jackson, it's an occupational hazard. Geologist talk. But really, I can't tell for sure if this turquoise came from the same mine, but it looks identical, and it seems too big of a coincidence not to be true."

She picked up the piece with the quartz and studied it again. She loved the play of bright blue on clear quartz. She'd only seen one other piece like this, or a picture of it at any rate. It came from the Bisbee Mine in southern Arizona.

"This is amazing. I can hardly wait until Gladys and Em see it. They'll..." Amy froze, staring at the specimen in her hand. She felt all the blood rushing from her head and she swayed slightly.

"What's wrong, Amy?" Jackson reached out and took her arm. Concern saturated his voice.

Amy looked at him, her wide violet eyes meeting his worried blue ones.

"When I was at the diner the first day I was here, before Carl died, I noticed that Gladys and Emily had some new turquoise specimens. I teased her about two-timing Nick, and buying the pieces from some other rock dealer. She was pretty cagey about it, teasing that a lady never disclosed her sources."

"What are you saying?"

"What if the other building isn't the town council hall like I thought, and instead is the diner. Gladys and Emily are pretty obsessed with their collection."

"So you're saying that one of those... ah... little old ladies...," Jackson paused when he caught Amy giving him the stink eye, then continued. "Okay, mature women of a certain age. You're saying at they're the ones who found the mine, and one of them killed Carl? Are you crazy?" Jackson looked at her with amazement clear on his face, and Amy started feeling foolish for making the suggestion.

"Wouldn't it be more likely that Emily or Gladys bought the turquoise from Carl, or the person who killed Carl, and that person swore them to secrecy?"

"Maybe. I hope so." Amy felt a flush of relief wash through her at the alternative explanation for Gladys' secretive behavior.

"There's got to be a good explanation. I just can't see Em or Gladys as murderers. But you know what this means don't you?" Jackson looked at her, excitement lighting his face.

"No... Wait. It means that one way or the other, Gladys or

Emily, or both, know who murdered Carl, even if they don't realize it." Amy felt the excitement building in her as well.

"Yes, well maybe not quite. If they bought the pieces from Carl, then they wouldn't know where he got them. However, I can't imagine Gladys or Em buying from Carl because they would have been suspicious of him having high quality turquoise separate from the shop. Besides, they didn't like him. I doubt they'd trust him to be honest about where the turquoise came from, and if you're right, provenance can be a large part of the turquoise price."

"It is. Those pieces that they have on their shelves had to have cost hundreds if not thousands each. Jackson, we've got to go talk to Gladys and Emily and figure out what they know. Or what they did."

Jackson glanced up at the clock. "They should be at the diner. Let's go. I'm hungry anyway, so no matter what it won't be a wasted trip."

Amy's stomach grumbled again in response, as if agreeing with what Jackson said. He laughed at the sound, and Amy felt her cheeks flush.

"You're on, Jackson. But we need to be careful. Emily asked me about a large Thunder Bay amethyst that Nick had supposedly gotten for her."

"The one that we think was used to kill Carl? The one that was broken up into pieces?"

"I'm pretty sure that's the one. Maybe it's just another coincidence, but I'm getting awfully tired of those. Maybe instead she was trying to determine if we'd figured out what she'd done with the one used to kill Carl."

"Sweet lil' old Emily," said Jackson in marveling tones. "She never seems like she'd raise her voice to the devil, let alone bash Carl over the head with a crystal plate." He shook his head, contemplating some image in his mind. "Not to mention, I can't picture her destroying an amethyst plate, especially one that she wanted as a display. That would have torn her up something terrible."

"Tell me about it. Let's go on down. Why don't I change back into my shorts, if you'd take the dogs out to take care of business, then we'll head out. You can ride with me if you want. I'll just leave the dogs here until we get back."

"Works for me." Jackson headed for the front door, whistling for Bess and Jynx, while Amy headed into Nick's office to change clothes.

A few minutes later the two were heading down Route 66 to the diner, the late evening sun turning the landscape around town golden. As they drove, Amy studied the buildings they passed, trying to verify where the tunnel truly ended. She could have sworn that the final set of turns would have taken them closer to the town council building, and it was the right age. Actually, it was even older than the rumors of the tunnels when it came down to it. The diner, on the other hand, was more modern. She was sure that it was built in the 40s or 50s, but maybe it was built on a foundation to an older building.

Amy tried to remember when she had explored the old building as a kid. She was positive it didn't have a basement. That was before Gladys Sanchez and Emily James had gone into partnership, bought the old building and started the Copper Springs Diner. Amy remembered that it had been a feed store, and then later a hardware store when she was younger. It also sat empty for a few years, as did so many of the old storefronts in town. The construction of I-40, and bypass of Route 66 had quite an impact on many of the small towns in that area, some of which had turned back into ghost towns, having first been abandoned by the depleting mines in the area, and then later the loss of tourist traffic. Maybe the new interest in Route 66 travel would revive some of them, but Amy didn't think it was likely.

The parking lot was nearly full with when Amy pulled the Wrangler into the parking lot, choosing one of the few spots left, in the second row straight out from the front door. A large group was just leaving, laughing and chattering in an unfamiliar language. Jackson caught the door before it swung shut and held it for Amy to enter. As they made their way through the vestibule, she could hear the mummer of happily eating people drifting out of the restaurant.

Amy and Jackson stood looking at the dining area, searching for a place to sit. It seemed that all the booths and tables were taken, but Amy spied three open seats down toward the end of the counter. One man sat at the very end, apparently fully engrossed in whatever was on his plate, and several tough looking men wearing bikers' leathers sat on the other side of the three empty spaces. Amy looked at Jackson and nodded toward the stools, and he started to walk in that direction, Amy close behind. He stopped briefly to say hello to Merri, who was carrying a tray full of food to a large table across the room, but in the babble of the restaurant, Amy couldn't hear what he said. He patted Merri on the shoulder and continued on to the turquoise naugahyde stools in front of the counter, sliding onto the one next to the biker, and leaving Amy one with a space between her and the man on the end.

That was fine with Amy, since that guy seemed to want to be alone anyway. He sat, keeping his head down, his kinky, steel wool gray hair falling forward hiding his face and reminding her of an angora goat she'd seen on the big reservation in the Four Corners area. He was dressed neatly for work, but reminded her of some of the hermit types who'd lived in the area when she was younger. They'd come into town occasionally to pick up things from Gleason's hardware store, or other supplies from Moira's dry goods, then disappear back out into the rangelands.

She slid onto her own stool and tried to ignore the strange man next to her. Meanwhile, Jackson had struck up a conversation with the biker on his right. They were talking about traveling Route 66 from one end to the other, and Jackson was quizzing the man on the places that the historic highway passed through, sounding ready to pack up his motor home and head out that moment.

She elbowed him in the side and he looked at her, a question in his eyes.

"What?"

"You're forgetting what we're here for," she hissed.

"No, I'm not. Gladys hasn't come out yet, so I was just talking to Duff about the..." Amy kicked him in the shin, causing him to jump.

"Will you...,"

"Hi there you two!" Gladys came popping out of the kitchen, looking cheerful and happy to see Amy and Jackson. "How are things going up at the shop? Are you ready to open back up tomorrow?" She beamed at first one then the other.

"It's been going great, Gladys. The shop is all cleaned up, and everything is back in order, so we should be open for business tomorrow morning."

"Wonderful, we'll have to come in and see how things turned out, won't we Em?" Gladys turned and looked back to the pass through, where Emily was peeking through, a huge grin on her face as usual. Amy just couldn't picture soft spoken Emily as a murder. Besides, Jackson was right, it was almost inconceivable that she would shatter a beautiful Thunder Bay amethyst plate just to hide the weapon.

"We, uh..." Amy looked at Jackson, unsure how to proceed. He looked back and shrugged, then tilted his chin toward Gladys.

"What can I get for you two today," Gladys asked, apparently unaware of the silent discussion going on between Amy and Jackson. Drawn back to her grumbling stomach, Amy decided that food was the first order of business. If they were going to catch a murderer, she'd like to do it on a full stomach.

"I'd like the Route 66 Burger and fries with an iced tea, please. Jackson?" Amy turned and looked at him. He gave her a *come on!* look, then turned back to the older woman across the counter.

"I'll take the same, Gladys. Thanks. When you get the chance, though, we need to talk with you a moment about those two new pieces of turquoise you have on your shelves."

"Well, certainly. Aren't they beautiful? I..." They all jumped as the man at the end of the counter accidentally knocked over his glass, flooding the counter with water and ice. Gladys' attention was immediately taken with her customer.

"Oh, my goodness, Scott. Let me get you some paper towels."

"No, it's fine. I have the napkins." A gruff voice emerged

from the hidden face, as the man mopped up the water. "Don't fuss. I'll take care of it."

"Let me fill your glass again at least," Gladys said, scooping the sopping napkins off into a plastic bag, and then picking up a pitcher of ice water to refill his glass.

"Thank you," came the mumbled reply.

"No problem. I hope your burger is okay?"

"Delicious as usual, Gladys. Thank you again."

Nodding, Gladys turned back to Amy and Jackson. "Let me go ahead and put in your order. We've been so busy this evening, I hardly know where my head is. Two Route 66 Burgers, two fries and two iced teas, is that correct?"

Amy nodded, and Gladys bounced over to the pass through and called out the order. She picked up two tall frosted glasses, and brought them over to Amy and Jackson. She picked up the pitcher of iced tea and filled them to the brim, finishing them off with a lemon slice each.

"There you go. Your food ought to be out in a moment."

"Thank you, Gladys," Amy said. "About that turquoise though..."

"Oh, yes. You wanted to know more about our new pieces? I'm... Just a moment." Gladys looked over to where Merri was waving at her. "I'll be just a moment kids. I've got to take care of something." She quickly walked out from behind the counter and over to where Merri was standing.

Amy and Jackson looked at each other, and Amy started to laugh. "We may need to nail her to the floor before we get to ask her anything." She spoke quietly, keeping her voice low so that the biker on Jackson's right couldn't hear her. She guessed he and his friends were just strangers passing through town, but there was no sense in taking any chances.

"Give her a minute. Most of these people are nearing the end of their meals, and it will calm down pretty quickly." Jackson spoke low as well, leaning in close so that Amy could hear him.

Amy nodded, and sat sipping her iced tea. Before long a waitress slid her and Jackson's burgers in front of them, and the next few minutes were spent feeding their grumbling stomachs. By the time they finished their food, the diner had started to clear out. The man at the end of the counter was still working on a piece of apple pie ala mode and a cup of coffee, but the trio of bikers had headed out the door, and from the sound of the engine roar, had headed off down Route 66, heading for California.

Gladys came back over to the counter where Amy and Jackson were sitting, and wiped the surface with her towel.

"How was your dinner?"

"Delicious as always Gladys." Jackson beamed at her, and her smile grew in response.

"Yes, it was wonderful. I wish I had room to eat another," Amy laughed, rubbing her stomach which was full to the point of bursting and no longer grumbling.

"Now what was it that you wanted to talk to me about earlier? Oh, yes. The turquoise. What did you want to know?

Amy wadded up her napkin and set it in the middle of her plate, then looked Gladys in the eye, praying she'd be able to read any signs of deception.

"You said they came from the Skystone Mine? How do you know?"

"Yes, they came from there, at least the person who sold the pieces to us says they did, and I have no reason to doubt him."

"This person, who is he? I... uh... Do you think he has any more? I might want to buy some for the shop. My understanding was that only one pack of the turquoise was ever brought out, and most of that has been lost or snapped up by collectors."

"That's what I thought too, honey. But our source told us that more has been found, and that there's no doubt that it's Skystone. The hardness is right, and the matrix is just amazing."

"Who is the seller, Gladys. Do we know him?" Jackson asked, keeping his voice conversational, as though it didn't matter.

"I don't know if you've met him or not, Jackson. I doubt you know him, Amy. Let me introduce you to him. Of course you may want to buy some from him for the shop. They are such beautiful stones. Right Em?" Emily, who had come out from the kitchen during the discussion smiled widely, and nodded.

"In fact, it's such good luck. He's here right now. Scott..." Gladys turned to the end of the counter where the man with the gray hair had been sitting a few moments before. "Well, he's left. I didn't see him get up, did you Emily?" Emily shook her head.

Amy looked down toward the end of the counter to the empty seat. The plate, with half a piece of pie and a melting puddle of ice cream was all that remained, with several dollar bills thrown haphazardly on the counter next to it.

"That's strange," Gladys said, a frown creasing her face. "He didn't even say goodbye. He always says goodbye."

"It's okay, Gladys. He probably saw that you were talking with us and didn't want to interrupt," Jackson said in soothing tones. "Who is he, though. You called him Scott, but Scott who?"

"Oh, Scott Branson. He's new to the town, only been here around a year. He's the town's code enforcement officer."

Amy felt like all the air had been sucked out of the room. She stared at Gladys in shock, all thoughts driven from her mind.

"He was in here one evening for dinner. He does that a lot since he's all alone, poor man. A different man had come in that day and tried to sell us a very expensive piece of dyed howlite, claiming that it was first quality Number 8 Mine turquoise. As if we were amateurs," Gladys continued, apparently unaware of the bombshell she'd just lobbed into the room.

"Scott overheard Emily and I talking about it, and mentioned that he'd recently found a cache of Skystone Mine turquoise and was needing to sell some. Emily and I were pretty skeptical, I'll tell you, but it was Scott. He's a nice man, even if a lot of people don't like his job." Gladys shook her head, apparently thinking about the struggles Branson had gone through trying to fit into the town.

"When we looked at the specimens, we could easily believe that they were Skystone Mine. They looked so much like that one Nick has in the shop, or the few pictures we've seen of collectors' pieces. Yes, I know that there are tests that can be run now, but we didn't want to bother with that. Besides, Scott was giving us an amazing price. He didn't want us to talk to people about the turquoise, or where we'd gotten it, but I'm sure he wouldn't mind us talking to you." Gladys beamed at Amy and Jackson, nodding her head vigorously. "After all, you're in the business, and you love the rocks as much as we do."

"Thank you so much, Gladys," Jackson spoke up from beside Amy. "I'm sure we'll be talking with Scott, although it will be Amy and Nick's decision about any purchases. I'm just the computer geek." He gave the older women a brilliant smile, and Amy was grateful that it took the pressure off her for a moment.

"Are you done with your dinner, Jackson?" Amy said, giving him a *let's get out of here* look.

"Yes. Thank you again, Gladys. Em. It was delicious." Jackson spun his stool, and slid off, then waited for Amy.

"Thank you for the information Gladys. I'll definitely talk to Scott about some of his Skystone Mine cache. It's an amazing find."

"It certainly is. Em and I were so glad to be able to get the two pieces we have. Normally we'd never be able to afford something like those two lovelies. Right, Em?" Gladys looked over to her partner who was nodding vigorously.

Outside the diner Amy stopped and looked at Jackson. The cool late evening air lifted her curly hair, and swarms of bugs swirled around the security lights that had come on in front of the building.

"What do you think?"

"I think that you may have the murderer," Jackson said, his voice as serious as she'd ever heard it.

Amy slid in behind the wheel of the Wrangler as Jackson walked around to the passenger side. She pulled out and headed back down the highway toward Stone's Gems and Minerals.

"I've got to call the sheriff's department and let them know about Branson. The door we found must open into the basement of the town council building. Branson must have found the door, and then the mine."

"You're right. Somehow he must have met up with Carl, they had a falling out, and Branson killed Carl, then started looking for the laptop. There has to be evidence on that computer that would implicate him. I'll bet the plan to condemn the building was concocted by him to keep anyone else from finding the mine. I have no idea how the Hazeltons got involved."

"He knows that we know about him, doesn't he?" Amy asked, feeling a shiver start deep down inside in spite of the hot late July weather.

"I don't see how he could possibly fail to know," Jackson said, a glum note in his voice. "We may not have been yelling in the diner, but we weren't being overly careful either. I'm sure that's why he disappeared."

"Do you think he'll make a run for it?" Amy said, focusing on the road as she pulled into the shop's parking lot. "He might be able to get pretty far before they start looking for him." She studied the front of the building. Something was different. Then it hit her; the front security light had burned out. *Great, just one more thing to do.* She sighed, adding replacing the front light to her to-do list.

"I don't know if he'll run," Jackson said apparently unaware of any change in Amy's attention. "Actually I hope he does make a break for it. I think that would be our best case scenario. He's smart, though, and I'm not sure he's going to do something that would draw attention. It would be smarter to get rid of you, reinforcing the idea that you killed Carl, and are running because you think the sheriff's department is going to arrest you. I hate to say it, but I'm not sure how safe we are right now. He must know we've got a pretty good idea what happened, but if you and I are gone, no one would be suspicious of him. There would be no reason."

"He doesn't know we've been in the mine yet."

"But he knows that we're aware that Carl's murder has something to do with the Skystone mine. Don't underestimate him, Amy."

"Okay, what are you suggesting..." Amy's phone's ringtone sounded. As she climbed out of the Jeep she pulled the phone from her pocket. "It's Maria Kissoon. She must be back from the canyon."

She hit send, and held the phone to her ear as she walked around the front of the Jeep. "Hey, Maria. How are you doing?"

"Hey Amy. Sorry it took me so long to get back with you. I went down to Supi to visit my parents for the weekend and I forgot my phone charger, not that I'd get much of a signal down there anyway. What can I do for you?"

"You know about Carl, right?"

"Yeah, I heard."

"It was looking like I was the chief suspect, and Tommy said I should talk to you. But, now I think I know who killed Carl, Maria. We have evidence that..."

A blow from behind sent Amy sprawling to the ground, her phone flying from her hand. She heard a sound as if from a great distance.

A yell.

Voices.

Jackson crashed to the ground next to her. She could see a trickle of blood running down the side of his face from a cut on his forehead. His eyes were closed and she couldn't tell if he was still breathing. Slowly she rolled her head to the left, the pain making her see spots. She squinted, trying to see who was there in the darkness. Slowly a face emerged as the shadowy shape knelt and grabbed her arms, pulling them together and running a roll of duct tape around her wrists.

It was Scott Branson. She struggled to get her arms loose and roll away, but a second blow to her head caused the world to go black.

Black Campan Marble

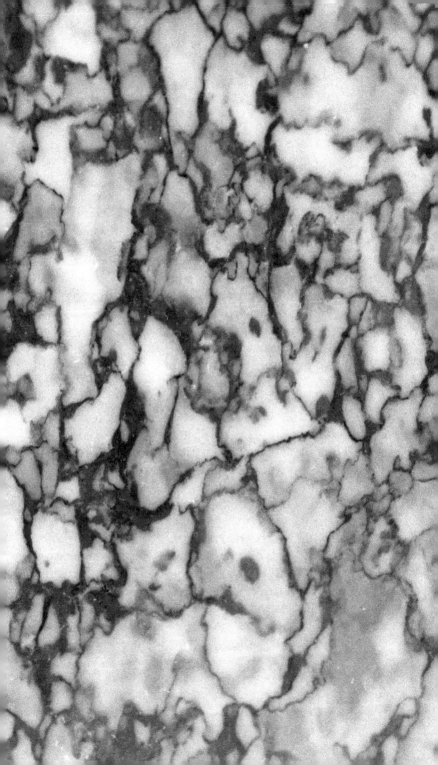

20

Amy felt herself being lifted and pulled. Someone's arms were around her chest, squeezing her uncomfortably and she started to struggle. Something bound her wrists and ankles. Tape covered her mouth and she tried to rub it off on her shoulder.

"Knock it off or you'll get it again," the gruff voice she'd heard in the diner spoke in her ear and she subsided. Branson was pulling her out of the back of a silver gray SUV behind a huge stone building; the Copper Springs town offices. A back road. No outdoor lights again and brush surrounding the property. Virtually no chance that some passerby would see what Branson was doing.

In the dim cabin light Amy could see Jackson still laying in the cargo area, arms duct taped in front of him, and ankles taped together just like hers. He was groaning and rolling his head, but there were no other signs of consciousness.

Branson dumped her in a pile on the gravel parking lot. Rocks dug into her shoulder, and she rolled trying to find a less painful position. He moved back to the SUV, and pulled Jackson from the cargo area, dropping him on the ground next to her like a sack of potatoes. Amy could see Jackson's eyes flutter open and he looked around. His eyes met Amy's for a moment, but he seemed confused.

"Wake up." Branson was standing over Jackson and Amy, holding a hose which was attached to a spigot on the side of the building. Their captor turned the valve, and sprayed both Amy and Jackson with cold water, and Jackson's eyes seemed to come into focus. He struggled for a moment against the duct tape on his arms and legs, muttering what Amy assumed to be curses under the tape across his mouth.

Thank goodness Merri wasn't here, Amy thought randomly. Jackson would probably be in time out for the rest of his life if his sister could hear everything he was likely saying, even if it was muffled by the tape.

"Lay still." Brandon's voice again. "I'm going to cut the tape around your legs so you can stand. Then I'm going to tie you together, and we're going to go into the building. You're not going to fight or try to run, because if you do, I will hit you again. This is easier on me if you can walk, but I'll manage either way." Brandon pulled out a large pocket knife and started to cut through the tape around her legs. She drew her legs back, ready to kick.

"Don't try it," Branson said without emotion. He picked up a long wrecking bar he'd set on the ground without Amy's noticing. She froze, then rolled her head so that she could see Jackson's face. He had become silent at Branson's words. Amy's eyes met his, and Jackson shook his head slightly. She relaxed and allowed Branson to continue to cut the tape. He moved over to Jackson's legs, taking the wrecking bar with him. He quickly cut through the tape, grabbed Jackson's arms and hauled him next to Amy, the gravel crunching underneath.

"Get up." Branson commanded.

Amy struggled to roll to her side, then forced herself up to a kneeling position, the gravel digging in to her knees. From there she pushed herself to her feet, her head pounding from the movement. Next to her she could see Jackson doing the same. Once both were standing side by side, Branson grabbed their bound wrists, and using his roll of duct tape fastened Amy's arms to Jackson's. That done, he moved behind and shoved them toward the back door of the town's government building a few feet away, prodding Amy and then Jackson in the back with the heavy wrecking bar.

Twice Amy ducked her head and tried to catch the edge of the tape against her shoulder, but Branson caught her, and jabbed at her even more viciously with the bar, causing her to stumble and pull Jackson with her. Branson was eerily quiet, having only growled a few words since the attack, and Amy began to feel as though she were captured by a poltergeist, rather than a flesh and blood man.

Nothing changed when they entered the building. Branson stepped forward, pulled the door open and prodded them through. Once inside the building, he locked the door.

"Down the hall on the left." Another prod in the back. Amy and Jackson walked the thirty feet down the hall to a narrow wooden door which was standing open. She looked at the stairs beyond and shook her head, trying to speak, but unable to make anything other than a muffled gargle due to the tape across her mouth. Branson poked her again, but she shook her head. Couldn't he see that the stairwell was much too narrow for two people to go down at once? She and Jackson would be sure to fall, and more than likely one of them would be hurt.

Of course, since he probably intended on killing them, keeping them from getting hurt prior to that might not be high on his priority list.

Jackson pulled back, recognizing the problem with the stairwell, and Branson raised his arm and brought the wrecking bar down on Jackson's shoulder, knocking him to his knees and pulling Amy down with him. A groan emerged from under his duct tape gag, and his face twisted in pain. Amy helped him to his feet, and looked back at Branson. For the first time she saw his face in the light, rather than the dim glow of the light of the cargo bed, or the dark shadows in front of the shop, and her eyes widened in surprise.

The face hidden by the wiry hair was flat and coarse, his nose misshapen. Mud brown eyes met hers with a look of loathing. Amy wasn't sure she'd ever been exposed to a look like that any time in her life.

"Get down those stairs," he said, the wrecking bar in his had swinging at his side. Amy had no doubt that if they didn't do as he asked, he wouldn't hesitate to use it again. Slowly she moved toward the steps, turning sideways and holding her arms up so that she wouldn't pull Jackson down on top of her. He followed, also turning to the side to avoid pulling her off balance. In that manner the two of them managed the steep staircase to the basement; a basement that was very similar to the one in the shop, except that in this case the walls were of stone and mortar, rather than brick.

The room was dusty, and Amy started to cough, choking under the tape, unable to catch her breath. For a moment Branson stood and watched her without reaction. Just when Amy thought she was never going to be able to breath again, he finally moved forward and yanked the tape from her mouth, turned and did the same for Jackson.

Amy took a deep breath, and coughed several more times, then finally stood and looked at Branson, who had taken a step back and was watching the pair.

"Thank you," she said, her voice still hoarse. She shifted her attention to Jackson, who still seemed slightly dazed from the earlier blow. "Are you okay?"

"I suppose. Although usually when I go out to dinner with a woman, I don't generally expect to get hit over the head and tied up." He gave her a weak smile. "Tied up, maybe, but..."

"Jackson!" She kicked him on the shin. Not hard, but it was enough to make him sway slightly.

Amy turned her head to look at Branson who'd been watching their interaction silently. "What are you planning on doing with us? Why do this?"

"You are going to disappear, Ms. Stone. You and Mr. Wolf are going to disappear, and it will be presumed that you realized that the sheriff's department was getting ready to arrest you for murder, so you and your boyfriend here decided to take off."

"Jackson's not my boyfriend. I just met him. I don't even know his real last name!"

"Really," Jackson said, looking at her in amazement. "The guy just tells us that he's planning on killing us, and what you're upset about is that he called me your boyfriend?"

"Sorry," Amy grumbled, then turned her attention back to Branson. "No one is going to believe we disappeared. My Jeep is still in front of the store. My dog..." Amy froze. She didn't want Branson to know that Jynx and Bess were still in the shop. It would be obvious to anyone that she'd never leave her dog in the shop and skip town. That alone would be enough to cause a search. Of course since no one knew anything about Branson, no one would know where to search, but at least they would be looking in the area, and not at the border to Mexico.

"Your Jeep will be taken care of." Branson held up the keys which he must have taken out of her pocket when she was unconscious. "There are a number of old mines out in the middle of nowhere. I'll simply drop it off in one of those shafts, and it will be a long time, if ever, before anyone finds it. Now, that way." Branson pointed the wrecking bar toward a doorway in a wall on the south side of the room.

Amy and Jackson moved in the direction Branson indicated, walking into a back room of the cavernous basement. Amy looked around noting the worn whitewash and cracked concrete floors. If she thought the shop's basement was creepy, this basement was downright hair-raising. It had obviously been used as nothing but a storeroom for years... or decades. The back room was filled with furniture; desks, chairs, filing cabinets and lamps. A narrow path wound back through the clutter to the back wall.

Suddenly a thought crossed Amy's mind, and she came to a stop, pulling Jackson with her.

"Move," came the predictable command from Branson.

"Wait a minute. The town had all this junk down here, and you've got the nerve to try and condemn Stone's Gems and Minerals. We've cleaned our fingers off the last few days to make sure that we get a clean bill of health. What the heck?"

"Move," Branson commanded again.

"If you're going to kill us, you should at least give us the obligatory final explanation first," Jackson said.

"Just move. Over there, behind the bookshelves."

Jackson looked at Amy and shrugged. He mouthed the words *I tried*. She nodded slightly, and the two moved in the direction Branson indicated. In the back of the room were two tall bookcases, covered with bits and pieces of office equipment. Amy came to a stop with Jackson, and stared at the blockage.

"Around the side. There." Branson was back to his "man of few words" persona and Amy gritted her teeth in annoyance. Jackson led the way around the bookshelves, and then stopped before a huge metal door. He looked at Amy and twitched his head, a question in his eyes. *Is this the door we saw from the tunnel side?* Amy nodded slightly, the movement didn't help her aching head. It seemed that both she and Jackson were in agreement as far as letting Branson know that they'd already been in the mines. Maybe, if they could get away from him, they could hide. It wouldn't be safe, but it was better than whatever plan he had for them. Better if Branson thought they were in unfamiliar territory.

Branson moved around Amy and Jackson to unlock the door and pull it open as far as the bookcases would allow, the door scraping against the floor and the old iron hinges making a squealing sound that Amy could feel all the way to her core, like fingernails on a chalkboard. He ushered them in, swinging the wrecking bar dangerously close to Amy's back.

"Watch it, would ya," she snapped as she felt the bar brush the back of her shirt.

"Sorry. I wouldn't want to hurt you," Branson replied with a sarcastic tone in his voice. He picked up a helmet with headlamp and a small battery powered lantern from the bookshelf and followed them into the tunnel, pulling the door shut with another screech and latching it behind them.

Amy pulled Jackson around bumping into the rough rock walls. They faced Branson, and Amy tried to reason with him. "Listen, I don't know what's going on, but there's no way you're going to manage to get away with killing us. What is going on?"

"Move. Down the tunnel. I'll tell you when to stop."

"No. Not until you tell us what's happening. Why are you doing this?"

Branson swung the wrecking bar menacingly.

"You're going to kill us anyway, and if you do it here, you're going to have to carry the bodies." Amy's temper was boiling over and Jackson jerked on her arm.

"Amy," Jackson hissed.

Amy turned to look at Jackson, taking her focus off Branson for a moment. "No, Jackson. He owes us an explanation, and I'm darn well going to have one before I take one more step."

Jackson shrugged and turned his face to Branson. "You heard the lady. We've guessed at a lot of things, but you're the only one who can fill in all the details, like what is this place?" He rolled his head, pointing with his chin at the tunnel surrounding them. Amy nodded slightly. The only card left in their deck was the fact that Branson didn't know they'd ever been in the tunnels before.

"You killed Carl Schrader, right?" Jackson kept his voice calm and matter of fact. "Why did you do it?"

"Fine," Branson said. "But you walk while I talk. That's the only way I'll do it."

"Compromise is a good thing," Jackson said. He pulled at Amy's arms and started walking down the tunnel, the narrow passage forcing them into an awkward position. They had only gone a few steps when Jackson stopped short. "You know, you're the only one with a light and we're blocking most of it. It will slow us down if we're walking into walls and tripping over rocks. Let Amy carry the lantern."

Branson looked at Amy and Jackson, the scowl on his face deepening in the harsh light. Finally, he reluctantly held out the lantern.

"Amy, take it. My arm isn't working so well right now." Jackson said, nodding toward the arm which Branson had hit with the wrecking bar earlier. With a concerned look toward Jackson, Amy reached out and took the lantern in her tied hands, pulling Jackson's up with hers. He winced at the movement and she could see fine beads of sweat glinting in the harsh light. They had to find a way to cut themselves free or they were doomed.

She and Jackson turned and started slowly down the tunnel, the light dangling in her hands, her hip bumping into Jackson's at nearly every step. Behind them, Branson began to talk.

"I heard you talking to the old ladies at the Copper Springs Diner, so I know you are aware that this all centers around turquoise."

"Yes," Amy said, "Gladys said you found an old stash of Skystone Mine turquoise. Was it down here in these tunnels?"

"Yes and no." Branson said so softly that Amy had to strain to hear his voice. Then he started speaking louder, his voice picking up speed as he launched into his story.

"I didn't find a cache of Skystone Mine turquoise, I found the Skystone Mine itself."

"Unbelievable. That's really pretty amazing." Jackson said, his voice sounding completely enthralled. Amy kicked him, afraid he'd lay it on too thick, and that Branson would feel mocked and retaliate.

Apparently Branson bought Jackson's admiration, however, and he continued without hesitation. "I moved here about a year ago to take the job of code enforcement officer for Copper Springs. It was a nice little town, and I wanted out of the big city. However, I found out there wasn't much to do in my off time. I'm a bit of a history buff, and it wasn't long before I heard the rumors of the tunnels under the town, as well as the story of the Skystone Mine, and a couple of other 'lost' mines in the area that had ghost stories attached to them. I began exploring any abandoned mines or caves that I could find, and that looked safe enough."

"Is that how you found these tunnels? You found an abandoned mine entrance?" Jackson asked, genuine curiosity in his voice and Amy could picture him searching out all the area's abandoned mines and caves at his first opportunity... that was if they survived tonight.

"I came across the door to the tunnel system a few months ago when looking for a filing cabinet in the basement. You might have noticed that the town has apparently saved every stick of furniture since the building was built, and I became interested in all the old pieces. I started exploring the basement, and came across the door. It took quite awhile to get it open. The hinges and lock were rusted shut, and the mortar itself was in pretty bad condition. Once I got the door open... well you know what I found. I started exploring the tunnels in my spare time, and that's when I found the Skystone Mine."

"This is it?"

"No. These are just tunnels. They join up with the Pipe Wash Mine, an old gold mine which was abandoned, and then collapsed back in the early nineteen hundreds."

"But how did Carl become involved?" Amy asked. "Did you contact him for help selling the turquoise because he's with the rock shop?"

"I wanted nothing to do with that slimy worm." The disgust in Branson's voice was obvious. It was equally obvious, Amy thought, that he ignored the irony of Branson, Carl's murderer, calling Carl himself a slimy worm.

"I was careless when I was exploring. I came to the brick wall, and was trying to figure out whether it was a buried leftover from another building, or one that was currently standing. By then I'd found the turquoise mine, and I didn't want anyone else coming across the tunnels." He snorted in disgust, and Amy turned to look over her shoulder at him. The harsh light of the headlamp made his already damaged face truly terrifying and she turned her head back quickly.

"That worm, Carl, was working in the basement; putting boxes down in storage he said. He heard me on the other side of the wall. He tried to find out where the sounds came from, and discovered the bricked in opening. He broke though that pretty quickly. I didn't want him exploring the tunnels and finding the turquoise by himself, so I confronted him."

As they walked, Amy was watching the walls of the tunnel, and knew they were almost to the large intersection. They'd already passed the inclined winze on the left, but Branson hadn't paid any attention to it. She desperately wished that she and Jackson had taken more time exploring the side tunnels that afternoon, not that they'd had the time to take of course. Still, if Branson took them down one of the side tunnels, they could find themselves up against the mine face, or a vertical shaft. She thought about running, but in the narrow passageways, tied together as she and Jackson were, and with Jackson injured, Branson would catch them easily, and wouldn't be gentle with the wrecking bar. He'd proven that already. Besides, Jackson had pulled the plywood back over the entrance to the shop, so they wouldn't be able to get out at that end.

Branson was apparently unaware of the thoughts going around in Amy's head, and continued on his narrative.

"That Schrader just wormed his way into my business. He said he could sell the turquoise online and get a good price. We'd split it fifty-fifty." The disgust in Branson's voice grew, if anything, more pronounced. "I did all the work. I found the mine and got the turquoise. All that worm was going to do was sell it, but he was going to get fifty percent."

"That doesn't seem fair." Jackson said, his voice dripping with sympathy. Amy gave him a look, but she wasn't sure if he was ignoring it, or didn't see it in the unreliable light of the lantern. "We found out that Carl had a lot of pretty sketchy deals going on, and was taking advantage of a number of people."

"Yeah, he bragged about how he was making a nice income from a lot of people in town. That car he drove sure wasn't paid for on what he made in a blasted rock shop."

Crap, Amy thought, *he's right. That car had to cost plenty, and Nick pays fair, but not nearly enough for that kind of ride.* She was furious that she hadn't think of that earlier, although with everything happening so quickly it probably wouldn't have made much of a difference.

"So where did the code violation warnings come into play?" Jackson continued. Amy could see him looking around as they walked and was sure he realized that they were nearing the intersection. She was sure that they would be taking the side tunnel, the one he called the Pipe Wash Mine. There was no reason for him to take them back to the shop when he could have left them there immediately after the attack.

"Carl found the tunnels. I wanted that entrance blocked permanently. The best way to do would be to fill in the basement, and the only way to do that would be to condemn the building, and demolish it. I know some contractors who would fill in the basement no questions asked in exchange for a few breaks on other construction projects."

"But the Hazeltons?" Amy asked, confused. They were intending to build a restaurant, not just fill in the basement. "They said that you were the one who'd told them about the place and assured them they'd be able to get a deal. They're not your partners?"

She looked over at Jackson. She was sure that the intersection was around the next curve.

Trip he mouthed.

Amy frowned and shook her head slightly, a questioning look in her eyes.

Trip! he mouthed again, *fall. Now do it.*

"The Hazeltons? Jon Hazelton and his snippy witch of a wife were a complication. Hazelton walked into my office one day and saw the paperwork that I'd started on Stone's shop. I didn't hide it quickly enough. I didn't assure him of anything. He came up with the idea of using the land for his wife's restaurant. Like anyone wants to eat something made by that sour..."

Amy tripped herself and fell to the floor of the tunnel, pulling Jackson down on top her. The fall apparently jarred his injured arm, and he groaned. The throbbing in her head increased.

"Get up. Come on." Branson commanded.

"I'm sorry. I tripped. These tunnels are too narrow for two people to walk side by side." Amy exclaimed, breathing hard from the fall. She struggled hard to get to her feet, Jackson pushing himself to his knees next to her. He sat for a moment, crouched over his arm, pulling her hands toward him in the process.

"Please, separate us from each other. Can't you see he's hurt. We're slowing you down, tied together like this." Amy pleaded, looking back at Branson. He narrowed his eyes as he studied the two on the ground in front of him.

"We'll be able to move faster if we're not tied together, especially when... ah," Amy started to cough, trying to cover the fact that she'd nearly told Branson that she and Jackson had already been in the tunnels and knew the narrower adits of the Pipe Wash were upon them.

Recovering, she continued, hoping that Branson hadn't noticed the mistake, "If the mines get any narrower as we go on."

Branson studied Amy and Jackson for a moment, obviously annoyed with the delay. Suddenly he made up his mind, reached into his pocket and pulled out the knife. Amy tensed for a moment, afraid that he'd decided to end things right then and there, but instead Branson grabbed her arms and started sawing on the tape connecting her to Jackson. It released with a snap, and Amy pulled her still bound hands back to her chest. Jackson sat back against the other side of the tunnel, hands in his lap, curled over them protectively. She could see beads of sweat popping out on his face again, and wondered how badly he was hurt.

"Now, get up. It's time to go."

"Just give me a moment," Jackson said. Amy could hear the strain in his voice and fought to think of something to distract Branson and give Jackson a chance to recover.

"I still don't understand about the code violations, though. Nick said they'd had some bats, and mice always manage to get into these old buildings, but it wasn't an infestation like the paperwork said. How were you going to make a health and safety violation stick?

"Schrader did come in handy setting up things for that. He found some packrat nests and the like out on the ranch where he was living, and had a plan to bring in containers of waste and dead rats and scatter them about just before the inspection. He even managed to catch some bats in a cave near his place and set them loose in the shop without Stone knowing."

"He did what?" Amy was appalled. "One of those bats may have been what distracted my dad and caused him to fall. He could have been killed." She felt more outrage at that betrayal than anything else that Carl had done to her father. The stolen specimens were money. This was Nick's life Carl had risked.

"Yeah, well, I don't think he intended for your father to fall. He just wanted vermin in the shop. Ideally customers would find them and complain, but that never really happened. I didn't need much, however. After all, I was the one in charge of the inspection. The hope was that your father would just decide that it would be easier to move the shop out of town, than to deal with constant town harassment"

"But why kill Carl? It sounded like working together was beneficial for both of you," Jackson said, his voice sounding stronger.

"That night when I went to the shop, it wasn't with the intention of killing Schrader, although I was getting pretty fed up with his greed. That night I went to take him some new turquoise pieces to auction off. Schrader started bragging about how he had started taking payoffs from the Hazeltons for the same things he and I had worked out, only instead of with the intention of condemning and demolishing the shop, the Hazeltons wanted their restaurant. Schrader started demanding more money from me, a larger cut. He was auctioning off his services, he said. He told me he'd inform Hazelton and the town council about the mine and my plan to condemn the shop. I pointed out that he'd implicate himself as well, and he laughed at me. He just said he'd tell the council that he heard me in the mines and found the doorway, and that he caught me coming through with the rodent droppings." The look on Branson's face gave Amy chills.

"I was so angry that I picked up the closest thing at hand and smashed him in the face. He fell and I hit him several more times. Then I realized he wasn't moving. I rinsed the geode off in the sink, and broke it up with a rock hammer. Then I kicked over some other trays of rocks and scattered the broken pieces in with them to make it look like a break in or a struggle. I took his phone because he'd said he recorded our meetings, but I could never find the laptop."

"So you broke into my parents' house and took the, uh..." Amy stopped, not sure if she should let Branson know that he'd taken the wrong computer."

"Yes, I took the laptop, and it and the phone are now where you're going to be soon," Branson said in ominous tones. Amy shivered.

"Why kill us, though? They're going to find out it's you, and you'll have three murders on your hands." Amy was frustrated at the man's lack of logical thinking.

"I don't think so. They're already suspicious of you, Ms. Stone. You'll disappear. The shop will be closed, and if necessary, I'll get it condemned. All the ladies at the diner know is that you were asking about turquoise, which would be normal for someone in your line of business. No one will even look twice at me. I've worked too hard to get this mine. I'm not giving it up." Branson swung the wrecking bar and hit the wall of the mine with a loud clang, making Amy flinch.

"Now get up. We're nearly there. "

Amy struggled to her feet, using the wall for support, then she moved over to Jackson and holding his uninjured arm, helped him rise as well. He gave her a ghost of a grin as he got to his feet. "You know, when you take a guy out to dinner, you do it right." He brought his head close to her ear and whispered, "Scream when we get to the intersection. Say you saw a spider."

Amy looked at Jackson, thinking that the blow he'd had to his head earlier had scrambled his thinking more than she realized. Why would he want her to scream? There was no one who would hear her. That type of noise didn't carry very well in the mines, and there was no one in either the town offices or in the shop. She gave him a *what the heck* look, which she was afraid wouldn't get through in the lantern's distorted light. It must have, however, since he gave her the *just do what I said* look right back. Amy shook her head and sighed.

"What are you whispering about. Just shut up and move. I want to get this finished." Branson snapped, again brandishing his wrecking bar.

"I'm going. Jackson was just telling me how much he enjoyed our dinner date, right Jackson?"

He nodded, only wincing slightly at the movement. "Yup, I can't remember the last time I was on a date with so much excitement."

"Yeah? Well, next time you get to plan the entertainment. Come on." Amy took the lantern and started down the passageway, Jackson following close behind. She glanced over her shoulder and saw Branson following closely.

Just as Amy suspected, as they rounded the next gentle curve, they entered the three way intersection. The tunnel to the mine led off to the left and Amy remembered those old, dilapidated adits she and Jackson had passed earlier in the day. If she was guessing, she'd say they were headed for one of those passageways.

Jackson bumped into her from behind, and she looked back. He nodded slightly and mouthed the word, *scream.*

Amy came to a stop in the middle of the intersection and suddenly took a step backward, and screamed from the top of her lungs, the sound echoing and reverberating around the tunnels, her head aching a thousand-fold from the effort.

Branson swung and struck the meaty part of her thigh with the wrecking bar, knocking her to the ground. "What the hell did you think you were doing?" he snarled.

Amy curled up in a ball as the pain washed through her body. His swing must have been blocked by the walls of the tunnel, and she didn't get as deadly a blow as she could have, but it still hurt like nothing she could remember. Tears pooled in her eyes.

Jackson dropped to her side, the light of the lantern showing the horror and concern in his blue eyes. "I'm so sorry, Amy. I'm so sorry."

"What were you doing?" Branson said again. Amy looked up at him as he stood, wrecking bar swinging at his side."

"I... I thought I saw a..." Amy swallowed as another wave of pain spread out from her thigh. She squeezed her eyes shut for a moment, then opened them. "A rat. A giant rat. I'm terrified of them."

Branson gave Amy a skeptical look. "A rat? Really? What do you think rats would be doing this far underground?"

"Well, I don't know where we are, do I?" Amy pushed herself into a sitting position, her leg screaming in protest. "It might have been a rat."

Branson rolled his eyes and gave Amy a disgusted look. Amy looked over at Jackson who had turned his head away from Branson. Amy could see him biting his lip to keep from laughing. Amy gave him an evil look that made Jackson chew on his lip even more vigorously.

"Enough of this crap." Branson growled. "Get up and let's get moving."

Amy sighed and started to push herself to her feet, her thigh throbbing. However, the intensity of the pain was fading, and she felt relatively certain that her leg wasn't broken. She had no idea why Jackson seemed to think she needed to scream, but she sure as heck hoped that it was for a good reason.

She stood for a moment, balancing on one leg, the other barely touching the ground. Gradually she put more weight on the injured leg. It didn't exactly feel wonderful, but the pain didn't become much worse. Weight evenly distributed on both feet, Amy took a deep breath and faced Branson.

"Are you two ready to go on?" The sneering tone in Branson's voice rubbed Amy the wrong way and she fought to keep her temper. If she and Jackson had any hope of getting out of the mine alive, she couldn't provoke the man any more. Her thigh was an ongoing reminder of Branson's instability. Before she could answer, however, Jackson spoke up.

"Certainly, Scott. We're eager to continue this tour of the netherworld." Jackson gave Branson a congenial smile. He squirmed around and struggled to stand, moaning softly when he jarred his arm and shoulder. "What's the next stop?"

"A very deep hole," Branson answered in terse tones.

Amy's heart sank. They didn't have long. If something didn't change quickly, both she and Jackson were going to die here, and no one would ever know what happened to them. Branson was right. No one would ever suspect him. He was completely off the radar as far as Carl's murder investigation went, and she and Jackson had never even met him before he knocked them out.

21

Amy hesitated, and glanced back at Branson, who used the wrecking bar to point down the adit toward the turquoise mine. Amy nodded sharply and started limping down the older passageway, the rough hewn walls closing in as they entered the older tunnels of the Pipe Wash. Jackson moved close behind her as Branson brought up the rear, once again silent.

This time when they came to the collapse, it felt like Mount Everest, her bound hands and bruised leg making the clamber over the mound of loose rock much more difficult. Once she was through, she turned back to see if she could help Jackson who was even more encumbered by his arm. The thought that she could run for it, after a fashion, crossed her mind. Branson was trapped behind Jackson and she could get a head start. Then she caught sight of Branson, impatience clearly written on his face, and remembered the blow to her leg, how he casually struck Jackson, and the sight of Carl, his face ruined. She was sure she knew what would happen to Jackson is she tried to run, and she couldn't do that to him.

A short distance later they came to the first intersection which Amy remembered, the adit to the left becoming even more constricted if at all possible. Amy turned to the right and started heading down the tunnel continuing toward the turquoise mine, but Branson brought down the bar, striking the wall with a loud *clang*. Amy momentarily gave thanks that the narrowness of these older mines restricted his ability to strike her at will.

"Not there. That way." He pointed toward the inclined winze on the other side of the intersection. Amy looked over at Jackson. Of all the tunnels they'd seen while down in the mine earlier, this was the one in the worst repair. Still, she didn't see a choice.

Amy hesitated a moment and walked into the old adit, the rough rock of the roof brushing her curly hair. She felt the weight of the earth over her head, and for a moment a slight feeling of claustrophobia trickled through her. She shone the lantern light on the rock and broken timbers lying on the floor of the adit and she was again sure that the various tunnels were of different ages. It started to dawn on Amy that even if these tunnels were dug at different times, there still should have been piles of tailings, or waste rock, somewhere to indicate where a mine was located. Often when she and her siblings were exploring with their father, they found the mines by examining the hillsides and looking for the tailings. Those piles of rock lasted for decades, well after the mines were abandoned. She still wasn't sure how extensive these tunnels were, but they were extensive enough to have produced a lot of waste, and Amy wondered where the entrance to the Pipe Wash had been and why nearby tailings didn't pinpoint the location of the tunnels for history buffs and mine enthusiasts. Still, Branson had said it collapsed. Maybe there was nothing left.

This new tunnel turned out to be a short one, ending in a small inclined stope, the miners having removed all of whatever ore they'd been after, leaving a gap in the earth. Several large chunks of quartz littered the floor, making Amy think that even if Jeb never hit gold, someone had. Poor Jeb may have died in the earthquake less than a mile away from his dream. Why had no one found Skystone Mine when these other tunnels were connected? Thick stulls, or timbers, held up the rock ceiling of the stope, but it was obvious that age was starting to wear on them as well. She saw some carving on the nearest timber. *Samuel Larson 1901.* A relative of Ms. Moira's? Amy came to a stop, and pivoted to look at Branson.

"What now. Are you going to beat us to death?" The sound carried strangely in the open space of the stope. She heard a sound in the distance and wondered if there really were rats in the mine.

"Keep going."

"Where? We're nearly at the mine face. Where do you expect us to..." Amy paused for a moment, sure she'd heard something, then shook her head. Probably just those strange vibrations that she'd heard earlier in the day. Branson didn't seem to notice anything different. Jackson was looking at her with curiosity. She shrugged, and lifted her hands toward her ear, hoping he would understand. She didn't dare mouth the words as Branson was looking right at her.

Branson seemed unaware, or didn't care, about the non-verbal exchange between Jackson and Amy. Instead it was obvious that his impatience to be done with them was growing. Amy had no idea what time it was since her phone had been lost in the initial attack, and she probably couldn't have gotten it out of her pocket with her hands taped together. She was sure that he was probably thinking he needed to get her Jeep, out of the parking lot, and into a nice secure mine shaft before long, since he'd likely have to walk home.

"Just move. You'll know the spot when you get there." Branson hit the wall of the drift again, only this time several small rocks fell out of the ceiling of the tunnel, pelting Amy and Jackson. Amy looked up at the stope and then along the drift to the adit, and wondered how stable, or rather unstable, they were.

She slowly moved a few feet farther down the drift, the passageway running parallel to the stope, looking for any way she and Jackson could possibly escape. The space was wider than the original adit, but it still wasn't large by any means. She wondered if she could climb into the stope, and surreptitiously tested the tape around her wrists for what seemed like the thousandth time. No more luck at wiggling lose than before, and without her hands she had no chance on the sharp incline of the stope.

A large column of rock protruded out into the drift from the wall opposite the stope, and when Amy moved around it, she was brought up short by a large pit where the stope continued down below the level of the drift's floor. The lantern light did little to illuminate the forbidding hole, and Amy found herself desperately wishing for her headlamp... or a flashlight, or anything that would tell her what was at the bottom of that darkness, and how far bottom was away from her feet. She had a sinking feeling that Branson intended for her to find out soon, and in person.

Amy turned, pressing her back against the rock wall, Jackson stopping right behind her. She could tell that he'd seen the lip of the hole, and knew what Branson planned. His eyes met Amy's and she could see he was trying to find something that would distract Branson and buy them more time.

Amy looked at Branson, who had just emerged from behind the column. "Ah... You never said where the Skystone Mine is in these tunnels. It's not here? Why wouldn't miners who came later, after Jeb, have found it? I'd like to know what I'm dying for."

For a moment Amy didn't think he was going to answer her, but then he drew a deep breath and began talking. "From what I can tell, both from looking at the old adits, as well as reading histories of the town and the area, this mine is younger than the Skystone, and the entrance was over northwest of the town, near the head of the Pipe Wash, hence the name. The miners came near to the Skystone adit, but apparently there was no indication of gold in that direction They followed the quartz veins, never realizing, or maybe caring, that the Skystone was there. The tunnels up top, near the town, are even newer, but since the gold was gone, they never seemed to want to dig deeper. At some point one of the timbers holding up the roof of the adit closest to the face of the Skystone broke and there was a collapse. It partially opened a connection to the Skystone, and I found it."

"So, just pure dumb luck that you found the turquoise mine?"

Branson's eyes narrowed, the light from the lantern and headlamp giving his features a ghostly illumination. Amy thought he was going to take offense at the term "dumb" and she stepped lightly on Jackson's foot to get his attention. She gave him a frown, hoping he got the idea that he needed to watch his mouth.

To Amy's surprise however, Branson didn't seem to be

angry... or at least any angrier than he was at any other time during this bizarre evening.

"I guess you could say it was dumb luck. Dumb luck that I found the tunnels in the first place, that they were in good enough condition to explore safely." Jackson choked at that, causing Branson to frown, but he continued. "Dumb luck that I found the turquoise mine. Maybe it was all dumb luck, or maybe it was because I do my research, and I'm smart. After all, I'm the one standing here, and you're standing on the edge of a deep hole."

"You've got a point there," Jackson nodded.

"Now, this has been fun, but I've a car to move." Branson raised the wrecking bar and started to advance on Jackson and Amy.

Amy prepared to rush Branson, sure she had nothing to lose. She glanced at Jackson and saw him bracing to do the same.

The next few moments passed in a blur, so chaotic that even afterward Amy couldn't remember exactly what happened. From farther down the tunnel she heard the scuffling sound again, and suddenly Branson was flailing forward, the light from his headlamp swinging wildly. Amy tried to duck out of his way, the wrecking bar giving her a glancing blow, causing her to take a step back. She slipped on the edge of the lower stope as Branson crashed into her, knocking her off her feet. As she fell, her arms flew up, and she lost hold of the lantern which spun off into the upper stope where it shattered on the rocks. In the bounding light before the lantern went out Amy saw Jackson thrown back onto the right side of the tunnel, where he'd landed on his injured shoulder. The flickering light showed something furry on Branson's back, but before she could tell what the animal was, the lantern went out, leaving them with nothing but the light on Branson's helmet.

A sudden high-pitched barking and howling, both human and animal, filled the air and Branson swung the wrecking bar again, his cursing blending with the animal sounds. The metal crashed into the floor of the drift next to Amy's head and she flinched and rolled away, her movement taking her legs and hips over the edge of the lower stope. She screamed as she tried to catch something to stop her fall. Her bound arms scrabbled in the rocks, and she caught her elbows on the edge of the drop off and dug them into the dirt trying to stop her backward slide. Branson continued to swing his wrecking bar and cursing. He turned his head toward Amy, and the headlamp blinded her.

Jackson apparently saw Amy's danger and threw himself across Branson's body. He used his good hand to grab the tape shackles trapping Amy's wrists, and leaned backward stopping her slide for the moment.

Pain shot through Amy's wrists and arms and she cried out again, kicking her legs.

"Amy, stop struggling. Can you pull yourself up onto your chest more? I don't know how long I can hold you," Jackson said, and she could see sweat popping out on his face yet again as he struggled to maintain his hold on the tape. Branson was continuing to flail with the wrecking bar, and in the bouncing light of the headlamp the walls of the stope seemed to be falling toward her.

"I can't, Jackson! I'm too far!"

Jackson tried to pull her back farther, but it felt like he was pulling her hands off at the wrists. The barking and snarling continued, making it sound as though the mine was inhabited by an entire pack of wild animals. Suddenly bright lights flooded the face of the drift, blinding Amy again, and a tangle of new voices filled the air.

"Amy! Hang on!"

"Branson put the wrecking bar down now!"

"Get these dogs away from here, dammit!"

"Here, let me have her."

"Dogs! Get away now! That will do."

Amy felt someone take her arms and pull her forward, away from the lower stope. Her hips and then her upper legs slid upward and onto solid ground. As her vision cleared, she saw Tommy Kissoon holding her arms. He finished pulling her over the edge and sat her on the ground. He squatted in front of her, studying her face with concern showing clearly in his eyes.

"Amy, are you okay?"

"I... I'm okay I think. Where's Jackson?" Amy looked around wildly. Branson was still laying on the ground, but now a sheriff's deputy had a knee in the small of his back, and it was his hands which were being bound; not with duct tape this time, but with handcuffs.

Jackson was leaning back against the rock column, his face pale in the brighter light, eyes closed. Jynx and Bess were laying beside him, eyes fixed on Branson. Every time he moved or made a sound, Bess growled.

"How did you find us?" Amy asked, looking back at Tommy in amazement. "Why are the dogs here?

"Here, let me cut that tape off your wrists first. Then I'll explain everything."

Amy nodded silently. She felt like she wasn't connected to the world any longer and that everything was spinning around her. The second deputy pulled Branson to his feet, which upset Bess. She barked, then dashed in to nip at his heels. Branson yelped and kicked out, which only made Bess more determined to get to him. Jynx started to rise as well, golden brown eyes fixed on Branson's face.

Amy shook her head, trying to clear it. "Jynx. Down. Bess. That will do." Jynx lowered herself back to the ground, but never shifted her focus. Bess, as Amy might have guessed, ignored her completely, and continued to try to get at Branson.

Tommy lifted Amy's hands and slid his knife between her wrists, slicing through the tape. Then he started to peel the tape from her skin and Amy came back totally to the here and now.

"What the heck, Tommy. I want some skin left on my arms!" She couldn't believe how much it hurt just to remove the adhesive.

Tommy chewed his lip, and she was sure he wanted to laugh, but was afraid to. "I'm sorry, Amy. The tape's been on too long, and he used that black duct tape that's extra strong."

"Just rip it off, then," she said, exasperated.

Tommy peeled of the tape in one quick move as Amy gritted her teeth.

"Better?" he asked looking at her curiously.

"Yes, much better. Thanks you. Please check Jackson. I think his arm or shoulder is broken."

"Oh, don't worry about me," said Jackson from his spot against the wall. "I'm thinking of planting myself here for a year or two." He gave Amy a half smile without opening his eyes.

Tommy moved over to Jackson, and cut the tape on his wrists as well, but when he went to pull it off, Jackson stopped him.

"Just pull it off the left side, okay? Then fold over the pieces that were pulled off so they're not sticking."

"Why," Tommy looked confused at Jackson's request.

"This arm's pretty messed up, and I'd sort of prefer not to put a lot more pressure on it right now."

Tommy looked over his shoulder at the wrecking bar that was still lying on the ground near the edge of the lower stope, then back at Jackson and nodded. He sliced through the tape at the top and bottom of Jackson's wrists, then folded the edge over on the piece left on the right wrist. Tommy then pulled the tape off Jackson's left wrist quickly, causing him to yelp in pain.

"Did you leave any hair?" Jackson studied his arm in the harsh light, then rubbed it on his jeans. He cradled his other arm carefully in his lap, the tape still dangling from his wrist.

The other deputy had Branson ready to take up top, and he looked back at Tommy, Amy and Jackson.

"Hey Tommy, let's get going with this guy. Are those two able to walk, or do we need to call the EMTs?"

Tommy looked at Amy and Jackson. "Are you guys up to it, or do you want us to call the paramedics? It will take them awhile to get here."

Amy pushed herself to her feet, hand against the rock wall for balance. "I'm fine. Jackson, how about you?"

"It's true that I've really gotten attached to this place, but there can be too much of a good thing, so I guess I'll come out with you guys." He gave Amy a smile that, while not as brilliant as his usual grins, still told her that he'd come through the day, if not unbroken, at least capable of bouncing back.

He rolled onto his knees and then rose to his feet, cradling his right arm and swaying slightly. "I do suppose I need to get a doctor to check out the wing, though. Hey boss, I'm not sure my typing will be up to speed for a few days."

"I guess you're fired, then, Jackson. I have to have some standards."

"Understandable." Jackson's smile came closer to its usual wattage.

"What happened?" Tommy asked, watching Jackson with a frown on his face.

"Branson was a little upset, and decided he had to get my attention with his wrecking bar."

"He confessed to killing Carl, Tommy." Amy said

"We'll have to get your statements later. Now, let's get out of these mines." Tommy started to walk down the drift.

"Wait. Let me borrow your flashlight for a moment."

Tommy handed it over, with a question on his face. Instead of saying anything, Amy took the huge light, and walked to the edge of the lower stope and directed the beam downward. She could see the bottom of the stope, approximately thirty feet below. Water covered the bottom, and it was impossible to tell how deeply. Amy knew that the odds were that she and Jackson would have drowned, or died of hypothermia in that pit if it hadn't been for Tommy and Deputy Arlen.

"Satisfied?" Jackson asked, watching her from where he stood next to Tommy.

"Yes, I'm satisfied. Tommy, how did you find us?"

"Come on, I'll tell you on the way out of the mine." Tommy nodded at Arlen who pushed Branson out in front, using the man's headlamp to help light the path as the group started making their way back down the drift to the adit. Periodically Amy could hear Arlen chiding Branson and telling him to move on. Branson would answer back in terse tones, but she couldn't understand his words.

"Maria called me, saying that she was on the phone with you when something happened. She said she could hear what sounded like an attack. Arlen, the deputy who is with me, was already on his way up to interview you about a break in at your folks, so he and I met in front of the shop. We found your phone under your Jeep, Amy. It must have been flung there when you were attacked. I'm assuming you were hit?"

Amy and Jackson both nodded in agreement

Tommy paused his story for a moment as they scrambled over the collapse between the older tunnels and the new one. Tommy's single flashlight making the movement slightly more difficult than it had been before, with huge areas of shadow. Amy's thigh, which she'd forgotten during all the chaos, had started to throb again, and Jackson was obviously struggling. Jynx and Bess bounded on ahead, and then returned to see what was taking the humans so long. Once through the loose rocks, Tommy began his narrative again.

"We didn't know where to go, but the lights were still on in the shop, so we broke the door and entered."

Great. Amy realized she was being a big ungrateful, but did they have to break the door? *Add get a glass company to the to-do list.*

Unaware of Amy's thoughts, Tommy continued. "The dogs were there, but no signs of anything else wrong, and we were just going to leave and call it in, when suddenly the Aussie... you called her Jynx... went crazy. She took off toward the storeroom and then out to the back door. The corgi took off after her barking and carrying on, and they both started throwing themselves at the back door."

Amy looked at Jackson in surprise. "Is that why you had me scream? Did you know the dogs would hear me?"

Jackson started to shrug, then thought better of it, his face twisting in pain. "I figured it would be a long shot, but we were pretty close to the shop at that point. Of course I didn't know the cavalry was coming behind the dogs. I was hoping Maria might do something when your call was interrupted so abruptly, but there was no way to know they were already in the shop."

Tommy looked at both Amy and Jackson and shook his head, then continued his story. "I let the dogs through, and they both ran down into the basement and over to the lumber rack. The corgi started digging at the board behind the shelves, and we could hear that it was hollow. Once we pulled the wood out of the way, the dogs took off through the tunnels, and we followed. They got a long way in front of us, and we got lost at the first intersection, but then Arlen saw the paint spots. I remember your dad always had you use that type of paint, so we rolled the dice and went in that direction."

When they got to the intersection Arlen pushed Branson toward the shop, none too gently, and he stumbled to his knees. As he rose, he looked back at Amy and sneered. "Are you enjoying this? The Skystone Mine belongs to me. You don't deserve it. None of you deserve it."

Arlen pulled Branson to his feet and pushed him down the wider tunnel toward the shop. Fifteen minutes later, the five were in the main showroom of Stone's Gems and Minerals and Tommy and Deputy Arlen were talking quietly out front, and Branson was ensconced in the back of the Mohave County Sheriff's SUV.

Amy sat next to the counter, head resting on her arm, eyes closed. Jackson was sitting on the floor with Jynx stretched out along his legs. His head was resting on the edge of a shelf. Several minutes later Tommy came back into the shop. Amy's eyes opened and she watched Tommy as he stood looking around.

"What's the next step?" She finally asked in a tired voice. Now that the stresses of the evening were over, she felt weighed down by exhaustion.

"EMTs are on their way to check out Jackson's arm and likely take him down to Kingman, since I wouldn't be surprised if it's broken. I'll help you board up the window. We're going to have to get statements from both of you, but I've got the basics and we can get the rest of it tomorrow.

Amy nodded. "It's over, then?" She raised her head and looked at Jackson.

"Yeah, it's over." He gave her smile, "At least for now. I'm not sure how I'm going to explain this to Ms. Moira, though."

Tommy looked at the two of them in confusion, and Amy started to laugh.

"Inside joke, Tommy," Amy said. She looked from Tommy to Jackson, who gave her a wink and a grin.

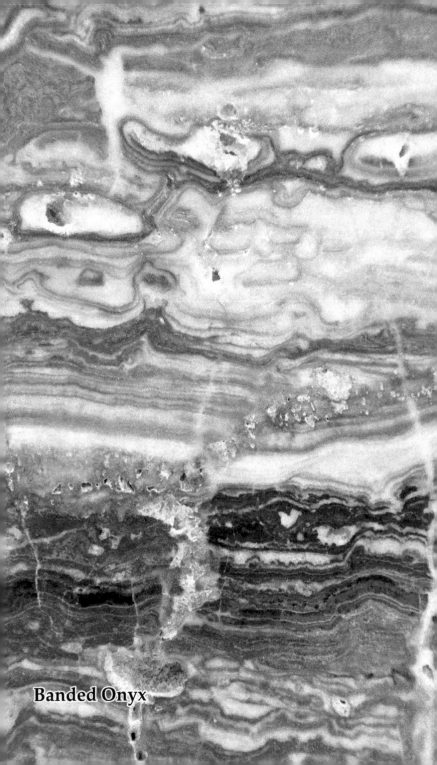
Banded Onyx

22

Wednesday afternoon Amy and Jackson made their way to Canyon View Rehabilitation Facility in Kingman to visit Nick. As they were walking up to the large single story stone structure, Amy drew a deep breath. How was she going to explain to her parents everything that had happened in the past week and a half?

Sunday evening had passed in a blur of activity. Both she and Jackson had been bundled into an ambulance and hurried to Kingman where they'd been checked for concussions. The doctors examined Amy's thigh where Branson had struck her with the wrecking bar, and determined that, while badly bruised, was going to be fine.

Just as they'd expected, Jackson's collarbone and scapula had been broken, the soft tissue badly bruised, and the muscles and ligaments torn. More fortunately, the doctors had been able to manipulate the bones back into alignment without having to perform surgery. His arm was immobilized, however, and he was milking that for all it was worth in Amy's opinion.

Amy pushed the button that released the front door, and she and Jackson entered the pleasant lobby. A large screen TV and several couches and chairs were over on the left side of the room. Several of the patients were either watching an old show, or talking quietly. Two others were playing a game of chess at a table set in front of the window.

Amy walked to the front desk with Jackson closely behind. She waited for a few moments until the older woman talking on the phone hung up the receiver. She gave Amy a welcoming smile.

"Hello. Can I help you?"

"Yes, I'm looking for Nick Stone. I'm told he's in A7?"

"Certainly. If I could just have both of you sign in here." She pushed a clipboard across the counter toward Amy, who signed both her and Jackson's names.

"If you'll just head back down the hall to the nurse's station, and then turn left, the 'A' hall will be immediately in front of you."

"Thank you." Amy turned to Jackson who'd been waiting patiently. "Are you ready?"

"Hmm. Let me think about the answer to that for a moment. Ready to meet my new employer, or ready to meet the parents."

"You're spoken for, remember? Ms. Moira is probably pining for you right now, wondering when you're going to get back..."

"To clean out the bunkhouse. Yeah, I know. When I talked to her Friday evening, I said I'd get out this week. I'll have to let her know it's going to be a little longer before I can finish that particular chore for her." Jackson said wryly. He twitched his arm, then winced. "That may be the end of the relationship right there. This will be the second time I've put her off."

"Don't worry. You got bashed over the head and the shoulder for me, the least I can do is help you clean a bunkhouse." Amy laughed at him.

"I get it," Jackson said with a grin. "You just want to make sure I'm not two-timing you with Ms. Moira."

"Yeah, right," Amy said with sarcasm. "As far as I'm concerned, she can have you. Are you really thinking about renting from her? She'll never leave you alone."

"I think if she and I can come to an arrangement, I will. I like my RV, but Merri is doing pretty well and doesn't really need me parked in her driveway any longer. Ms. Moira's bunkhouse might be a good spot until I find some land."

"You're going to stay then?" Amy paused as they entered the central hub of the facility. She looked to the left, and headed down the hallway the receptionist had indicated.

"Are you kidding? Of course I'm staying. I've told you that. Repeatedly." Jackson shook his head. "Stop worrying about it, okay? Besides, you're giving me a spot to display my photographs. How can I turn down a gallery of my own?"

"I said I thought it sounded great, but that it's up to Nick. With all that's happened, we haven't had a chance to talk about it." Amy studied the room numbers mounted beside each door, finally stopping in front of the one labeled A7. A sense of deja vu washed over her. Once again she knocked on the half open door, then stuck her head into the room.

Nick was propped up in his bed, watching a western on the small flat screen TV mounted on the wall. The other bed in the room was empty and there was no sign of Crystal. Nick looked up at the knock and grinned at Amy.

"Amethyst, come on in! I'm bored out of my mind sitting in this place with all these old people. There's this old woman down the hall who keeps hitting on me. Your mom is having to stand guard."

Amy sighed and pushed the door the rest of the way open. She walked over to the bed, closely followed by Jackson.

"Please, Dad. It's Amy. Everyone calls me Amy, why can't you?"

"Gladys and Emily call you Amethyst," Jackson chimed in from the foot of the bed.

Amy turned an evil eye on Jackson, making him laugh.

"Hey, I was just pointing out that not *everyone* calls you Amy." He gave her a completely unrepentant grin, then turned his attention to Nick. "Hello Mr. Stone. I'm Jackson Wolf. Amethyst.. Ah Amy, your daughter..." he gave Amy a sideways look and she was sure he was checking to see if he was getting to her. "Your daughter hired me to take Carl's place."

"I've heard a lot about you, Jackson. I'm told you can tell an agate from obsidian."

"I can do that, although if you throw too many jaspers at me, I might not do so well."

Nick nodded, his eyes sparkling. Other than rock club meetings, and the times he talked to Amy, he didn't often find someone who was ready to talk in depth about his passion.

"You'll do fine, Jackson Wolf. I'm glad to have you in the shop."

"By the way, Dad, I told Jackson that we'd try and set up something so that he can also display some of his artwork. He's a photographer."

Nick's eyes sharpened as he looked at Jackson with intensified interest. "What types of photographs?"

"Landscape and wildlife primarily, although I've also got some macro shots, mainly of various stones and minerals."

"I think it sounds like a wonderful idea. We can rearrange the display room so that the walls are exposed and you can hang them there."

Amy thought of all the work they'd just done cleaning the shop and groaned inwardly. She caught Jackson's eye and knew he was thinking the same thing.

Oblivious to what was going on, Nick continued. "I really want to thank you Jackson, for all your help this last week and a half. I know Amethyst probably hasn't told me everything, but it's enough to know that her mother and I owe you a huge debt of gratitude."

"No worries, Mr. Stone."

"Nick."

"Nick. I've really enjoyed what have probably been the most exciting two weeks of my life, although I'll have to admit, I could have done without the wrecking bar to the shoulder." He nodded toward his immobilized arm. "I'm looking forward to working at the shop. Maybe you'll eventually be able to teach me how to tell all those jaspers apart... and the agates as well." He gave Nick and Amy his brilliant smile.

Just at that moment Crystal walked into the room carrying a brown bag from a local fast food restaurant. She stopped, apparently surprised to see Amy and Jackson.

"Hello, you two. You must be Jackson. I'm Crystal, Amy's mother. I want to thank you for helping her out in the shop and... well, and with all the other things that have happened. If I'd known you'd be here, I'd have brought more food."

"Don't worry Mom. Jackson and I have to be getting back to Copper Springs anyway."

"Before you go," Nick said, "What is happening with Scott Branson and the Skystone?"

"Branson is locked up, and is going to remain locked up. He confessed to Jackson and I that he killed Carl in a fit of rage, but he's not talking to the police at all. They've got the shop's laptop, and they're trying to compare the SBSM listings with his bank records, but I haven't heard the results of that investigation. Right now it looks like they're going to charge him with murder, assault and kidnapping, as well as a few other things. The tribal council has been notified about the location of the Skystone Mine, although I guess they're going to have to do some surveying to make sure it's actually on the tribal lands. It turns out the old entrance was, but the actual turquoise itself is very close to the border between the tribal and Bureau of Land Management lands. If it's BLM, then we can file a claim if we want. I've already sent them a letter letting them know about the situation."

Nick nodded. "What about the Pipe Wash Mine?"

"Most of that is on hold at the moment. The situation with the mines is complicated. There's some talk that they should be labeled as historic structures, even though the old gold mine is considered depleted. There are still some useable minerals down there, but it's only been a few days. Have patience." Amy grinned at Nick, knowing that patience was not one of his strongest areas.

"Yeah, my luck the dang town council, led by that blasted Hazelton, is going to have the mines declared a town asset, and make them into a tourist trap and want my shop as the kicking off point for tours."

"I think the Hazeltons have a few other things on their plate right now. Especially since Branson told us about how they'd planned to use eminent domain to take your shop for their own benefit, and we found records that seem to show them paying off Carl... those lines labeled BJH stood for Bea and Jon Hazelton... at least we think so. I hear some people are talking about getting a recall petition going."

Nick snorted. "Good. The sooner the better."

Amy looked at Jackson and he nodded. "We've got to get going Dad. We're finally opening the shop tomorrow, and

I've still got some stuff to do."

"It was great meeting you, Nick, and you, Crystal. I'm sure I'll be seeing a lot more of you at the shop once Nick has returned to work."

The two headed back out of the room and down the hall to the lobby where the receptionist pressed a switch to let them out.

Jackson looked at Amy. "So are you planing on staying after your dad gets better? There's that high class apartment upstairs from the shop. I'll even spring for the exorcist."

"I don't know, Jackson. Maybe. After all, my portfolio is at the bottom of a flooded stope and it will take awhile to re-build that. Not to mention that my professional reputation is in the toilet thanks to my ex-boyfriend and his father." Amy scowled at the thought of Jeff.

"Yeah, like that's a convincing argument. Come on, admit it. You want to stay. Shrug off the corporate life. Get out of the packrat race, like me!" Jackson was so deeply into his soliloquy that on the word "me" he tried to throw his arms open wide. His face twisted as his broken shoulder damp-ened his passion.

Amy started to laugh. "You know, you and I would prob-ably be heading back to the hospital right now if it weren't for the way they strapped that arm."

"Is that why you told them to tie it up extra tight?"

Amy was glad to see that Jackson's cheerful nature had come through their ordeal undiminished. "You bet. I figured you'd be off on some other adventure and end up falling apart again."

"Me? You were right there with me, Ms. Stone," Jackson said with mock seriousness. "Stop avoiding the subject, though. This is the life for you. You've got rocks and mines and other places to explore." He gave Amy an ingratiating smile as they reached the Jeep.

Amy stopped and looked around at the mountains sur-rounding Kingman, and thought about Copper Springs and all the places she'd never explored. Jackson was right, there was a sense of freedom at the thought of working with Nick at the shop. Freedom that she'd never had working at Gila Geologics.

"I'll think about it, okay? Dad's in this place for another month or so, and I'll be able to make up my mind by then, that is if he wants me. Is that good enough for you, Mr. Wolfart?"

"Really, Wolfart?" Jackson looked at her with admiration. "I'm impressed. You're still wrong, but this one may have made it up to tepid, instead of 'plunging the icy depths of the Arctic Ocean' wrong."

Amy grinned back at Jackson as she climbed into the Jeep. "Well, that settles it. I have to stay until I guess your name."

"Glad to have you on board, Ms. Stone." Jackson laughed as he gingerly maneuvered himself into the passenger side of the vehicle. "Now, do you think the yellow pages has a listing for exorcists?"

Amy shook her head. "There's something seriously..."

"Wrong with me. Yeah, we've been over that." He settled back in his seat, and made a shooing gesture with his left hand, as if telling Amy to "drive on."

She rolled her eyes, put the Jeep into gear and headed out of the parking lot, back on to the road to Stone's Gems and Minerals.

Glossary

Adit - An adit is a horizontal, or a mostly horizontal entrance to an underground mine. Adits may be used to haul ore out of a mine, and may have rails for ore carts. They can also be used for drainage, ventilation, exploration for mineral veins, or a combination of all of the above. Often in old or depleted mines the rails for the ore carts are removed and sold as scrap metal. Adits often contain either wooden or masonry supports to help protect against collapse.

Agate - Agate is a translucent form of quartz with an extremely small crystalline structure (cryptocrystalline) There are many different forms of agates depending on the other minerals in the area, and how it was created. Agates usually display bands, plumes, dendrites, or inclusions, and these various patterns make it colorful and popular for jewelry. It is often cut into cabs, beads or carved into different forms. There are many different forms of agates around the world.

> **Crazy Lace** - Crazy lace agate has a pattern of bands that looks like lace, including shapes such as eyes, swirls and zigzags. Much of the crazy lace agate comes from Mexico, although there are other lace agates around the world.

> **Plume** - Plume agate has patterns that look like small plants or ferns. These are caused by formations on the outside of the rock before the agate developed. When the actual formation eroded away, the inclusions remained, leaving patterns inside the rock.

Amethyst - Amethyst is familiar to many people and is one of the most popular gemstones. It is a transparent form of quartz and is usually found in colors from light lilac to deep purple. It is found around the world.

> **Thunder Bay Amethyst** - Thunder Bay amethyst is amethyst which has been found in Thunder Bay, Ontario, Canada. It is known for its hematite inclusions, which may give it a red cap, or in other cases, give a reddish cast to the entire gemstone.

Azurite - Azurite is a dark blue copper ore, although it's considered a minor one. It may be cut as a gemstone, although it is opaque, and it may also be used as a pigment. It's often found with malachite and chrysocolla.. It is a soft mineral with a Mohs hardness of 3.5 to 4.

Cabochon (Cab) - A cabochon (often shortened to a 'cab') is a gemstone cut with a flat back and a convex front surface. It is not faceted.

Chatoyant (Chatoyancy) - Chartoyancy refers to the way a band of light reflects off parallel tubes, fiber or other linear inclusions in a stone. This creates a band of white light, which moves back and forth beneath the surface of a stone as it is moved under a light source. It is a primary characteristic of tiger's eye, but may be seen in a number of other minerals.

Chrysocolla - Chrysocolla is a green to blue-green minor copper ore that forms during the oxidation of copper deposits. It is often found with malachite. It is a soft mineral, and some people may mistake it for Turquoise.

Citrine - Citrine another transparent variety of quartz. It's color can be golden yellow to yellowish orange to golden brown in color. It is often cut as a faceted stone. Natural citrine, which is created by the heat of the earth versus the heat of the lab, tends to be more uniform in color. Most citrine on the market is either heated amethyst, or treated smoky quartz, which causes the minerals to turn yellow.

Chalcophyllite - Chalcophyllite is a rare secondary copper mineral occurring in the oxidized zones of some arsenic-bearing copper deposits. Another name for it is copper mica.

Drift - A horizontal tunnel driven along the strike of an orebody

Druse (Drusy) - Druse (or Drusy) refers to a coating of small crystals on another rock, or within a geode. Druse can be found worldwide, and is frequently seen as quartz located in voids in chert or agate. Garnets, calcite, dolomite and a number of other minerals can be a druse coating.

Epidote - Epidote is calcium aluminum iron silicate that occurs as green prismatic crystals.

Flash - The term "flash" in labradorite refers to labradoresence or schiller effect. These bright colores are not actually part of the rock, but are reflected light, and may only be seen at certain angles as the stone is moved.

Epidote

Fluorite - Fluorite is an important industrial mineral composed of calcium and fluorine (CaF2). It is used in a wide variety of chemical, metallurgical and ceramic processes. Specimens with exceptional diaphaneity and color are cut into gems or used to make ornamental objects.

Geode - Geodes are roughly spherical stone nodules which may be formed in either volcanic or sedimentary rock. Some of them started as gas bubbles, and eventually their cavities may be filled with either crystals or other minerals.

Hematite - Hematite is an iron ore that is usually red, reddish brown or gray. Inclusions of hematite in quartz crystals usually add red or reddish formations.

Howlite - Howlite is a white calcium borosilicate mineral found in the Mojave Desert of California. It is soft (3.5 hardness) and easily shaped and dyed. Turquoise imitations are often dyed howlite.

Inclusion - An inclusion is any size or fragment of one rock inclosed within an igneous rock (cooled magma)

Jasper - Jasper an opaque variety of chalcedony (fine grained quartz) that comes in many different patters due to various impurities and inclusions. Most jaspers are red, brown, orange, yellow, gray, or green or mixtures of those colors. High quality jaspers take a polish well and are frequently used for jewelry and other items.

> **Imperial** -Imperial jasper is known by its varying shades of green and pink or mauve, shading from dark to a lighter exterior. Some pieces of imperial jasper appear to be shaded with a paintbrush.

> **Polychrome** - Polychrome jasper may also be called desert jasper and is generally a very colorful stone. It includes red jasper, pink jasper, brown jasper, and grey jasper in colorful swirls.

> **Willow Creek** - Willow Creek jasper is found in Idaho, and is known for its subtle pastel colors, squiggly lines, and orb patterns.

Unknown

Kyanite - Kyanite is a metamorphic mineral. It is found in both blue and green, from opaque to translucent or "gemy."

Labradorite - Labradorite is a gemstone variety of feldspar that produces flashes of iridescent blue, green, yellow, orange, or red when moved under light. This luster is known as labradorescence or flash.

Magnesite - Magnesite is a magnesium based mineral that is off white in its natural state, but may often be dyed to resemble other more valuable stones such as turquoise.

Malachite - Malachite is a minor copper ore that is bright green. It often shows beautiful banding, swirl, and eye patterns. Because of this it is a popular gemstone, although it is soft and breaks easily.

Mineral - A mineral is a naturally occurring, inorganic solid with a definite chemical composition and an ordered internal structure. If it isn't grown, it is probably a mineral that is produced from a mine.

Mohs Hardness - Mohs Hardness is a scale of mineral harness based on a collection of minerals ranging from very soft to very hard. Using items made with these various minerals, or other testing devices deliberately created with the corresponding harness , one can try to scratch the unknown mineral. If it scratches, then the unknown mineral is either softer or equal in hardness to the testing mineral or device. From softest to hardest, the ten minerals are: talc 1, gypsum 2, calcite 3, fluorite 4, apatite 5, orthoclase 6, quartz 7, topaz 8, corundum 9, and diamond 10.

Obsidian - Obsidian is a glassy igneous rock with a composition similar to granite. The glassy texture is a result of cooling so fast that mineral lattices were not developed. There are several different varieties of obsidian, depending on what type of inclusions appear.

Ore - Ore refers to any rock that contains a mineral that can be mined profitably.

Pietersite - Pietersite is the trade name for a combination of primarily hawk's eye and tiger's eye. It's usually a dark blue-gray, swirled with other colors such as gold and red, and embedded with fibers of silicified mineral. It is a chatoyant mineral.

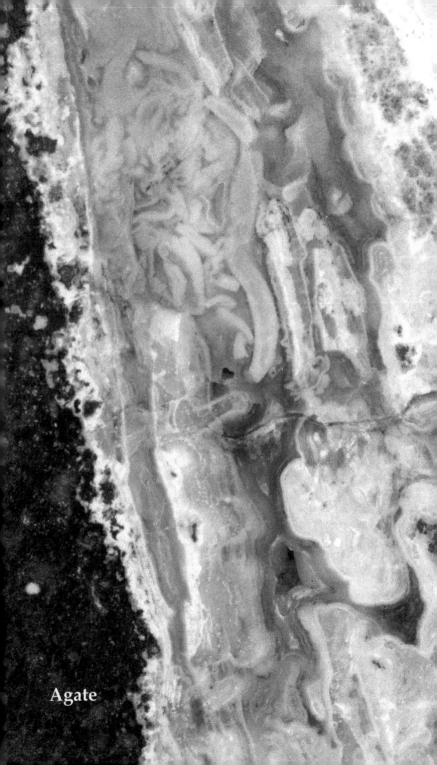
Agate

Calcite Geode

Point - A single crystal from a group of crystals

Quartz - Quartz is one of the most abundant minerals in the Earth's crust. It is the index mineral for a hardness of seven on the Mohs hardness scale. Quartz can be found in sedimentary, metamorphic, and igneous rocks and a number of popular gemstones are colored forms of quartz, such as rose quartz, smoky quartz, amethyst, and others.

> **Rutilated** - Rutilated quartz are a clear quartz which have needle-shaped inclusions of rutile, usually gold or silver. This makes them look as though there are hairs frozen in the quartz crystal.

Rough - Rough refers to minerals or rocks that have been collected, but have not yet been cleaned, cut and polished.

Stabilized - Stabilized refers to a process of impregnating fairly porous or low quality minerals with another substance, such as epoxy or liquid glass, making the mineral stronger, and better able to be cut and polished.

Stull - A stull is a timber that is used to support a rock ceiling or a hanging wall in a mine.

Stope - The stope of a mine is the cavity or void left after the ore or mineral has been removed.

Tailings - Tailings are the waste rock that has been removed from a mine, but that do not contain ore. One will often be able to identify where a mine is by looking for piles of tailings which are left near shafts, open cut workings, and opposite the mouths of adits.

Turquoise - Turquoise is a copper mineral with a bright blue to blue-green color. The color is so familiar and liked that the word "turquoise" is used in the English language as the name of a color. In the United States, most of the turquoise is found in the southwest.

Tourmaline - Tourmaline is a silicate mineral that can be found in man of attractive colors. It is a very durable gemstone that is popular with jewelry makers.

Vein - A vein is a fracture in the rock that has been filled in with a desirable mineral. At times a piece of the surrounding rock may be cut out with a piece of the mineral and presented that way. The surrounding rock at that time is called matrix.

Winze - A winze is a vertical or inclined shaft driven downward from the interior of a mine. In may mines they may become places where water collects, or dangerous heavier than air gasses. These gasses are odorless and colorless and are one of the dangers of the older mines that may not be well ventilated.

Zoned - A crystal that does not have uniform color or composition can be said to be zoned.

Calcite and Barite Geode

Also by Cheryl F Taylor

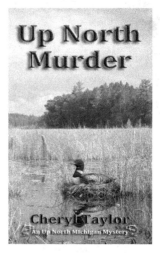

A phone call can change your life forever...

Abigail Williams gets that phone call. Gordon Dorsey, Abby's uncle and last living relative has drowned in the lake on his property, and Abby is his sole heir.

There are a few complications, however. Abby's inheritance is a trout farm in Michigan, but she's a city girl from Phoenix, Arizona. In addition, Abby doesn't believe the official story of her uncle's death. And the biggest complication... the four-legged furry owner of the farm who seems to have her own ideas about how things should be run.

Culture shock is the least of her worries.

This is book 1 in the Up North Michigan Cozy Mystery series

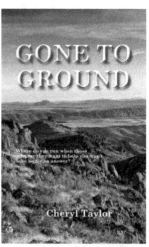

Following a deadly outbreak of influenza which decimates the population of the planet, the government issues orders that all remaining citizens are to report to designated Authorized Population Zones so that resources may be fairly distributed.

Journalist Maggie Langton, determined not to let her son, Mark, grow up in the dangerous environment of the APZ, decides to run for the empty ranch land of northwestern Arizona. When she runs into O'Reilly, a fugitive ex-Enforcer, she grudgingly admits she needs help developing those skills needed to live on a small ranch camp. What she doesn't expect, however, is that with knowledge of how to live rough, O'Reilly also possesses a darker knowledge: knowledge much more dangerous, and knowledge which the government will do anything to suppress.

Maggie and O'Reilly find themselves in a fight to keep their newly formed family safe and secure, and out from under the rule of the controlling new government. At the same time they discover a conspiracy much deeper than anyone had believed possible.

CPSIA information can be obtained
at www.ICGtesting.com
Printed in the USA
LVHW021809020521
686267LV00010B/811